TRAVELLER

THE RÍONA KILBRIDE TRILOGY: BOOK ONE

CAITRÍONA PAGE

WINTER ROSE PUBLISHING, LLC

TRAVELLER

CHAPTER 1

"Mum, we need to talk," Ríona sullenly informed her mother, who sat across the overly large and perpetually empty kitchen table. Behind her, the kettle whistled its high pitch scream.

"I best get the tea ready. I have a feelin' this is gonna be one o'hose talks 'gain," her mother softly laughed, using both the sturdy table and wobbly high-back chair to lift her fragile body upwards.

No matter her health, her mother always insisted she do as much as she could herself. There was no need, as Ríona was always around to help. But there was comfort in routine, even something as meaningless as having tea shortly after the sun rose over their fields.

"Are ye gonna wait until we both die o' old age?" In all the years here, her mother never lost her accent. It bemused the locals at first, but later when they laid her to rest, those who spoke at her eulogy would share inside jokes about their inability to understand her brogue, often turning to the "wee one" who chased her mother's shadow to translate.

"I think it's time to leave."

It was. It wasn't that she was unhappy with her life or felt the sting of her latest heartbreak that acutely. She told herself over and over, that it wasn't because of *her*. Though she still couldn't bring herself to mention her name for fear that it would just pour more salt over that wound. No, it was bigger than that. It was *more*, but...

"Hmmm," her mother replied, always a sage of unfathomable advice. Somehow, unbeknownst to her, her mother had lived a life beyond the fences that kept them safely entombed in their idyllic farm life. "And where ye think' o' running off to eh? Omaha?"

Truthfully—she didn't know. Her lust didn't specify a destination, only a need. It wouldn't be until the snow finally melted that she would have her answer.

"No, not Omaha. As much as I love playing there," she let her voice and thoughts trail off, finding their way into forlonging memories.

"But she's there."

"I want to say that's not why."

"I's okay." Her mum said. She always understood when the words failed.

Ríona watched as they lowered her mother into the ground, all six feet deep. Once the crowds left, obligatory hugs and condolences long gone, she stood there over the loose mound of dirt. An empty patch of earth that would soon be over-grown with buffalo grass that would dance in the prairie winds like her mother used to dance when she thought she was alone at night while Ríona slouched under the handrail, hiding in the shadows of the balusters desperately believing if she fell asleep she would wake surrounded by the itchy black smoke again, the heat of the flames pouring through the open doorway as her mother screamed for her from the other side of the impassable fiery wall.

That was the first night her life was taken away from her. Too young to put the scene into words adults would understand, but old enough to bear the scar on her arm for life. The forever reminder that in one night her family of three became a family of two.

The day her mother was buried she laid a single black rose on her grave, one of many traditions her mother insisted her only daughter keep alive. Back home traditions were essential to a happy life, her mother would often say. They made the world make sense. That even amongst all the chaos the modern world could bring, tradition was what held them together. A single rose was all she asked for, in all its glorious irony. *Róisín Dubh*, her mother called it.

Her mother didn't want her death to be a festival of mourning filled with bereaved friends and acquaintances. Instead, the *Róisín Dubh* would be Ríona's reminder not of her mother's death, but the day she truly become free.

"When ye think ye might leave?"

"I don't know, ma. Not far, I guess. I don't want to be far from you."

"I can take care of me self." As if the universe wanted to tell them both a message neither wished to hear, that was the final tea her bone china kettle would pour. After that incident, they used the cheap electric kettle Ríona brought back from her college dorm. Her mother called it an abomination to proper Irish teas, which she still imported as religiously as some attend their churches. It lacked the Celtic knots that ringed the heirloom kettle, but it worked.

Their talk ended as awkwardly as she had started it, leaving much still stagnant in the air never to be shared. Although, she knew her mother understood, even when she herself couldn't put it into words.

Instead she poured her feelings over the sinewy strings and bow of her fiddle. A sweet romance of lonely notes leading a tale of unspoken melodies singing the feelings her words couldn't. Her father's fiddle, meticulously restored after the fire, became her gateway drug. Not only to the world of music, but the world in general. When she outgrew the neighbour's rudimentary fiddle skills, her mother took her into Lincoln to find a proper music teacher.

It was a vibrant scene unlike the endless stocks of corn that was her childhood. There were coffee shops, libraries, and a college— places she only knew from television shows featuring friends who'd meet on the regular at such places to share their city lives so far removed from her fields. It was here she met her first violin teacher, a sweet college student in her senior year—and almost a decade her senior.

She did more than instil a deeper love for the smooth curves of her fiddle that nuzzled her thin, soft neck. Her delicate hands would often guide hers, coaxing her fingers into the proper arches needed to draw the correct pitch from the fretless strings. Then one day her teacher enthusiastically broke the painful news that she had accepted a position with a company out west. It sounded glamorous. A life she yearned to live for herself, but that day she learned more than advance fingering techniques.

She learned what heartbreak felt like. Her mother was so patient as she laid in her lap, a broken twelve year old yet to understand the nature of emotions. Years later, she would repeat the same process of crying into her mother's comforting lap as yet more women, women actually her age, would break her heart with a far more malicious intent. It was also how she accidentally came out to her mother before she came out to herself.

"Rí," her mother cooed, "'tis okay. Tell ye mum about the beuor who stole me cailín's heart."

"Me heart?"

Ríona only knew she wanted to be everywhere the other girl in class was. Whether they were at lunch, or at recess, the two of them were inseparable. Deep down she knew there was something different about their friendship, about the way Jolene lit up her world, or how her world would turn into dark clouds the days Jolene would miss school. The teacher always telling her to not worry, that Jolene was fine.

She wasn't, but her fifteen year old self hadn't understood fully how insidious diseases can be. Or how cruel other humans could be towards their own.

It was the day she returned from being absent for two weeks. While her other friends had text messaging, Jolene's family were "old school", cutting their daughter off from the world the moment she hopped off the school bus every afternoon. When Ríona bolted across the room to hug her friend, Jolene held her hand out, stopping their embrace. From that day on, the two would remain silent beacons, broadcasting their light for the other to gaze upon from a safe distance only.

One day, Ríona caught Jolene in the hallway, alone. Summer break was fast approaching, and all their classmates were exchanging phone numbers and social media profiles to hold off the hiatus of friendship. These summer months could be excruciatingly isolating as their parent's lives became busier during the prime farm months, leaving their children prisoners of loneliness and menial work.

"Rí, we can't be seen together," Jolene painfully pleaded, her eyes refusing to meet her own.

"But why? What changed?" She grabbed her friend's hands, their younger innocence returning for a fleeting moment.

4

"People are talking about us."

"So? You're my friend, Jojo."

"They're saying you like me."

"Yeah, I like you! You're my friend."

"More than friends." Jolene raised her eyes to meet Ríona's, a sad smile twisting the corner of her lips. Her eyes hid a truth that would only be told over a round of IPAs in some dive bar the college kids would pass fake IDs to the bartender.

"As in love? Of course I love—" Jolene cut her words short with a peck on her lips.

That simple kiss, awkward and cold, would careen her high school life. That dark cloud would rain on her every day until she came to forget why her world turned black.

That was the second time her life ended. The first in a roaring inferno. The second... on the lips of a girl who thaught Ríona heartbreak. Standing over her mother's grave was the third, and she swore final, time her life would end.

"Rí, promise me you'll go."

"I will." They both understood she didn't have a choice.

"Have I ever told you the story of the Selkie?"

She had. A million times, actually. It was one of her mother's favourites. Having grown up in County Donegal before meeting her father further south in Galway, never returning back to the parish she was born in, let alone the homeland that had rejected their family.

"You have black hair like they do. And your heart is trapped in longing, like theirs. I's only when they make it back to the sea are they free again. Free to be who they are inside. Like ye."

CHAPTER 2

Tuesday night came and went like any other Tuesday night in Lincoln. Outside the streets listlessly waxed and waned between busy and utterly desolate depending on how cold the breeze turned. The snow had melted, for the most part, leaving the concrete sidewalks a mixture of wet and slick, forcing everyone in their party to mindfully push their way through the crowd spewing out the pubs. Or bars, as they're more commonly called here.

There were a few words she still needed to adjust to. Starting off in another country, even if it spoke the same general language, leaves a mark on you. Not just in the scar wrapping your left arm, but in the words you use. Some of them she kept for the sake of being a little different, but others she'd only resort to after having one too many whiskey shots.

Tonight there would be no whiskey. Instead, she kept her head clear as the night's sky, the stars raining down through the foggy light pollution marking the progress of every great flyover state's city. An hours drive and it would be nothing more than an annoying glimpse on the horizon, but inside, it blanketed you in its modern comforts.

Much how the stage would blanket her as her band would take the stage again, the "usual Tuesday performance" as Zach would call it. She didn't care much for their drummer, his messy brown hair always masking his pestering eyes. *How can he see where he's going,* she always wondered to herself. It didn't make sense, but that hair annoyed her to no end. Standing a head and shoulder taller than her measly five foot three inch self, he had an uncanny ability to see only her and his sister Jordan, who also stood her height. He used that superhuman vision to torment the two of them every moment neither held their bows, an expensive weapon of personal defence against the annoying brother.

Taking her jacket off, she appreciated the warmth of the pub, her long sleeves not providing the same warmth her leather bomber did. In a way, this felt like a home to her, especially since her mother passed. Its familiarity and scent seeped into her memories and gently tugged them to the surface.

This Tuesday was unseasonably busy, likely due to the college students not travelling as much during break. Something about a downturn in the economy, or at least amongst the farmers.

"Whatcha havin'," Zach flirtatiously asked her, as if he was being a gentleman by paying for her free drink.

She rolled her eyes and pushed past him deeper into the bowels of the backstage where the other musicians were. Guitars lined the wall, their warm amber and deep mahogany woods a stark contrast to the pitch black and pearl white banjos haphazardly breaking up each bands setup. A mandolin sat idly on the table, one of her more favourite instruments to listen to, although she had no interest in learning that one. Watching others play it, though, brought a lot of awe and respect from her; their fingers flying across the strings with a graceful ease.

"Zach, leave her alone," Bryce chided him. Of the three guys in the band, he was by far the most reasonable. He was almost as tall as Zach, but unlike him, Bryce was built like a farm boy. Thick torso, even thicker arms. He kept his hair clean and short, and his beard even shorter, despite his five o'clock shadow appearing as if he sported a full beard at all times. She was told he was handsome, and from the stories she'd heard of his younger years, it clearly was true he had no trouble in finding partners for the night. But unlike the stories every frontman hypes, his truth was far more tame. If one were to pay close enough attention, they would notice the tan line on his ring finger.

7

But rings don't sell fans, Zach would say.

"I'm just offering her a drink. What's the harm in that?"

"Enough."

"Fine. Whatever dude," Zach stormed off to hunt for a bartender. He wouldn't be gone long, she lamented, noting on their way in that the usual busty bartender wasn't working tonight. Unlike most of the students here, she actually went home for the week. Wherever that tiny town was. Even if she could remember the name, she wouldn't begin to know where to find it on a map that generally only listed two cities out of the fifty-odd something ones dotting the state.

Zach returned in as much of a huff as he left, her prediction proving true. "I got you this," he announced forcing a fizzy towards her hands.

"I didn't ask for anything." She ignored his offer, turning back towards her violin case, popping open the latches to reveal the prize of her life.

"It's just pop, calm down." He continued to hold it out, as if by some chance if he kept dangling the fizzy she would turn into a prized fish and bite.

"If I wanted a fizzy, I'd ask for it."

"It's pop. When are you—," his sister punched his arm, forcing him to retreat holding his now bruised arm. "God. No wonder you can't get yourself a man."

"I'm sorry," Jordan pleaded with her, as usual.

"Why are you apologising? I'd have given him a swift one in the bullocks."

"I just feel bad."

"Well, stop it. He's a, and it's questionable, a grown man."

Jordan went quiet, turning her attention from defending her repeat performance towards her own fiddle. It was pretty enough, if to Ríona a bit non-traditional. Ríona enjoyed the bright electric blue colour, with he hints of metallic finish glinting in the spotlight, but to her, it lacked the appeal of a more traditional, acoustic fiddle. Here in the flyover states, acoustic still ruled the roost, as the locals would say.

Jordan's electric violin had its perks. Mostly that her parents couldn't stand hearing her practice and they "worried" about her practicing alone in the shady storage units skirting the outside of town. The rusty walls and broken chain link fence didn't speak highly of the security, but her brother was permitted to practice alone there courtesy of their fathers "allowance".

Ríona pulled her Perry fiddle out of its case, the soft amber glow of the worn wood sparking the usual love she felt when playing, the only moments in her life she felt that deeper emotional attachment. Settling the instrument in the crook of her neck, she pulled the bow drawing out a simple scale, her usual practice of testing each string's tonality. She already tuned before leaving her flat, preferring the quiet solitude to bond with her fathers instrument, a relic of a past she would never remember.

"You guys go on in five," a large man announced from behind a curtain, disappearing as quickly as he appeared to bark his six words.

The night passed quickly in a breathless frenzy of sweat and joy. Within the first few bars her mind wandered, chasing after the flighty sixteenth notes and long drawn out passages. The crowd vanished behind the fog of artificial smoke and cheap stage lights that left her pale skin feeling like it was kissed by the sun. Rowdy drunks sang along with stomping feet, their voices a far cry from Bryce's angelic southern draw. Even their timing lacked the fine tuned finesse Bryce would carry the chorus with.

In her own little world, the time passed by before she could start to truly enjoy it, yet it left her coming down from an nearly orgasmic high, her body sore but limber. Although they performed similar numbers every week, she still felt as if she was giving herself away, note by note, to the liquid filled crowd. But the moment she stepped off that stage, the lights quickly dimming, the filaments leaving a trace glow as they cooled, that world left her and she re-emerged into a world of... existence.

"Good show guys," the same man from earlier congratulated them flatly, his regular meaningless praise he ushered onto any performance that wasn't absolute rubbish. Theirs rarely was, which earned them the not so coveted position of Tuesday night that guaranteed the pub a profit but lacked the prestige players desired. "Friday you play a double. Jason's band bailed on us again."

Being a "house" band gave them a nice sense of stability in their musical career, a bonus few turned down, but it meant they only ever opened for other bands. Their lyrics and licks the main attraction those who paid their cover fee actually came to see, unlike her band's tried and true standards that were a mere appetiser.

"Sis, you really need to step up your game," Zach chided his sister as they filed into the "green room" behind the stage. He wrapped a sweaty and foul smelling arm around Ríona's shoulders, which she quickly tried to shrug away from. His hand grasped her arm quelling her escape. She shivered, repulsed not by the stench alone, but the mere fact it was Zach touching her.

"Let go of me," Ríona demanded, grabbing his hand and prying it off her arm, freeing herself from his moist prison. "Gross, dude." She didn't only mean the sweat soaking his graphic tee, but his... his everything.

"I'm hungry," Paul, their banjo player, plainly proclaimed, the first words he'd spoken since they arrived.

"You don't want to watch the other players?" Jordan asked, a mouse within a stampede of a single stagehand, and gruff owner barking at the next set of performers, and said performers frantically tuning their instruments as they pushed past the departing set.

"We saw them the other week," he shrugged. He only cared about his own performance. While showcasing some talent, it lent itself the air of extreme hobbyist with too much money and time than the rail thin country emo boys filling the stage.

Paul won the argument. Both Zach and Bryce nonchalantly following whatever suggestion satisfied the baser need needing quenched at the moment. Jordan gave her a pleading looking, but Ríona couldn't decipher what her silence was actually asking her.

She tried to silently question her meaning, but Jordan simply rolled her eyes and agreed that she was hungry. They all knew she wasn't, nor would she actually eat anything, complaining that the food made her nauseous.

"Dude," Bryce cooed lovingly as they filtered out into the street. Zach whipped his head around, quickly scanning all the rear ends walking the street, desperate to spot the same woman that elicited such an excited response from their singer.

"That would be a sick way to tour," he continued, leaving everyone else still confused about his intentions.

Paul caught a glimpse of the rusty bucket of steel across the street parked haphazardly along the curb, the driver long past concerning themself with keeping within the white paint. Without missing a beat, he skipped across the road, ignoring a childhood of training to check for oncoming dangers for the allure of a wishful fantasy.

The rest of them followed, closing in around a horrendously painted van that conjured images of the Beetles and Rolling Stones touring before they became the cultural icons they are today. It weathered a large swath of black grey skulls with bright garlands of hibiscus, daisy, and sunflower. Peering in the cracked windscreen the van looked empty, almost soulless, except a mattress topped with a loose blanket and pillows in the back.

"You like," a slow coastal voice called from behind them.

Ríona jumped, taken back by the sudden intrusion of another male into the group. Jordan reflexively grabbed her arm. The owner introduced himself as "Goat", an unusual name none of them assumed to be his real name. However, the boys took to it quickly, introducing themselves proudly, casually mentioning that they were a band in the process. Bryce even casually slipped in he was considering picking up a van like Goat's to take them touring.

There was no hope of that happening. His cutesy "I don't need feminism when I have a good man" wife would never let him out of her sight. It was already a battle to get him out to gigs let alone a gig a thousand miles away in a city known for its "wild nights".

Goat, the slender "dude" standing before them gave them a quick once over, pausing too long while examining her body, "might be small for all of you."

"It would just be to get us from point A to point B," Bryce tried to rationalise. "We wouldn't need to sleep in it."

"Why not," Goat pushed back, his surfer dude vibe washing out the incredulous questioning. "I live in mine. The road is my home. Hakuna matata, man."

"Did—did you just quote 'The Lion King'? A children's movie?" Jordan spit at him, somehow appalled by the childhood reference they were a decade too late to truly enjoy.

11

"Yeah. It's not about the corporists exploiting the animators and traditional African stories, it's about the message."

At that point, Ríona and Jordan tuned out, physically distancing themselves from the boys who animatedly chatted profusely about the van. According to Zach's loud voice, the van was a "classic". To her, a "classic" was any car made before she turned sixteen and was given her mother's plain but functional Ford half-ton pickup truck. A perfect workhorse for a farm, but by no stretch what an aficionado would call a "classic". Old and barely holding itself together, yes, but not a classic.

"Would you really travel with them," Jordan started, her voice a little shaky.

"With them? I don't fit in."

Jordan's face soured, "what do you mean? They love you. I'm pretty sure Bryce would happily leave his witch of a wife for you."

Ríona laughed even though she knew she shouldn't, but Jordan's disdain for the woman never failed to amuse her. Mostly because she agreed with the sentiments, only she felt bad for speaking of another woman in such a way. Her mother made sure that was one habit she never picked up, warning her that picking at your fellow woman is what *they* want.

"Awww, you don't see me shagging your brother instead?"

"Oh god, gross, no!" She punched Ríona in the arm, but not nearly as hard as she hit her brother whose bruise was already turning a deep purple. "I would kill you."

"Why not him?"

"Friends don't date your family. Plus, I'm stuck with him until someone else kills him first. If you married him, I'd never get rid of him."

"You make me glad to be an only child. I'm not sure I could handle that kind of sibling love."

"Anyway...," she made a nudging face towards Bryce, as if Ríona only causally forgot about her comment rather than intentionally steering it away from the topic.

"He's not my type." She shrugged, hoping the conversation would quickly turn before the boys finished their rabid gossip session. "This van however..."

Wistfully she slid her hand across the rough painted surface, feeling the papery texture of spray paint art. Part of her flickered alive at the thought of travelling in a van like this. Only, just her. Maybe Jordan could come. Just the pair of them, like sisters, touring the long empty roads over desolate sandy deserts with the occasional cactus leaping from the dusty earth. Her long black hair billowing out one window while Jordan's bleach blonde hair out the other.

The lack of air conditioning just a story they could tell the server at the little dying diners along Route 66. Pulling into cutely named towns like Shamrock and Peach Springs and pretend they're from a time long paved over by massive eight lane interstate highways where people miserably waste an hour of their morning only to waste another hour later cursing at the driver in front of them.

"You need freedom," her mother had told her. It was after she pulled her electric kettle out of the box of dorm goods she brought back with her when she switched to online classes.

"I am free, mum. I can come and go as I please here just the same I could back in the city. It's only thirty minutes way."

"That's not freedom," her mother chided before taking the kettle, her cold fragile hands brushing against Ríona's strong, ring cladded fingers.

"Don't tell me you were serious about my brother?"

"Oh feck no. No offence, but your brother is the first person I'm sacrificing to the zombies."

"Paul?" When Ríona returned a scrunched up nose, Jordan threw her hands up. "You need to date, woman!"

"Yeah... I agree."

Their imaginary road trip came to a terror inducing halt.

"What are you two girls gossiping about?"

She glared at Zach. "Jordan, meet the definition of 'irony'. He lives and he breathes, and can't figure out how to tie his shoes so he only wears thongs."

"What? I wear boxers you dweeb."

"They're shoes, eejit."

"She means your flip-flops, Zach. Don't be an ass."

"You two are are so gay," Zach huffed. He turned back to the other boys, "hey, food?"

13

CHAPTER 3

*R*íona's iPhone buzzed on the table adjoining her bed. Her instinct was to ignore the digital intrusion into her world, instead preferring the oppressive pillow smashed against her face, arms draped over it in defeat. It was her last semester and her homework was butchering her free thoughts, torturing them with conductors and distant history and baroque versus romanticism and *too much*. Too much of everything. The black on white words on her MacBook screamed at her. Even the forever blinking cursor blistered her ears with its visual assault. There, not there, there, not there, there—*why is the world like this?*

If she closed her eyes hard enough, perhaps university would vanish in a haze of forgotten memories and take her along with it. Again, her iPhone buzzed, almost angry that she ignored the first notification.

"Ugh, what time is it," she complained to her empty studio flat.

Reaching over, she begrudgingly rescued her phone from its forced solitude. Up until now she was being good and avoiding what little social media she engaged in. Truthfully, she worried more about the time waster games she, and most of humanity, seemed to enjoy too much when her reward centre wasn't flagging "homework" as the epitome of pleasure.

SORRY ABOUT MY BROTHER. HE'S A JERK, the message from Jordan read, trailed with a string of crying emojis.

She considered ignoring her message, but the animated ellipses shoved her previous message up, a warning that Jordan knew she had read her message. Likely, she imagined, Jordan sat on the other end, laying in her frilly bed at her parent's house, watching her phone for any indication that Ríona lived.

I KNOW YOU HATE IT WHEN PEOPLE MAKE FUN OF THE WAY YOU SPEAK.

Ríona sighed. She knew she was being baited into a conversation, yet she couldn't wrestle an excuse that wouldn't haunt her later.

SERIOUSLY, FORGET IT. She couldn't tell Jordan why she was actually upset.

"Don't say that," Jordan snapped at her brother.

"What's your problem," her brother defended himself, his nervous energy radiating from his body. "I'm not the one who uses stupid words to say normal things."

"You're such an ass," Jordan complained.

"Zach," Ríona pleaded, paranoid about the direction the conversation would head, "just stop it. Let's go get dinner."

BRYCE CHEWED HIM OUT AFTER YOU LEFT.

BRYCE? WOAH. ALMOST SAD I MISSED THAT SHOW.

WE MIGHT NEED A NEW DRUMMER...

WHAT???

YEAH... ANYWAY. I SAW THE WAY YOU LOOKED AT THAT VAN.

"And," she whispered out loud to herself as she stared at the ellipses, waiting patiently for Jordan to hit send and silently hoped she hadn't simply hit a random letter by accident. "You and your slow ass fingers, I swear."

MY COUSIN HAS ONE LIKE IT. I FACETIMED HER EARLIER AND SHE SHOWED IT TO ME. SAYS IT'S BEEN THERE FOR A WHILE NOW BUT IT RUNS. JUST NEEDS SOME WORK. SAYS YOU CAN HAVE IT IF YOU PUT THE WORK IN.

She couldn't be serious? Could she? The thought of running away in a van was just wistful thinking, a little pastime of "what ifs" not a tangible reality she could sit in, wind whipping through her hair.

WELL, Jordan prodded when Ríona failed to respond immediately, still recovering from the fantasy.

Her gut reaction was to say "yes", that she would absolutely take it, but the rest of her reeled at the reality of it. Could she?

I'M GOING TO TELL HER YES.

WHAT? NO! MAYBE...

RÍ, I LOVE YOU, BUT DON'T BE YOU FOR ONCE.

"I can't," a sixteen-year-old Ríona cried into Jordan's down pillow, darkening the thin white cotton with her tears.

"Rí, you have to." Jordan pulled at Ríona, carefully dragging her off the bed and onto her feet. "You're gonna mess up your makeup."

"I don't have to go," Ríona pleaded, her puffy eyes still threatening to overflow. "I can't."

"Sweetie, you are one of the best fiddle players I know. No one is going to make fun of you there. All they'll see is a beautiful blue-eyed girl playing her nervous little heart out."

Jordan wasn't wrong. She nailed the interview, a rather progressive event given the controversies swirling around the news sites over gender biases and racism. Ríona sat nervously behind a blank wall, nothing but a comfortable performance chair and a sealed envelope holding the sheet music she would be sight reading. The assistant gave her strict instructions to not speak.

When the indicator light turned yellow she opened the packet, sliding the stiff sheets of music into her free hand. She was given a minute to read over the test given her. She skimmed over the piece—her voice humming a trail of notes—she quickly spotted the transitions that would trip her up, making mental notes how best to avoid making a fool of herself. One such transition she knew she'd had to fake.

Six agonising tear filled months later the hanging cloud over her was lifted. Her mother casually strolled into the kitchen, holding a pile of mail collected from the post office on her last trip into town. Normally her mother would set the mail on the edge of the counter where it would go unchecked for days before finally Ríona became annoyed with its presence and sorted through the junk mail to pick out that one bill notification that marked they paid their electric bill online.

"Subtle, mother," she snidely remarked, pulling the stack of papers towards her. Starting from the bottom, she started pulling out each letter, checking who it was from before sorting it accordingly. With two pieces of mail left, she pulled the second to last.

"You knew I'd start from the bottom, didn't you?"

Her mother just smiled proudly, waiting like a dam eager to burst. It was the college. Carefully tearing it open, her mother turned and put the bone china kettle onto the stove, turning the gas to high before retrieving the tea and cream.

"I got in."

FINE. YES. TELL HER YES.

GOOD. YOU CAN RIDE DOWN WITH ME THIS WEEKEND.

This weekend? That was more sudden than she expected, but then again, so was Jordan texting her with news that her cousin, the one she would visit on occasion but never introduced her to, had one just sitting around waiting to be rescued.

CHAPTER 4

"Hurry up woman," Jordan called to Ríona, "we were supposed to leave already."

"Listen, I fed you. You can be a wee bit patient eh?"

"I don't know if pouring water into a jug of pancake mix counts as 'making breakfast' but just hurry. You're meeting my cousin, not your future husband."

Truthfully, she didn't understand herself why she was so nervous. All she needed was a pair of jeans, a few flannels, some underwear, to refresh her stash of girl things, and her brush. She kept most of her toiletries in her bag because she never knew where'd she'd wake up the next day. The joys of college life, she guessed.

"There, done," Ríona announced as she flicked the lights off in her tiny flat. "Windows shut. Fridge closed this time. Clothes packed. I think we're good to go."

"Seriously? We're staying one night."

Downstairs Jordan's two-door Ocean Blue Wrangler sparkled in the early morning sun, the top pulled back and the windows already down. Ríona wouldn't call the area around her flat the most dangerous city in the world, but her heart still skipped a beat every time Jordan left her Jeep wide open. Of course they never left anything valuable inside, but there was something about the trust that didn't settle well with her.

Storing her weekend bag and fiddle case inside the custom-built boot, Jordan started up the Jeep and started a playlist she particularly enjoyed on their longer road trips. Ríona had failed to ask just how long of a trip she was in for.

"Two hours, there about," Jordan answered, unfazed by the answer. "Wanna grab coffee?" Jordan clearly didn't need any coffee, her normal perky demeanour already annoyingly chipper.

"Absolutely," she moaned pitifully. After the previous night's double performance, she needed more than a strong, almost black coffee.

Jordan pulled onto Eighth Street and parked in front of the five story red bricked Apothecary, taking one of the many open spaces on a slow Saturday morning. The crisp chill of a late Friday still scaring away those not adventurous enough to wait outside a coffee house until the owner opens the door at last. Soon the college students will fill the smattering of work friendly watering holes, intermittently complaining about shoddy Wi-Fi connections and mid-terms or research projects.

This one was their little haven of reclusion. "Moon", as they short-ened the name. A mixture of nerdy, hipster, and genuine uniqueness underneath the historic district. It was a hard mixture to achieve, that ideal sense of organic and trendy. Unlike the neighbour coffee house with their Instagram perfect white washed "reclaimed" wall boards and exposed industrial chic tables. It felt like a place you rushed through coffee and lunch with a business associate, unlike Moon.

Today's coffee specials were all Game of Thrones houses, each loosely connected to the "mood" of the Houses if you squinted enough. None of which enticed her, although Jordan thoughtfully perused the menu she wouldn't order from before snapping a picture of the sign. Her favourite was Dany, the tiny but fierce woman born through fire. On occasion Jordan would call Ríona her Khaleesi, a pet name she wasn't sure was a positive thing or disturbingly negative. A woman born of fire; only she didn't walk through her fire unscathed. Unconsciously she pulled down the long sleeve of her flannel button up, hiding the already hidden scar.

"Mornin' ladies," the barista greeted them, somewhere between Jordan's chipperness and Ríona's bitterness at being awake. She was a cute thing, even in that boring maroon T-shirt sporting their branding. Her face was perfectly made up, her brows looked professionally done and her thin but brightly painted red lips standing out on her flawless foundation.

Ríona had taken special notice of her since she started frequenting Moon in the mornings in addition to random open mic nights when both of them would play original pieces for the small crowd.

"Morning, Ashleigh," Ríona answered with a slight smile to her tone. "You know me, Ethiopia, double cream. To go though."

"You two ain't stickin' 'round?" Ashleigh leaned on the counter, her slender hand buried in the crook of her neck as her elbow bore the weight of her body against the counter, bringing her closer to Ríona's height.

"We're going to visit Jordan's cousin down in Kansas." She couldn't help but stare at Ashleigh's deep brown eyes, made almost black by the dim lighting.

"Awww, that's a shame. Jordan better bring you back in one piece," she sweetly cooed.

"I will."

Jordan seemed unaware of the redness building in her pale cheeks. Was Ashleigh flirting? No... she couldn't be.

"Coffee for...," the other barista, Ana from Ríona's recollection, fumbled at seeing her name written on the cup.

Ashleigh giggled, a disarming habit of hers when someone made a mistake, "It's pronounced Ríona. Ree-nah." She took the coffee from Ana and gave it directly to Ríona, "here you go, honey."

"If you two are done flirting...," Jordan interrupted, tugging on Ríona's belt from behind.

South 81 was empty. Not just the road, but the boring expanse surrounding the divided highway. Just empty fields waiting for their caretakers to avoid the possibility of a frost destroying their crops. Some farmers seemed confident enough that the increasingly warm yet volatile winters had thrown its worse at them this year. February had seen the most snow in a single month than they had the past three years so it was understandable that many farmers played it cautiously this year. Many started new crops they were entirely unfamiliar with as a last ditch effort to avoid the same fate her mother's farm faced.

Maintaining their farm had been a long and painful process, and in her opinion, one of the main factors to her mother's rapid deterioration. Others had said it was fortunate timing, that her mother had wanted Ríona to leave their farm and pursue her own life, not follow in her family's footsteps alone.

If she had siblings, or even an extended family that hadn't disowned them, they may have continued to fight for the farm and stave off the encroachment of the larger agribusinesses that were foaming at the mouth to take advantage of the overwhelming downturn in trade.

Already several of her friend's parents had committed suicide, realising their future no longer existed outside their life insurance policies. Many still had no one, much like her mother, to help care for the family farm.

"Rí, me sweet baby girl, you needn't cry," her mother hugged her tightly, the brief letter pushed aside angrily. *"This is a good thing!"* Her mother kissed her forehead, the same way she always had since she was a wee babe.

"I don't want to leave," she pleaded with her mother through a stream of tears.

"I know ye do, Rí, it's all over ye face every time we go into the city. I cannae blame ye. So much glitz we never had back home. Oh and the people. I seen ye lookin' at the lasses too."

"This is me home," her own accent came out despite her efforts to blend in, her emotions always coaxing it out like sweet honey to a mischievous piskie.

"And when I'm gone?"

Silence fell between them both, the weight of her mother's words sitting uncomfortably on Ríona's heart. Jordan belting out the chorus of her current favourite billboard single brought her back to the expanse of road rolling out before them. Their ponytails whipping around in the chilly air mixed with the blasting furnace.

"You're gonna love my cousin," Jordan started when the song finished, bored by the silence between the two of them. It would be another hour before they reached her cousin's farm, according to Siri who stopped giving directions nearly an hour ago when they turned onto the highway. "She's a little different, but she's so cool."

"Oh really? Do tell," Ríona played along, letting her friend joyfully brag about her family.

"She owns her own business now. Working on vintage cars, which is why she has that van. She used to be an amateur race car driver when she was in the Air Force. She tried out to be a pilot for a few years but never made it."

"She's a veteran?"

"Yeah... but it's a sensitive topic. She was dishonourably discharged."

"Oh." She didn't actually know what that meant, but it didn't sound good. *Air Force...* Her father was in the Royal Air Force when he met her mother while on leave.

"Otherwise she's a cool chica. After her discharge, she moved back and bought herself a small farm just outside Wichita. She started tinkering on some vintage cars and next thing she knew people were bringing their barn finds to her. Some just dump them at her place; others actually pay her to restore them so they can relive their teenage years."

"That's pretty cool that she found her way."

"Yeah... it is."

IN TEN MILES, TURN LEFT, Jordan's phone started instructing. Not that Jordan needed the directions at this point, but there was some comfort in knowing a higher power was guiding them when they were no longer aware of their own actions.

CHAPTER 5

"𝒥'm so glad you didn't bring that asshole of a brother of yours this time," the tall, muscular dirty blonde woman started.

"He's your cousin too," Jordan defended her absent brother.

"I don't claim that one—only you," Tomi laughed as she grabbed her smaller cousin for a forceful hug.

Pulling away, Tomi eyed Ríona, giving her a slow yet appreciative look over. "This your friend?" Her voice was far from the hyper-feminine singsong of Jordan. Instead she carried a gruff voice. Almost too stereo-typically "military" with her forcefully enunciated words mixed with a hint of myriad accents she couldn't place outside that faint tinge of a Midwest twang.

"Yeah. Hi, sorry," she stammered, hopping over to the other two. "I'm Ríona," she held out her hand towards the muscular arm holding Jordan's shoulders hostage.

"Ríona," Tomi tested the name, turning it over on her tongue with ease. "Not Scottish, so must be Irish?"

"Tá," she teased in Irish. Her mother insisted she at least become conversational in their language, despite it essentially being dead at this point. "Means, 'I am'."

A smile broke out on Tomi, who finally took Ríona's awkwardly airborne hand. Her grip was firm with a touch of roughness she'd expect from someone who worked with their hands. Unlike the other two women, Tomi's hair was short, the left side cut to a fade, the centre slicked back with an ample helping of moose.

"So you're here to see that van, huh?"

"Yeah," she shyly replied.

"I think you're intimidating her," Jordan teased, knocking her shoulder against Ríona's.

"Uh... no. I—," she stopped herself.

"At least she's cute," Tomi joked to her cousin who merely rolled her eyes.

"You can't have her."

"You're no fun. Anyway, let's give our girl here the tour."

Tomi's house was small by farmhouse standards. Unlike the massive two and three story "traditional" homes many people built in the nostalgic sense of a long-gone Midwest style, hers was actually old. First built in the late 1800s, Tomi explained, it retained much of the original styles that most would find cramped or stuffy. No massive open floor layout, no half baths in every room.

It was adorable in its simplicity. Two bedrooms, two baths, a basic kitchen with a natural gas stove. It was remarkably remodelled inside. The hardwood floors professionally restored and refinished. Compared to her mother's house, which kept that vintage country chic, Tomi's felt modern... like the Instagram coffee shops but with a touch more heart.

"I'm half expecting a 'Live, Laugh, Love' sign somewhere," Ríona teased, still appreciating the touch of details in the adjacent dining room.

"Oh, I keep that out in the shop."

"Really?"

"I use it as target practice for my nail gun."

"Oh..."

"You're a mess, Tomi."

"Let me have fun with the girl. She's cute when she blushes."

"Anyway," Jordan loudly announced, her face scrunched up in disgust. "If you show her your bedroom, I'm gonna vomit."

"Way to kill the buzz, Sunshine."

"Sunshine?" The nickname piqued Ríona's interest.

"She's too damned chipper, ya know?"

"Oh god yes, do I ever! You'd think after twelve years I'd have developed a tolerance for it, but nope, she's a tiny ball of kinetic energy every morning."

"You should have seen here when she was younger. I'd babysit her and I about died."

"I'm right here you know," Jordan's tone shifted from amused to developing a tinge of anger, which at the moment only incensed her cousin to tease her more.

Afraid to see her friend lash out and leave her behind with this unusual woman, Ríona started asking about the rest of the property. "If I'm not mistaken, that was a horse enclosure I saw out there, no?"

"Yeah, although sadly no horses of my own at the moment. I do let some yuppie 'horse girls' board theirs here. If you're keen, I can give one a holler."

"No... I don't ride much."

"And you grew up on a farm?"

"Well, yeah. We use tractors nowadays. Not sure you old folk know about them yet."

"Ouch, Jordan didn't tell me you have a tongue on you." Tomi gave her a sideways look, implying somewhere in her words she buried a secret she expected Ríona to understand.

Hesitant to respond, still puzzled by the taller woman whom she found oddly, if unconventionally, attractive. She looked nothing like most of the women she'd ever met. Almost a novelty of sorts one finds at those weird stores along the highways pretending to be the interstates crisscrossing the Bread Basket.

Her hair... her voice... Even her posture deviated so fiercely from the "norm" she found herself almost staring. Tomi returned her quasi-stares with a small sensual smile, a truth hidden in her thin lips she beckoned Ríona to take. They would be warm with a hit of forceful tenderness—

"The van?" Jordan tapped her foot impatiently, refusing to hide her annoyance that her cousin and best friend were quickly bonding. "We came for the van, not so you can seduce my best friend."

"Is that why you've never brought her around, Sunshine?"

"What? No! It's not that..." Jordan suddenly turned sullen, her words remarkably soft for the already tiny voiced woman. "It was a rough night."

Sensing Jordan struggling to justify her odd behaviour, Ríona offered an explanation. "Zach ditched us last night."

"Ah. Told you, he's an asshole." Without a hint of hesitation, Tomi grabbed Jordan again, pulling her into a tight hug that they both held onto, Jordan resting her head against Tomi's collarbone as a young daughter would with her doting mother. "Sunshine, you need to let him go. You can't cure him."

When they continued their embrace, Ríona started shifting uncomfortably, both jealous Jordan got to take in Tomi's woodsy aroma so personally, but also with a painful longing.

The last time she could rest her head against her mother's chest so comfortably she was still a wee lass, barely old enough to be trusted with "the good plates". It was shortly after... after *that*. Burnt wood lingered on their clothes for months afterwards, the woodsy aroma forever seared into her olfactory memory. Shortly after, the comfort of her mother's embrace waned until she grew too tall to embrace her shorter mother the same.

"The bus," Tomi announced, relieving Jordan of her embrace. "It's out back."

She walked them around the back of her shop; it humming with the whirling of fans and the occasional regeneration of the air compressor. Behind the large steel building sat a row of blue tarps wrapped up like Christmas presents without the bow.

"It's one of these. Guy up a town over had it sitting in his garage, so he traded it for some work. I had planned to get her purring again as a side project, but real work has kept me too busy to give her the love she needs. Here, Ríona, help me with these ropes."

Quickly the two of them untied the ropes holding the blue plastic in place, unveiling an unexpectedly pristine looking Volkswagen Kombi. She had seen them in all the hippie movies as the preferred transportation of the stoned and free loving types. Except... it looked different from the one she saw earlier in the week. She didn't fully understand why, her knowledge of automobile history as fluent as the next college kid focused on passing standardised tests instead of trivial pleasures like rebuilding vintage cars.

"Last of her kind, sadly," Tomi said ruefully, running her hand along the smooth clear coat.

She knew enough to know the van didn't need painting, but beyond that she couldn't begin to imagine what needed to be done. "Is it that old?"

"I wouldn't call her old. She's younger than you, actually."

"Really," Ríona was surprised. When Jordan first texted, she imagined a run down pile of rust being held together by peace signs and garland. Instead, what sat before her looked like a showroom piece. The powder blue paint job still looked new.

"I'm baffled by it, honestly. I don't think the guy who gave it to me actually understood what he had. That's rich men for you—buying shit just because they can."

"So what's wrong with it," Jordan asked as she peeked into the windows, the glare of the rising sun reflecting painfully off the windscreen. "Oh."

That "oh" deeply worried her. Her own curiosity bursting at the seams, she looked to Tomi for approval, who gave it to her with a small smile and a nudging tilt of her head. Inside it was... empty. It looked as if someone had stripped it down of everything but the powder blue leather driver's seat, shiny steering wheel, and—"is that?"

"Never drove one before?"

"Not really. Me mum's truck—my mother's truck," she caught herself slipping out of her trained speech, "is an automatic. Just press the pedal and point it away from other cars. And trees."

"I'm not even going to ask," Tomi shook her head, her fingers pinching the bridge of her nose. "So we need to teach you to drive a stick, eh?"

"I guess?" She took in Tomi's bemused, knowing smirk. "It can't be any harder than driving a tractor."

"Likely not. Just know this thing has the power of a field mouse compared to a tractor. If you think you're going to be cruising the highway at ninety, you're going to be disappointed."

"Next you're going to tell me I shouldn't go muddin' in it."

"Don't," Jordan snapped, a fierce finger pointed threateningly towards her cousin.

Tomi held her grease stained hands up, silently pleading her innocence. "I wasn't going to say anything."

"Sure you weren't." Jordan rolled her eyes. "Why is it empty though?"

"My guess is the last guy was planning to do what our Irish lass here wants do: make it into a camper."

Her interest peaked, Ríona tugged on the passenger door's handle, "is that a thing people do? Last one I saw just had a mattress tossed in the back."

"Oh totally. Back on base we had a few who converted some box trucks, one guy converted an old school bus, and one woman just set out in her SUV on the weekends. Here, let's head inside for lunch and we'll talk."

Over a lunch of square cheese and sliced meats that she traded for biscuits, they would discuss Ríona's vague dream. A feeling, really, compared to anything solid like Tomi's spoiled dreams that brought her back to her hometown in the middle of northern Kansas. Ríona detailed the state of her mother's truck, the one reliable enough to make it around town with only a handful of unexpected repairs and as comfortable to drive as riding a wooden rollercoaster.

Jordan had urged her to spend some of her inheritance on a new car, one that didn't require the occasional two in the morning rescue, but Ríona insisted on holding out until she figured out what her path would be after finals.

If her mother had held out for another few months, she could have watched her only child walk the uncomfortable aisle crammed with thousands of other graduates, the School of Music a short but excitable crowd in the grand scheme. Her plan was never to be taking her mother's truck into her next life, but the doctors missed spotting the lump in her scans.

Tomi sat a warm mug in front of her, the thick condensation wafting into her still face. A draft twirled the green tag of a generic store bought tea. It wasn't the same...

"Sorry, it's the only tea I have." Tomi sat packets of sugar on the edge of the saucer. "Now that you've seen her, what are you going to name her?"

"Name her?"

"She thinks naming cars is weird."

"You named yours 'Barbie' so I wouldn't talk if I was you."

"What's wrong with that?"

Both of the other women gave Jordan the same knowing look.

Tomi continued, "yes, you need to name your ride. Cars with names aren't just how you move from one place to another. They became an integral part of the journey—wherever that may lead you.

"The love of your life isn't named 'person'. She has a name that you awkwardly have tattooed on your back. That's how you know the car is right for you: she has a name."

Ríona pondered her monologue. A name... "Roan Inish."

"Sorry?"

"Roan Inish. Me ma loved that story and would call me her Selkie. This way, I have a part of both my parents with me."

Jordan was still staring at her cousin, "you never told me you had her name tattooed on your back!"

CHAPTER 6

*S*unday afternoon arrived quicker than Ríona anticipated. Tomi told her she was lucky the snow melted that week, the warmer weather blowing through the Fly Over States calling the early end of winter. A few weeks prior they wouldn't have been able to get the van started, let alone give Ríona a few driving lessons.

Those lessons had been painful. Tomi decided, with her vast wisdom, that it would be best to teach Ríona how to drive a manual transmission on an old Celica she had laying around. It amused Ríona to no end to watch Tomi climb in and out of the tiny car, her five foot ten inch height plus western boots making her a head too tall to comfortably drive the older import. But, as Tomi reassured from the passenger seat, "you ain't gonna eff her up."

It was somewhat sweet the way Tomi had stopped cursing around her, although no one asked her to. She must have noticed over dinner Saturday night that Ríona never cursed, despite the occasional foulness of Jordan's wine induced tirades. Whiskey sours—the sour mix made from scratch using the fruit from a pair of trees grown inside her small greenhouse—weren't enough to loosen her vocabulary.

"This is soooo much better than Bob's. No offence to Bob," she slurred, feeling lightheaded after only two stiff drinks. Her legs dropped onto Jordan's lap. "I could come just for this little taste of heaven."

"I would not be opposed to that," Tomi mischievously agreed.

In a few hours her shifting skills transcended from drunk almost-college-graduate to "I wouldn't want to be behind you but you'll pass". It would be another week, Tomi broke the news, before she would get a chance to drive Roan though. The engine was delicate, it was explained to her, and could be finicky at times despite its comparative youthful-ness. "I wouldn't trust you out on the road with one of those vintage seventy-two ones you thought you were getting."

"What's the plan," Jordan asked sullenly over the loud hum of the road and wind, the top once again down so they could enjoy the breeze in their face.

When Ríona didn't answer, Jordan smacked her thigh, "Earth to Rí."

"Sorry...," she wasn't, but it felt like what she was expected to say; years of "girl conditioning" once again rearing its head.

"Well, what *is* your plan now that you've seen the van." Jordan kept looking towards her furtively between vaguely keeping her eyes on the straight road.

"I... I want to travel?" Why was she asking? She shook her head trying to eject those hounding questions.

"You mean like touring?"

"No... not touring. I guess I don't know how to explain it? It's just a feeling, you know? Something inside me is drawn to—"she fumbled for words, desperate to recall meanings and phrases, even idioms or anything—"something."

"Something? That's descriptive."

The two went silent for a few miles as they both mulled over what "something" could mean.

"Will you come back? When you're done, that is?"

Ríona turned her body in the seat, forcing herself to face her friend, the wind surging through the open window pulling at her hair fever-ishly, a low drum beat breaking through the silence. "To visit you, of course!" How could she not?

"Visit? I know your dream is to play music... and there's no future for that here," she swallowed a lump in her throat. A sliver of light bounced unsteadily between the large sunnies Jordan hid behind and her moistening eyes.

"Sunshine," she teased, testing out the new nickname she learned, silently hoping Jordan wouldn't notice its growth, "you know I love you. Deeply."

Jordan bit her lower lip, "I know—I'll miss you is all. I'm just being selfish, I guess. I want to keep you here with me." Jordan took her hand out from underneath her leg and grabbed Ríona's.

Her normally frigid hand felt nice, a soft gentle warmth the near opposite of Tomi's rugged hand. Jordan slid her hand underneath Ríona's, intertwining their fingers together. An electric current rode down Ríona's back, flutters filled her abdomen, her breath caught in her throat.

"And I love you too, Rí. I just don't want to lose you to some boy who knocks you up before leaving you, never speaking to you again."

"Trust me," Ríona laughed, "I'm not gonna shag some bloke and ruin my life like that."

Ríona watched Jordan's face, their hands still melding into one, like they used to do so often as young teens. Back when they would share beds on most weekends, alternating between whose parents would suffer the brunt of their endless antics and questions, begging all night for a later bedtime or more triple chocolate fudge ice cream.

In those days, no one thought much of the two girls holding hands while roaming the dying mall, half the storefronts long vacant since the rise of internet shopping's dominance. Mall security often shooing them along rather than allow the two to occupy floor space near the abandoned hallways.

Leaving home meant leaving Jordan. There would be a life for her here still, her family well off enough to survive the economic crush so many were suffering through. Regardless of how the world around them would change, Jordan had a place here, she had a path already planned out for her. She was happy staying.

In their first few weeks of college, they laid in bed one night discussing their after college plans, Jordan describing the idyllic family where she would have four or five children by the time she was thirty, a budding law career like her mother, likely at the same office where she currently worked as an aide, and her general sense of perpetual chip-perness.

No matter how many times Ríona was asked, even then she couldn't articulate an answer, an emptiness somewhere inside her sought comfort in the unknown. Ríona would entertain Jordan with stories that her mother once shared with her, of the Cliffs of Moher south of where she was born and how her mother and father used to go there to watch the sunset while her father improvised lullabies on his fiddle. On her fiddle.

No where in Nebraska would she ever see such a sight. Jordan, she didn't understand, seemed content with that. Always answering that she was happy wherever her family was. Deep down, Ríona knew what she really meant was she felt obligated to watch over her brother and keep him out of trouble.

As children, Jordan practically raised Zach as her own child. Both her parents investing their time on their law firm rather than investing it in their children. It wasn't until college did Jordan taste a hint of freedom, even if overshadowed by the fact her brother played in the same band as she did. Ríona often wondered if she only joined the band to watch over Zach.

As freshmen, the two of them would explore the college campus together and the neighbouring downtown. Walking the empty streets late into sunrise underneath buzzing sodium lights, their orange hue casting deep shadows over their faces as they shared hushed secrets. Over time those walks quietly ended.

"You know I've never kissed a boy, right?"

"How? You're eighteen! Pretty, petite, popular. I can't imagine a boy some-where hasn't fallen in love with the handsome Jordan McGraw."

"God, I hate my last name," she would whine. "I would much rather have yours. Jordan Kilbride. Has a much nicer ring to it, wouldn't you say," she softly pleaded only a hand's distance between their faces, the sheets underneath Ríona's body cool and sensual to the touch.

Jordan propped herself up on her elbows to hover over Ríona's nearly naked body, only the thin silk pyjamas protecting her goosebump laden skin from the heat radiating from Jordan's body, only a small tank top and cotton panties deco-rating her milky flesh.

Jordan's luscious lips touched hers, the lips Ríona jealously wished she had.

The touch of her lips intoxicated her. Much like Tomi's whiskey had the night before.

"I think I just need time to find myself," Ríona answered at last, Jordan's fingers slipping from her own as Siri issued a command to turn.

"You can't do that here?"

"I don't think I can."

After Jordan kissed her, for what felt like an eternity she wished would never end, she ran. It would be a week or more—they could never agree on how long it really was—before Ríona could look Jordan in the face again. She had gone back home, to her mother, and hid there until her mother forced her to go back to school, warning her that if she missed anymore classes they would fail her.

When she returned to their shared dorm room, Ríona was greeted by a notecard telling her a pint of triple chocolate fudge waited for her in the dorm room freezer.

"Hey, wanna go get ice cream," Ríona asked. "I don't want to go back to my flat just yet."

"Um," Jordan glanced at the clock display, "yeah." She turned to Ríona with a warm smile on her face, "it's been a while, hasn't it?"

CHAPTER 7

"*R*íona," Jordan cried her name over the phone, waking her from her groggy midday nap. "He's in the hospital."

Alarmed, she sat up quickly, desperate to gain her bearings. "He who?"

Her first instinct was to think of her own father, to panic that something tragic had happened to him. But as quickly as that traumatic worry appeared, it was shooed away by the more traumatic reminder why that was never a worry.

As soon as that rush passed, she knew who it was.

"My brother. He's in the hospital again. They found him last night."

She fought back letting out an exaggerated sigh. Right now it wasn't what Jordan needed to hear. Zach's been in the hospital before. This wasn't new, yet, something about Jordan's panic worried her. This wasn't her usual resignation that her brother's habits were causing him harm.

"Sunshine, where are you?"

"Work."

"Okay. Let me get ready and I'll be there as quick as I can. Ten minutes, promise."

CHAPTER 8

*B*oth of them rushed into the hospital, the automatic doors almost too slow in recognising their existence. Ríona fell back, allowing her friend to frantically squeeze her way through first.

Inside was frigid and dry, the benefits of a modernised hospital, along with the open brightly tiled rooms echoing loudly every sneaker squeak and dress shoe hard sole. In what felt like an awkwardly distant corner, they found the receptionist busy on the phone, who with a single finger warned them to hold. Jordan's patience long thinned out. She tapped her foot loudly and fidgeted with her phone, repeatedly checking for new messages that never arrived. She sent another, the swoosh sound verifying that the lack of response wasn't her own doing.

"Maybe they don't have signal up there," Ríona tried to reassure her friend, resting her hand on the small of Jordan's back.

"This is so frustrating. Why hasn't anyone texted me back?"

Behind the receptionist a scrolling billboard of hospital events ticked by, advertising weight loss programs, knee replacement surgeries, and counselling services. Occasionally it would list the purpose of each floor, a useful feature if it stayed on the screen long enough for them to read anything.

At last the receptionist hung up. Immediately Jordan burst with a flurry of questions, practically on the brink of violently demanding the hapless woman answer a litany of unknowable questions.

"He's up on the fifth floor, so you can't see him at the moment. They're in the process of transferring him still. You are welcomed to wait upstairs, if you are family that is."

"I'm his sister—we're his sisters," she corrected herself giving Ríona a half smile, a reminder that she wasn't forgotten.

"We don't accept *that* kind of 'family' 'round here. She can wait down here." The receptionist turned her attention from Jordan with her amber skin and sandy brown roots and gave Ríona a *look*. The kind of look she knew and understood deep down inside the core of her essence.

Ríona was lost for words. She wanted to speak, to offer some form of protest, an explanation, or even a denial, but only silence fell from her agape mouth. Fire burned in her cheeks, a mixture of emotions dominated by a profound sense of revelation she wanted to keep even from her diary.

"She's adopted. Just because she's not blood doesn't mean she's not family," Jordan lashed out without hesitation. It was as if she planned that excuse from the beginning and practiced it in her mirror before Ríona's pickup rolled to a stop on Jordan's dusty gravel driveway.

"Oh," this time it was the receptionist's leathery face littered with wrinkles and pronounced crows feet that burned hot with embarrassment. "My apologies. I thought—"

"What room is our brother in," Jordan again demanded, still frantically checking her phone furtively from the corner of her eyes, fingers tapping erratically on the glass-topped receptionist bar.

Wordlessly, the receptionist tapped the "must show ID" sign before turning to her computer, entering unseen commands before taking their IDs one at a time, sliding them back along with a nameless keycard and a room number adorning a bright yellow sticky note, the thin kind used to mark your place in a book rather than the large mass of papers framing the receptionist's monitor with indecipherable scribbles.

"Sisters, huh," Ríona teased as the elevator door closed, securing their ascension to Zach's floor. Much like the main lobby, the air tasted different, as if it was a highly processed knock-off store brand alternative to actual air. Hints of chemicals she couldn't begin to name let alone gander at what purposes they served swirled in the air.

Two floors up the rear doors opened, exposing a busy floor filled with nurses, doctors, families, machines, noises, and another influx on uncategorised scents. It smelled like the proverbial "old people smell" she'd heard used frequently amongst her peers but never truly understanding just what the smell encompassed. She could safely say she understood at last, ensuring that white card would carry this memory every time they played that game.

An orderly, or was it still 'nurse', rolled a man in on a wheelchair, his IV swinging gently. No one spoke a word again. The remaining two floors passed quickly, albeit awkwardly, until they all exited onto the same floor, both women gracious enough to let the patient exit first.

"Dad?" Jordan rushed forward to embrace the large man, his clothes wrinkled and hair no longer the well-groomed prize of a man long since recovered from male pattern baldness.

"Baby," he sweetly replied as he embraced his daughter, his head resting on top of her.

Pulling back from their hug, Jordan began to cry. "Daddy, what happened?"

"He's fine. The doctors say he was already stable before they transferred him here. We just have to wait for him to wake up." Mr McGraw turned his eyes towards Ríona, an odd mixture of disdain and approval in his dark brown eyes. "Thank you for bringing my daughter here. I'm sure it means a lot to her."

"When can we see him," Jordan pleaded.

"Doctor says another hour or two." In the meantime, Jordan quizzed her father. *Why hadn't he answered his phone? Where's mom? Where had Zach been? When did this all happen and why were they just now finding out?*

The last questions caught Ríona off guard. Over the years she had grown close not just to Jordan, but also Jordan's family. In particular, her mother who would often come by to check on her own sickly mother. In those final days, Jordan's mother was instrumental in arranging her mother's affairs.

"Are you sure you wouldn't rather be at the hospital," Delilah McGraw

asked her mother in hushed tones, believing that if she whispered softly enough that their morbid words wouldn't reach Ríona in the living room, headphones draped over her neck.

"This me home, Delilah. It is where I'll leave this world." Mrs McGraw sat with her mother until they said their final goodbyes.

So why hadn't she'd known Zach was missing? Jordan never called her, never mentioned it over lunch. Jordan's guilty looks told her the truth that she was hiding.

"Jordan, why didn't you tell me?"

Both McGraws went quiet, Jordan's father clenching his square jaw bitterly, vicious words teetering on the edge. "This isn't any of your concern," her father finally snapped.

"We've been trying to keep him missing a secret, Rí," Jordan walked over to her, grabbing both of her hands gingerly.

"Even from me?" She pulled her hands back, stuffing them into her shallow jean pockets. "Why me? Who would I tell?"

"Rí, it's not like that. This is..."

"This is a private family matter," her father finished for her.

"Sisters, huh?"

"Rí..."

"Just because Zach and I don't get along doesn't mean I don't care what happens to him. Sure, he's an ass most of the time—"

"Excuse me, you will *not* talk about my son that way."

"Honey," the tall, lean bleach blonde cooed as she strolled out of the nurse's office. "Zach's an asshole, we all know that. Especially towards the girls," she smiled at Ríona before enveloping her within her yoga toned arms.

"Well," Mr McGraw pleaded with his wife, an unspoken question lingering on his singular word.

"It's taken care of. Our Zach was the unfortunate passenger."

Their dad looked suddenly relieved. Creases that defined his rough face melted away. "I'm sorry, Ríona." He took a moment to collect himself, his chest collapsing. "I'm just worried about my son."

"Understandable, Mr McGraw. I am too. I just thought... you know, that I was *family*."

"Mr McGraw," a petite nurse beckoned, her plain blue cotton scrubs only slightly hinting at her curvy figure underneath. "You and your family can follow me."

The inside of Zach's room was cramped, leaving little room for all of them to squeeze their way in past the beeping equipment. The heart beat monitor increased in frequency slightly, a good sign the nurse told them. Although Zach wasn't awake, or conscious really, the nurse reassured them their voices would be good for Zach. But she warned them to keep their voices low and to keep it brief.

"Thank you, Maddie," Mrs McGraw sweetly thanked the young nurse. "Tell your mother I said hi."

"I will, ma'am," Maddie replied with a small curtsey then faded into the hustle of the ICU wing.

While Jordan's parents hovered over Zach offering him a litany of prayers, Ríona pulled her to the corner of the room. She didn't even need to ask, the look on her face did.

"He never came home last weekend." She paused, seemingly hoping that would satisfy Ríona's curiosity. "I don't think he missed our gig on purpose."

"What do you think happened to him then?" Zach had always been like that though. Disappearing for a few days at a time before reemerging, his family in an angry tizzy over his absence but soon forgetting about it like some unspoken open secret.

"Rí..."

"Jordan, what is it?"

"You know the rumours."

Of course she did. She was too close to the family to not have heard the multitudes of supposed drugs Zach was into. In a way, she expected some of them to be true, in particular his frequent use of alcohol and marijuana. But that wasn't peculiarly remarkable amongst their age group. Most of the time, she felt as if she was the only one who hadn't smoked.

"They're not even half of it. His, um, habits have gotten worse over the years. I've tried keeping him out of trouble and I thought he was just being his moody self Friday ditching us like that."

"There is definitely a 'but' in there."

"But instead his other friends introduced him to... other things."

"That doesn't explain—." It did, though. Jordan didn't need to at this point.

"He was in a car accident sometime between last night and this morning. A patrol officer found him and his 'friend' in a ditch. They had been there for hours. They took him to the nearest hospital but since Zach didn't have anything on him, they listed him as a John Doe. Wasn't until mom started calling around did we find out."

"Oh God, Sunshine..."

Ríona grabbed Jordan and held her tightly. Jordan slipped her hands around Ríona's straight but narrow waist, her face nuzzled into the crook of Ríona's soft neck. Is that what her mother meant...

What else didn't she know about her friend, or this town?

"Can you two not do that," Mr McGraw barked. "It makes you look gay."

"Honey, they're girls. That's what they do."

"I don't care. This is bad enough," he motioned towards Zach's motionless body, "but I don't need her also ruining my chances."

Ríona felt distant at that moment, as if she had been circling their lives from afar rather than sharing meals at their dinner table, or forced to attend Sunday church services with them every time she spent the weekend.

"My dad decided to run for mayor," Jordan explained quietly, another family secret she was late learning.

Her family never held any secrets. Not that they could, at this point. Her only secret her mother pried into with hawk eyes before she knew. Since then, there wasn't a single facet of her life she could keep secret from her mother, even that growing hunger for something bigger than a slow rural town.

"Oh, sweetie," Mrs McGraw gently floated over, "don't worry about your performances. I'm sure the boys will understand both of you needing to take a few weeks off."

"Seriously mom?"

"Yes, baby girl. I'll speak to your professors. I'll get you a week off so you can focus on helping your family deal with this." She rested her hand on Ríona's shoulder, lovingly massaging her tenseness away. "We'll also continue to paying your show fee."

"Mom! Stop, please." Jordan took a panicked turn, pushing her mother away. "We get it."

CHAPTER 9

STILL ON FOR THIS WEEKEND, Tomi texted her.

OF COURSE! I CAN'T WAIT TO DRIVE HER. After Tuesday's mayhem, and Wednesday's and Thursday's marathon post-break class schedule, she had forgotten about Roan, and the tall, muscular woman who plied her with one too many whiskey sours.

MY COUSIN BRINGING YOU AGAIN?

HAVE YOU HEARD?

HEARD WHAT? She could almost hear the confusion in her text, and imagined her rolling her eyes in disdain at her relative's antics.

ZACH WAS IN A BAD ACCIDENT. THEY MOVED HIM TO OBSERVATION YESTERDAY.

OH GOD. WHAT HAPPENED?

I'LL FILL YOU IN WHEN I GET THERE TONIGHT.

TONIGHT?

She forgot Tomi didn't know, or at least, somehow expected her family to fill her in on her cousin's condition. Without Jordan, or her Friday night performance, there was nothing keeping her from driving down.

IF THAT'S ALRIGHT WITH YOU.

OF COURSE IT IS.

SHOULD I EAT FIRST? Ríona texted back, adding a pizza and whiskey emoji for effect.

IS THAT YOUR CUTE WAY OF ASKING ME TO TAKE YOU ON A DATE?

She blushed. NO...

YOU'RE CUTE, TINY. WAIT TO EAT HERE.

WHEN?

I GET HOME BETWEEN 6 AND 7. I NEED TO SHOWER FIRST... UNLESS YOU WANNA JOIN ME??

YOU'RE TERRIBLE!

GIRL CAN TRY LOL

I'LL SEE YOU AT 7, she added a kiss emoji, although she couldn't tell herself why. It brought a smile to her face and left a flutter in her heart.

Checking the time, she was disappointed by the quick math. Her usual spot at campus was its typical busy self, a constant flow of students and staff rushing between classes. Ever since she moved back home two years ago, this spot became their routine, her always waiting patiently for Jordan to escape from her boring law classes before they head towards the pubs.

It felt odd being alone, but not lonely. She had expected an emptiness without her routine, the predictable events that gave her something to look forward to during the week. Perhaps it was the butterflies of what the weekend would bring, or even the flirty texts Tomi was sending, but it felt... okay.

Not wanting to wait around campus for another couple of hours, she made her way towards Moon. Her truck idled heavily underneath her, the heater refusing to provide much heat at the moment, making her grateful for now that warm weather was returning.

In front of her, the cars came to a slow stop a distance from the light. A pair of people her age hopped out the back, crossing the street with their instrument cases slung over their back. Unlike the locals, the girl's cutoff shorts and bohemian tunic adorned with turquoise stones caught her attention. Not for the elfish figure underneath, but their sheer oddity.

Her male companion sported a jet black mohawk and leather studded jacket overtop jeans that were tighter than any she had ever worn. Like the woman, he wore black leather combat boots, their distinctive yellow thread around the sole. Hers shone with fresh polish while his could benefit from desperate repair.

They both entered an abandoned building where a handful of other *uniquely* dressed people her age idled about on the wide sidewalk, some curled up against the red brick wall, keeping a steady beat on their lap drums while a woman strummed her guitar to his beat.

"What the...," she muttered to herself, the horn behind her startling her into hitting the gas pedal with a rough start. Without much thought, she flicked her blinker on and turned onto a side street. Before the dinner rush, most side streets were easy parking.

Tossing the truck into park, she grabbed her fiddle case and backpack, not wanting to chance the side street's other reputation.

"You one of the players," a young man asked walking up behind her, sending her heart racing. Instinctively, she gripped the keys between her knuckles.

"Woah! Sorry, didn't mean to scare you."

"What did you expect?" She relaxed a little, the stranger taking a wide step back.

"Fair." He dropped his raised arms, a silly show of innocence.

"What players?"

"Oh... sorry, I thought you were one of the players. So many have been calling me lost. They keep ending up on K street."

"K street? But that's a few blocks over."

"Right?"

"So what is going on? I saw some people hanging around and got curious."

"I'm Yi, by the way," he held out his hand, a mixture of nervous and awkward in his weak grip.

"I'm Ríona."

"Ha! So I'm not the only one in this city with a weird name. Not that... you know."

"That my name is weird? Thanks. Maybe I should change it to Becky or Karen?"

"Oh please, I doubt you could pass for a Karen. Not unless you called the cops on me."

She laughed. Although she vaguely kept up with social trends, some were just too well known to miss.

"I do have a phone. I have time."

He stared at her, calling her bluff. It didn't take long before he burst into smiles, announcing she was the victor this time.

"What do you play," he asked, motioning for her to follow.

"Fiddle."

"Ah. Ashamed to call yourself a violinist."

"What? No! It's totally different."

"But it's a violin."

"You really want me to become a Karen, don't you? 'Hello, officer, some crazy rich Asian is calling me fiddle a violin!'"

"Hmmm, perhaps I underestimated your average white girlness. Are you hiding a pumpkin spice latte in that case as well?"

"Gross dude. It's all about the white chocolate mocha."

Yi escorted her to the front of the abandoned building, an old factory building once filled with sprawling early century technology, now just an empty shell of a long-gone discount department store. Yi greeted the street musicians and burrowed further into the cavernous space.

Inside sat several long tables covered in random fabrics from burlap to the sheets stolen from grandma's attic. Off to the side a makeshift dance floor and stage had been rudimentarily built, a handful of spotlights haphazardly illuminating the stand-ins.

"This is a 'pop-up'," he said, opening his arms wide like a conductor pulling together a crescendo.

"And that's not some pervy pick up line?"

"What? No! It's an unofficial official event that people throw together without any official sanction or cause. People bring food, or music, or money. We put a sign out front inviting the public in, they donate if they can, and in the end we give the money to the local homeless shelters."

"What do you get out of it?"

"Nada. That's why it's wonderful."

"And stressful," a girl chimed in with a surprise hug, Yi happily lifting her off the ground with a quick twirl.

"Hey girl! Been too long," Yi eyed up, taking in her still youthful appearance but clear signs of mature adulthood. "You've grown."

46

"I'm finally getting boobs."

"I can see that. Must be exciting."

"Dude, you have no idea. No more flat-chested Mary." Mary turned to Ríona, "is that a fiddle."

"Why yes, it is indeed a *fiddle*," she jokingly hissed in Yi's direction.

"Oh, don't mind our boy here. He wouldn't know a trumpet from a bassoon."

"I know what a trumpet is thankyouverymuch."

Ríona paid little attention to Yi. Mary absorbed all her attention at the moment. Her blue eyes a match for her own, her flawless skin with hints of masculine touches hid behind awkward dyed black bangs, the light sandy hair showing through at the roots.

This girl sat somewhere between Jordan's perpetually youthful, childlike beauty and Tomi's serious, mature definition. When she spoke, a dark sultry voice oozed out with a seductive timbre, lingering somewhere in the word of androgyny.

"Why don't you play something for us," Yi asked. "On your *fiddle*."

"I... uh. I only brought it because I don't trust it alone in me truck."

"Oh, please, I'd love to hear you play. No one here plays fiddle. It's all emo acoustic 'I hate the world and the world hates me' around these guys."

"I... I guess."

Mary introduced her to the circle of musicians sitting on the floor around their instrument cases, most as Mary joked were guitar players and drummers. Mary was the only one with neither. From the size of the case, it looked to be a clarinet or possibly an oboe. Both capable of beautiful music, whether solo or in a quartet. Which she mentally noted, often involves a violinist.

Quietly she pulled out her father's fiddle and bow while the group set aside their own instruments as if they were readying themselves for an official Ríona Kilbride concerto. Embarrassed by the thought, not for having it, but for enjoying it so lovingly, she put the fiddle in the nook of her neck and begun playing.

First she started them off slow with well-known passages of Bach and Beethoven, easy staples most any layperson remotely familiar with classical music would know. She knew Mary and Yi wanted to hear something more passionate, something that earned the title of a fiddle player with the slight Galway accent.

But she wanted them to taste the full range of her instrument, and her talents. Like the guitars that lined the hipster and grunge crowd, the fiddle could dance with any style, and transition between them quickly.

Sensing the first sign of boredom, she drew out one last long note, giving it just a hint of vibrato before jumping into a livelier Irish jig called "Blaydon Races", while it sounded better with a walking bass line behind it, it was still a popular enough solo tune to get wake up a throng of pub goers.

At the switch Mary took the lead to start clapping and stomping in time. Mary's enthusiasm brought a smile to her face. Many of the others played along clapping in beat, bored expressions slowly turning to appreciative smiles.

Mary jumped up, almost causing Ríona to scratch her bow. She turned to the girl who had been sitting next to her, pulled her to her feet and started twirling the giggling girl. Seeing the cue, Ríona switched to a dance jig called "Blackthorn Stick."

Both girls hopped and danced their worst impression of claddagh dancers that they could. They weren't the finest dancers she'd seen, but the joy lighting up their eyes made it worth it. This was the joy she missed.

"Pa, play another," Ríona would hound her father, her pastel skirts like dervish dancers.

"Okay, but on' one. Then it's off to bed with ye."

She was also a terrible dancer, stumbling over her feet as if they were tied together, but also bouncing off the ground in a fit of laughter. Her father dancing around her, his bow string a burning fire of sound, hopping from one steel wound string to another, his notes sharp and precise, his mind elsewhere as his daughter lost herself.

"Oi, 'ou two. Rí, off ye pop now. Teeth then sleep."

As quickly as the two girls swirled energetically around each other, they relaxed to catch their breath, chests heaving from the sudden exertion.

For fun, and perhaps to get a rise out of the more stoic metal boys, she switched to "Whiskey in the Jar." Yi yelped in excitement at recognising the tune while the metal boys gave her a smirk of approval. One grabbed his guitar and started playing rhythm, his mate grabbing his lap drum off the floor.

Slowly a crowd formed around them, Mary's friend taking up singing the familiar tune, her voice a sweet alto with plenty of vibrato. For the next two minutes the world around her melted away, no longer in the middle of wheat fields or the empty house on the hill. Right now she could be anywhere in the world, chatting with strangers in G-Major.

As they collectively played the last note, the definitive end to her impromptu performance, clapping erupting peppered with whistles and whoops of praise.

Mary rushed over, still sucking down air in large gulps, "you just have to play with us tonight." A few affirmations from the crowd followed, including the metal boys who quietly set their instruments aside.

Mary's dancing partner joined her, her hand slipping between the pair and grasping Mary's. "I'm Renee, Mary's girlfriend."

"Oh, um, I'm Ríona."

Girlfriend... She couldn't help but take a peek at their hands, a butterfly of embarrassment fluttering in her stomach. A phantom warmth spreading where Jordan had grabbed hers this past weekend.

"Well," Renee inquired with a hint of jealousy.

"Oh I'd love to..."

"But you can't. So much sad face."

Ríona couldn't judge if she was being sarcastic, or if that was Renee's normal demeanour.

Mary elbowed her, "be nice."

"What?"

Mary rolled her eyes, "you can't make an exception for us?"

"I'm going down to Wichita."

"She better be cute," Yi joked, "otherwise she's not worth it."

"She is," Ríona blushed. She didn't know why she felt comfortable admitting that to these absolute strangers she only met an hour ago on chance. Words like that stayed secret around here, never daring to pass from her lips or even from her pen to diary. Instead, she bottled them up and let it explode in her passionate playing.

49

Yi wrapped his arm around her shoulder, "do tell."

"Um... what do you want to know?"

"How long have you two been dating?"

"Dating! Oh no, nothing like that," her cheeks continued to tattle on her, "I only met her last weekend."

"So you're on the uHaul date," Renee teased, her demeanour much more amicable.

"The what?"

Mary lit up, "I think we have a baby dyke on our hands. This is exciting!"

"No no, she's just helping me convert a van."

Yi pulled away, but kept his arm around her, "a van? Like, to travel?"

"Yeah... actually."

"You're already leaving us, how sad."

"Yi," Mary chastised, "you can't have her. I saw her first."

"What? No you didn't! I'm the one who found her wandering around the street like a lost kitten."

"What are you planning to do," Renee asked with genuine curiosity.

She shrugged. Honestly, she still hadn't thought that far. It was still too sudden for her to process.

"You should head out to Cali. Big Sur is the bomb this time of year. Killer surfing, the mountains, and the to-die-for music scene. Huge pick-up scene that would murder for someone like you. Hey babe, phone."

Mary handed her girlfriend her phone who then breezed through pulling up various photos of the coastline, ocean slamming violently against jutting pillars of rock, another that she recognised as the Santa Monica Pier. Flipping through, there we dozens of photos of the two girls kissing in front of the Golden Gate Bridge, or making silly faces with groups of lavishly dressed drag queens. More still of just random life— pubs, decorative park benches, beautifully designed graffiti, skateboard-ers, and so many odd foods. One, she stopped to drool over was called poke, some Hawaiian dish quickly becoming the go to fad.

"And the gay bars," Yi added. "So many gay bars."

"You?" Ríona looked at him with a surprised look on her face.

"Me? No. I'm boring. I just go for the free drinks guys buy me. What bear could resist a twink like me?"

CHAPTER 10

*E*xcitement still buzzed in her ears, the tinnitus accompanying a hard earned performance. It tingled through her body; the rough ride of her Ford keeping her cloud nine grounded in reality. Her stereo hummed along softly, the playlist feeding her hunger with more Irish jigs— the perfect soundtrack for a wandering mind tainted by a lustful soul.

At her speed, if traffic held out and the threat of rain tonight waited its turn, she'd be to Tomi's by seven. Perhaps a little earlier, but she could always busy herself with reading. She still had a few hundred pages left of the latest novel she picked up from one of the coffee shops. A local mystery novel with that small town charm and gunslinger ghost hunters. It was cheesy, poorly written, and clearly in desperate need of an editor, but it brought her joy. When she was done with it, it would find its way to another store where she'd leave it to fate to locate a new home.

"California, huh," she whispered to herself, a comforting discussion where all parties always agreed.

"Hurry up child," her mother sighed from her doorway. "You needn't pack a whole house in 'ere."

That was the last trip they had taken together. Prior to that they had made "local" vacations, always staying close enough to the property should anything happen. Outside of planting and harvesting, the farm stayed relatively mild but always in constant need of attention. The cows needed milked, the chickens fed and eggs harvested, tractors needed oil, and a fence always needed mending. If you left a fence alone for a day, the entire thing would disappear into a void of entropy.

Neighbours would volunteer, since they had no kin other than each other. But their good nature would only last a handful of days at best, never long enough to take a month's holiday back home like they had before her grandparents passed.

"California," her mother told her. "I's not far. A night and a day of driving. I'll pick you up from school."

All day she couldn't keep her excitement contained, much to the annoyance of her teachers and classmates. Jordan was of course sad she couldn't join them. Her family had their own holiday plans up in Banff and a town named Whistler. Jordan couldn't stop daydreaming about the Fairmont Chateau and how wonderful it would be to fall in love in such a romantic place. Ríona only rolled her eyes at her enthusiasm.

As promised, her mother sat idling the truck in the excruciatingly long pickup line as most other families planned the same summer escape they had. Pick up their child and make a break to chase the sun as it set over the horizon.

They had no intention of driving the twenty hours straight through, despite Ríona offering her assistance. Her mother assuring her she was fine to drive. They would stop over in Sterling along the South Platte River. They had reservations booked at a cheap motel, three stars on a good day her mother joked. She assumed that meant bad or average, but clean enough to survive the night.

When they arrived, the sun grazed the tops of the distant mountain ranges still hidden behind the curved earth and hazy ozone. Their motel was certainly worth the stars it received. It's glowing back-lit sign sat broken and sun-bleached. The building was in desperate need of a pressure washing, and a few shutters groaned against rusty bolts as they joined the lonely breeze coming over the water. Dirt and algae grew in spires where the rain gutters leaked. From the looks of it, even the algae was browning under the drought conditions threatening the small farm town of just under fifteen thousand, according to the "Welcome to the Town of Sterling, Colorado" greeting them as they pulled off 76.

Inside the night desk greeted them with a loud, "howdy y'all". He made small talk with her mother, asking all about their trip, their plans, what they do *for a living... so many personal questions it made her uneasy, but her mother answered them with vague pleasantries.*

Her bed was stiff with an odd odour, a weird staleness she couldn't describe other than wrinkling her nose in disgust. Her mother laughed at her, telling her she better appreciate the last night in a proper bed. "Af'er tonight, we'll be sleeping on the ground."

"Yeah... I know. At least the ground won't smell. And we'll be near water-falls and mountains."

Redirecting her thoughts, her mum excitedly pointed towards the wall. "Hey look, they have a window seat. You've always wanted one of those. And it over-looks the river."

Her remaining waking hours were spent there, watching the highway fade into the distance towards the ever darkening horizon, copper streaks turning into a faded glow then an inky black stillness perforated by billions of tiny lights. If it wasn't for the lingering glow of Sterling, she could enjoy the view of the Milky Way stretching from one end of the heavens to the other.

Despite losing herself in her novel, she woke up in her bed, firmly tucked away from the chill permeating the thin window. Her mother already finished her morning shower, her thin grey hair still dripping on the floor, a pillow of steam billowing out of the freshly opened bathroom door.

"Yer turn, lassy. If ye hurry, we can still catch breakfast."

The diner was tucked away in a small open plaza, two glass doors begrudg-ingly greeting them, a flag waving on the top like a cake topper. It felt like she had stepped back in time to another era. Faux wood panelling on the half wall between the kitchen and dining room, chairs with red pleather cushions, and horribly laminated menus showcasing the usual fare mixed with the "trendy" foods such as chicken and waffles.

Everywhere tiny ads tucked themselves neatly into your view, business cards tacked on top of business cards on the "community board" everyone but those tacking business cards wilfully ignored. Even the coffee mugs couldn't help be contaminated by the same litany of ads.

Judging by the older demographics, the diner was high-end when they were first old enough to drive their beat-up-hand-me-down trucks, now replaced by gigantic shiny behemoths sprawling across multiple parking spaces.

Some still wore their baseball caps, a mixture of camo and sporting teams, while more "polite" gentlemen, likely the parents of the baseball cap generation, sat their wide brim tan hats at the edge of the table.

"Howdy," an older, plump woman greeted them as they took their seats, emerging from the thin stagnant air, a hint of grease and cheap smoke following.

"'ello," her mother greeted back, forgetting to tone down her brogue.

"You musn't be from 'round here, huh," she asked with a smug look on her face like a modern day crime detective.

"Nebraska."

Her mother's matter-of-fact answer knocked the woman off tempo. "Ah, you sounded Scottish."

"Nah, we're a wee bit more civilised than 'em."

"We're Irish," Ríona corrected with a proud smirk.

"My family is Irish."

"Oh, when'dae come o'er?"

"I'm fourth generation."

"I'll have the two eggs and salted ham," her mother ended the discussion, annoyed. "Eggs hard fried. White toast."

"Coffee?"

"Please."

"And you lil' miss?"

"Scrambled eggs and English muffin, side of hash browns and coffee as well."

"Aren't ya a little young for that, sweetie?" She stuck the tip of her pen in her mouth, leaving another tooth mark in the cap.

"No, I'm too young for Irish coffee."

With a huff, "what meat would'ya like?"

"No meat."

"It comes with it."

"Just give me fruit or something. I don't eat meat."

"A'ight. Let me go grab that coffee. Creamer?"

Absentmindedly, her mother replied, "double cream if you have it." She never looked up from her phone, or she would have seen the puzzled expression on the server's face.

"You call it heavy cream here."

"Oh, well, we have that. Sugar too?"

"Mum doesn't take sugar, but I'll take whatever fake sugar you have."

Her mother's face soured, a displeased turn on her lips.

"What's that look for," Ríona asked, suddenly concerned. Her mother was never one for playing on her phone, let alone losing herself so intensely.

"Huh? Oh. Sorry baby girl, nothin'. Just'a lookin' at weather forecasts."

Her mother had lied to her, a rarity between them. Of course it would be years before she knew the truth behind those secretive eyes. That year did prove to be painfully dry, the forecasts a worrisome facet of farm life.

But what her mother hadn't told her, not until the day the hospital called her to inform her that her mother had been rushed to the E.R., was that on her phone was the X-ray results that foretold how many years she had remaining. Not until she died in her bed, but until she could be of any use around the farm.

Or on a holiday. Her mother's friends pushed her to take this holiday, Mrs McGraw offering to pay for the entire trip, while others took turns offering to watch over the farm. But that would be the last holiday her mother's body could endure; an almost whirlwind trip. Their first few nights would be spent in Estes Park, Colorado before making their way to Joshua Tree.

A beautiful mountain top town on the edge of a large crystal clear lake, a bicycle path circling close to the water's edge. More often than not they had to wait for the elk to clear off the path, their enormous bodies standing at least twice her height. While they seemed friendly enough, they had been warned by many locals to stay clear of them. Especially during the seasonal Elk Jam. Named not for any music festival, but the sheer number of elk that brought the roads to a standstill, backing up traffic for hours every September or October.

She would love to revisit those places that her mother took her to that trip. Only, perhaps, spend more than a day or two at each place. It was exciting, she would never deny that, and she would cherish those two weeks until the day she died, but it left her hungry for more.

You ALMOST HERE? Tomi's text lit up her phone sitting on the dash, propped up by the suction cup phone cradle.

Using the voice to text feature, she did her best to reply. Siri managed to only butcher a handful of words, but enough survived that Tomi should be able to decipher her intent.

SWEET.

"Who says 'sweet' still?"

JUST GOT OUT OF THE SHOWER. HUNGRY?

CHAPTER 11

$\mathcal{P}$ ulling onto the dark dirt road, her foggy headlights weakly lit the way. With no more oncoming traffic, she flicked her brights on, dimly showing her the full length of road before her riddled with washboards. Her truck's loose suspension bounced like a listless ship in a rough sea over the tiny ripples of dirt, the torment left over by others driving way too fast on these rural utility roads.

After what felt an unusually long time, much longer than the first time she came here as a passenger during the day, Tomi's porch lights came into view through the trees lining the edge of her property.

COME ON IN, Tomi texted before she could put the truck into park in the empty gravel driveway.

Ríona grabbed her backpack and fiddle, absentmindedly hit the lock button on the doors, and walked up the creaky steps. At the door she hesitated, weirded out by the thought of just walking into a stranger's house unaccompanied. The McGraw's house was one thing, having spent most of her early teenage years running in and out of their door, but Tomi's, although related, was an another world entirely.

She was an adult now, much too old for the primary school antic excuses afforded a twiggy twelve-year-old desperate for validation. Hesitantly she twisted the doorknob, the wood and glass door creaking open, the next best thing to an annoying door chime hanging over the small country store doors.

"Heya, be out in a second," Tomi's sultry voice called out from the bedroom, hints of shampoo and steam lingering.

Unsure what to do, or where to wait, she eyed the couch for a moment before deciding to set her things down on the kitchen table, the scent of Pine-Sol still powerfully present. As she made herself comfortable, she noticed a few other small details were tidied up since her visit the weekend prior.

"There," Tomi announced with a rushed flourish. "I picked out this wonderful barbecue place in Wichita. It's literally nothing but meat."

Ríona stared at her blankly, unsure if the woman was teasing, or an arse. Tomi gave no clues, merely searching for her wallet and keys on the little table next to the door.

"You locked your truck, right?"

"Yeah...," she replied suspiciously, silently watching her for clues.

"Not really worried around here, especially with the sheriff living a few miles up the road. No one really wanders around here with ill-intent. Why are you staring at me like that?"

At last Tomi's face betrayed her with a hint of mischief.

"You really are too easy."

"Hey now! I thought you might be serious," she whined, sinking into the soft couch that she offered to sleep on before Jordan told her they'd share the bed in the spare room.

"Don't worry, hun, I noticed you and Jordan trading food."

Ríona threw a throw pillow at her.

"Did you just throw a throw pillow at me," Tomi said slowly, emphasising the word "throw" as painfully as possible.

"For that I should throw the table at you."

"I like it when they fight back."

Ríona went quiet and sank back into the couch, completely at a loss how to respond. Tomi, sensing her uneasy frustration, walked over to her; a tower of lean, muscular feminine prowess—freshly cleaned. Her woodsy scent mingling with perfumed soap and a hint of cinnamon spice cologne.

Her aroma immediately intoxicated her, tingles of attraction that would pass and fade every now and then staunchly heightened, as if the tall dirty blonde held some electromagnetism over her untouched libido.

"Come," Tomi commanded firmly, hands held out for hers.

"Ma'am, yes ma'am," she teased before Tomi lifted her easily, standing her dangerously close, that spicy scent an increasingly potent danger.

Normally she'd shy aware from these feelings, pulling herself further into a lonely abyss safeguarded by her mother's carefree embraces. Normally... there was no normal anymore. All she could manage was a painful bite on the inside of her lower lip, a small prick to dull the arousal in her chest.

"So where are you really taking me?"

"It wouldn't be any fun if I just straight up told ya."

Inside the garage, the one she had only seen vaguely on her last visit before being ushered into Tomi's much larger shop, the lights flickered on with the loud clack she imagined military bases all sounded like when someone walked in. Only, all the lights turned on at once, a rather anti-climatic reveal of the canary yellow Mustang Fastback, two bold black stripes racing down the centre front to back.

"She's a beaut isn't she?"

"Well?"

"Well what?"

"You made me name Roan. I assume you've named your pretty little car here."

"First off, she's not pretty. She's killed women for less. Second... her name is Mariam."

"Was not expecting that," she gave Tomi an odd look, surprised by the rather mundane name. She had expected something like Bumble Bee, or She-Hulk, or a name befitting a mean looking puppy that's best known for their sloppy kisses and hiding from bad electrical storms.

"She's a fighter pilot." She paused, shoving aside a past she wasn't ready to share with a girl she'd just met. "She's a badass. Shall we?"

"Yes, we shall indeed," Ríona giggled before being escorted to the passenger side. Tomi opened the door for her, an unexpected gesture she'd only received from some of the guys in town who often fought over who was more of a "gentleman" yet always expected gratitude or more in return. Tomi didn't seem to want either, instead she seemed pleased by Ríona's surprise, her smile its own reward.

"Buckle up. She's not the smoothest ride."

With a thunderous roar, Mariam came to life, her purr amplified by the steel building. Underneath, the gravel moaned as the meaty tyres rolled over, their tread better suited for mud and rough terrain than the slick city streets of drag racers.

Once they pulled out of her driveway, Tomi let out a mischievous grin. A Cheshire Cat with a treat too good not to share. A rocket ignited behind her, slamming her body against the black leather bucket seat as it tried to race past her, annoyed that the hundred-something pound woman was still there.

Unlike her truck, the Mustang sported a series of round racing lights that brilliantly illuminated the length of the moonlit dirt road, dust wafting through like London fog. Beside her the fence posts darted by in a frantic blur, a scary reminder that caused her hands to instinctively dig into the armrest, the lump in her stomach threatening to drown her lungs in panic.

Suddenly her body lurched forward mimicking the whole muscle car, a playful laugh on Tomi's grin as she slammed the shifter into second gear then took off again, the clutch catching instantly unlike her poor attempts. Again her body slammed into the seat as it embraced her, holding tighter as the world buzzed past her, a rocket of adrenaline coursing through her pounding heart.

"That explains the washboards," she joked to herself, her mouth unable to overcome the roar of more horsepower than she could comprehend.

Then Tomi stopped, nearly sliding as the reflective red stop sign came into rapid view. As Mariam purred, panting with excitement, Tomi turned to her with a sideways smirk.

"She's pretty badass, right?"

"Terrifying, yes. I felt like I was going to die. I still think I did."

"Oh, it gets better."

"I hope not. All I want is some food. A nice little meal free of me turning into a pancake every time you hit the gas pedal."

"Well, good news: you won't have to wait very long."

"Oh god... Tomi..."

She braced herself, ready for Tomi to launch them down the black abyss of lonely bitumen. Perhaps the smooth tarmac would prove gentler on her nerves. After all, she did close to the eighty-five speed limit in her F-150 and that didn't scare her. Jordan scared her, but her cousin...

Tomi turned onto the road slowly, checking constantly for any distant lights coming over the long rolling hills cresting on either end of the road miles away. Mariam came to a slow stop, purring hungrily.

"You ready?"

"No... but I have a feeling you don't care."

"Eh, I don't. But I'm a gentlewoman, so I had to ask."

Tomi revved the engine, loud pressure waves galloping around her delicate ears, the distinctive sound she knew meant there was an incredible amount of power hiding underneath the bonnet. Yet something felt different about the sound, something that told her this was uniquely vintage, a relic of a time prior to other one of them being born, the raspy yet throaty sound a staple during the vintage car shows popular in Lincoln and Omaha.

As if answering her unspoken question, "this is why I love her. You don't get this with modern cars. They may be better is so many other ways. Better reliability. Better fuel economy. Safer... but they lack that experience.

"And I get to pop that cherry for you."

Ríona could only glare at the rugged woman, her wicked smile luring her in.

"You might want to lean back."

As commanded, Ríona leaned back, relaxing as much as she nervously could against the cool leather.

Mariam exploded in a exhilarating blur of speed. The yellow and white stripes the only consistency Ríona could focus on as the world disappeared, the sky a bleak blank canvas of twinkles kept safely from view by the g-forces slamming her body. With a furtive glance, she watched the illuminated speedometer needle bolt from zero to twenty to thirty to fifty to seventy only to slowly even out at eighty as her body turned weightless, the velocity evening out as Tomi oddly respected the Kansas rural highway speed limit, if ever so barely.

Inside the canary yellow rocket the engine still roared, or as she was told later, it was the turbo charger bulging from the bonnet that deafened her. Tomi's pride and joy modification, turning her father's classic "lady killer" into her personal nightmare machine.

For a few moments they were no longer on the ground, speeding along solidified petroleum and aggregate, but in the cockpit of an F-16 Fighting Falcon, much the same as the real Mariam would fly years after Tomi turned her wings in for civilian life.

Music was her escape, the bow and fiddle the last refuge of her sanity when the world around her no longer made sense. This was Tomi's. The speed, the danger, the rush.

The control.

Once their speed evened out, maintaining a new perfect "just under", Ríona could melt, letting her worries dissipate into Tomi's capable control. Much how Tomi enjoyed the control Mariam brought her, Ríona was consenting hers away.

"*Giorraíonn beirt bóthar,*" Ríona mused aloud, a soft wish towards her companion.

"What does that mean?"

"It's just something me ma would say every time we started a new adventure. Always when we've gotten into the truck and turned onto the road, heading to some destination she wanted to surprise me with."

"Ah. It's like a good luck wish then?"

"Something of the sort. Mum first taught me it when we landed in Wichita of all places. We had just met my father's parents at the airport. They loaded our lightly packed suitcases into the back of their SUV—I was crying my little eyes out. Me mum bent down, kissed me on the forehead and told me, '*giorraíon beirt bóthar mo cailin*'."

"How old were you?"

"When we finally made it to the states, I was only nine. We had moved around for a couple of years, from one family member to the next before my grandparents offered us their farm. And now here I am."

Two people shorten a road, her mother explained. They had each other, no matter what, no matter where they were. Their journey would be easy so long as they were together.

Only now they would never be together again. Her grandparents passed a few years after they arrived. Later she found out that's why they agreed to give them the farm, not just guilt over what happened to their eldest son and how her mother's family eventually abandoned them, but because they feared losing the farm.

Her mother feared the farm would cause Ríona to lose who she was and agreed to sell the farm without telling Ríona she had already signed it away upon her death.

They passed the "Welcome to Wichita" sign, a city not terribly far away but one she seldom visited. As the traffic thickened, Tomi slowed Mariam down, downshifting with an ease that left Ríona amazed and jealous.

"Something for every vegetarian in your life," Tomi announced as the engine bitterly turned off.

"I'm the only one you know, aren't I?"

"Eh. You think you're special, don't you?"

"I'm told I'm 'cute' at least," she shrugged. "Perhaps it's gone to my head."

"Ugh. You are, but that's not fair."

They had a short walk before standing in the middle of a nicely redesigned plaza, the efforts of a massive city revitalisation to attract more of the tech crowd that has been filling the city over the past two decades.

"Latin food, huh," Ríona gave Tomi a suspicious look.

"They have food you can eat, I promise. And it's a nice night so we can sit on the patio."

The hostess quickly seated them, warning them that their server would be a minute as they were short staffed.

"It's okay," Ríona assured.

"If you could let Michael know I'm here, I'd appreciate it."

"Sure, if I can find him, that is."

"Either you're popular or you can't cook," Ríona deadpanned.

"You're full of all sorts of challenges, aren't you?. And I can cook... mostly meat. I don't do veggies."

"Why am I not surprised, huh?"

"Tomi," a Mexican accent called out suddenly. "Leah told me you were here, but she didn't tell me you came with a date. I thought you were on sabbatical since you and Jessica split?"

"We're not," Tomi corrected him. "She's my cousin's friend. I'm helping her with a project."

"Uh huh," he winked at her, setting down the largest Sangria Ríona had ever seen.

"Seriously, Mike, she's just a friend."

Michael turned to her, asking her with his eyes, "I'm innocent in all this."

After dinner, which Tomi paid for despite Ríona's protest, Tomi grabbed her hand and started directing her off the patio and onto the streets, assuring her the next stop will be "loads of fun". Although, "my friends can be a pain," she warned.

It was a short drive through the suburbs. The bedroom communities where those too afraid of city life lived in hopes of enjoying the city when the mood strikes while vaguely feeling as if they were distanced from their neighbours whom they avoided at all costs, erecting large privacy fences and only exploring the "great outdoors" when they took the rubbish bin to the curb once a week. Bins still lingered on the curbs as the owners avoided driving home after a long Friday at work.

Soon they turned into a fast food parking lot, or perhaps the road leading behind those glowing arches surrounded by a slew of lesser-known drive-thru's still serving lines of cars.

"Are those dumpsters where you ditch the bodies?"

"Those? No. Too easy to trace. The neighbour has hogs and they eat everything. Just need to dispose of your clothes, which I could just pass off as Jordan's. You two are the same size."

"So you're not murdering me. Check. Then... is that?"

"Yelp. Never been to one?"

"Me? Why would I?"

"Because you'd fit in," Tomi gave her a puzzled look. "You're serious? You've never been?"

"Not that I know of. I don't think we even have one in Lincoln."

"You're more the coffee shop kind, aren't you?"

"Well...," her face turned red. "Jordan and I—"

"My cousin," Tomi cut her off with a surprise outburst.

"Yeah, that Jordan. We play the open mics a lot, just the two of us."

"Oooooo that makes so much more sense now."

"I don't think Jordan would be caught dead anywhere with an army of Pride flags waving from the roof and a giant rainbow painted on the door."

"True. Her parents are what I call 'Grade A Homophobes'. Only Jordan is cool with me. The rest of them... meh. Don't need 'em."

Tomi found a place to park Mariam in the crowded lot before checking out the other cars, naming their human owners and who their likely companions would be. Approaching the door, Ríona felt the familiar tinge of anxiety building up. Glancing over her shoulder, she watched the yellow Mustang disappear and kept vigil for any prying eyes amongst the crowds mingling between cars and puffs of vape smoke.

Tomi took her soft hand into her worn hand, the callouses scratching her skin in an oddly comforting way. Looking down at her hand, Tomi gave her a gentle reassuring squeeze, a small affirmation that her anxiety was ill-founded.

Inside the pub it carried a distinct mixture of stale alcohol, too much oestrogen, and the lingering effects of decades bygone when people smoked real cigarettes indoors with a rabid, lung burning passion. Like those outside, more inside puffed clouds of vape in scents of blueberry and banana, and one the distinct smell of something far more... elevating.

"They're all staring at me," Ríona whispered privately to Tomi. She felt as if every eye watched her, like an outsider accidentally traipsing into unfamiliar territory not realising they were nothing but a helpless lamb.

It felt like stage fright, a sensation long since holding a deep grasp on her chest, yet always present waiting for the opportunity to strike her down. Only it was, at least, making its move, grasping her like a terrified child hiding in her mother's shadow, all the new faces staring at her, whispering about her... *I can't do this.*

Tomi pulled on her hand, pulling her closer to her cinnamon musk. "It's okay. No one is judging you for being here."

"Oh god," a woman exclaimed excitedly as they approached a table towards the side, "you didn't tell me she was a cute little femme. Ain't she the cutest thing. I love the flannel," the woman picked at her sleeve feeling that it was indeed a flannel shirt, not just a plaid button up.

"Brie, this is Ríona. Ríona, this is Brie." Brie was a larger woman, standing somewhere between the two in height, but carried much more weight on her frame hidden behind her baggy jeans and baggy button up dress shirt. Her hair was cut short, a flat top buzz cut and a tattoo peaked from underneath her collar.

"And that's Brie's wife, Julz. That's Rebecka and her girlfriend, Mandi. Where's Juli and Bette?"

"On their way," Julz answered, her face buried in her phone. "Toni's driving; so they'll be here sometime next week."

Brie walked closer to Ríona, her voice that of a smoker, her clothes hinting that she might be. "How'd our Tomi land a cutie like you?"

"You know how it is—nice car, fabulous hair" Ríona tried joking, unsure how she fit in. When no one laughed, her nerves got the best of her.

Like a frightened animal, she quickly flitted between the butch women, her gaze desperate for a sign of validation. Then, with a practiced cue, they all burst into boisterous laughter, except Julz who still pecked away at her phone.

Julz finally unburied her head, looked directly at Ríona's terrified face, "you've passed test number one."

What, she angrily complained to herself, Tomi's hand still firmly holding onto hers.

"You haven't run off yet," Julz explained, "so I think ya might'n survive this bunch. Think of it like basic. But for Tomi's love life."

CHAPTER 12

*R*íona woke slowly in an unfamiliar room, one that wasn't her own brick walled flat above the small leather worker who made a variety of wallets and purses, and as a late night hobby, medieval armour. This room, much too dark to be her own, lacked the distinct earthy and slightly sweet smell of freshly tanned leather.

No cars passed by below, the college boys revving their engines when they see a girl they find attractive, which if by the nonstop harassment she witnessed from her window was essentially every remotely feminine person. As a rooster crowed in the distance, others of his kind joining in like a call and return chorus. She almost wished for the now familiar sound of passing vehicles than the reminder of the farm she grew up on, her mother's own roosters perpetually confused about the task society laid out for them as an alarm clock.

Unlike her lonely flat, this room was filling with the smell of coffee and fried potatoes, and a hint of greasy bacon and eggs. Curious, she begrudgingly zombie-walked over towards the ajar door to peek her head out. Her reward was a stronger call for breakfast, her stomach growling angrily at her, demanding the long night's fast be broken.

"Morning," Tomi called out without looking up from the skillet demanding her full attention. "How do you take your eggs?"

"Hard fried."

"I'm guessing that means I don't feel bad about breaking your yokes then," she chuckled. "Cream's in the fridge and sugar is on the table."

"What's on the agenda today?" Ríona grabbed the cream from the fridge, then playfully peeked over Tomi's arm to inspect her breakfast, her cheek gently pressed against Tomi's arm.

"Nothing special. Just getting your van drivable," she replied, shooing Ríona away from the popping grease. "Can you put the toast in?"

"You mean put the bread in the toaster?"

"I have a spatula and I know how to use it," Tomi threatened, holding the potato and eggs covered spatula up threateningly, a playful scowl on her face.

"Fine. Toast it is. Toast into the toaster," she announced cutting slices off the sourdough loaf Tomi had picked up for the weekend.

"I think I already regret letting you stay the night."

"No you don't. I'm cute, remember?"

"I really regret ever calling you that," she muttered loudly.

"If you weren't holding a scalding hot cast-iron skillet and twice my size, I'd tickle you right now."

"Sorry to break the news to you, Tiny, but I'm not my cousin. Unlike her, I'm not afraid of a gentle breeze."

"Did she ever tell you about the time she was nearly knocked over by a gust of wind getting off the bus?"

"No! I will definitely ask her about it though," she said with a devilish smirk on her face.

With the food plated, they sat for a relatively quiet breakfast. Ríona didn't realise how much of an appetite she had worked up the night before singing karaoke with Tomi's gruff friends, none of whom could match a pitch let alone keep time. Ríona quickly became a darling as their small group grew when more of Tomi's friends appeared at the tiny lesbian bar.

"First things first," Tomi began the tour of chores with the Cajun fried potatoes still lingering on her tastebuds, and a cool breeze weaving through the shop, "we need to change those tyres."

"Why? They looked fine to me." She at least knew that vintage cars had those large white stripes on their tyres, white walls she thought they were called, but the ones sitting at the edge of the shop looked "normal".

Explaining in lengthy detail, Tomi instructed Ríona on how to judge a tyres condition, showing her how to measure tread depth, which the original tyres had plenty left. Seeing the question, Tomi then pointed out the small cracks forming along the sidewall.

"That's tire rot. Tires age even if you're not driving. And these sat still for too long and started flattening out. Useless at this point."

"I'm guessing I'm not supposed to be impressed yet?"

Tomi fumbled her words before pinching her brow, "you're killing me, Tiny."

Ignoring the use of the pet name, "how do we change them?"

"That's the fun part. You're about to learn how to jack up your van. You might wanna roll up your sleeves of else you'll get grease all over them."

"Eh, it's okay. This is a junk shirt. Got plenty leftover from working on the farm."

"Suit yourself."

Tomi seemed impressed by her ability to dive into greasy work, pulling out the heavy car jack, and her reliance on kicking the tyre iron to loosen the lug nuts. After she removed a wheel, Tomi took over and placed the wheel on her workbench and using a series of hand tools, parted the tyre from the rim with ease only to slip on the new tyre, still glossy black, on with the same practiced ease. Each tyre made the same terrifying "pop" as the bead set into place, the air compressor quickly recharging behind her as Tomi balanced them, the rubber that would carry her spinning at frightening speeds.

"You forgot one," Tomi chided, rolling the fourth wheel back to Ríona.

"Huh? There's a—dammit."

"Now that your girl has new shoes, time to get her purring."

"I sometimes forget you're older than me. Then you remind me that, yes, you indeed are."

"Ya remember what I said about those pigs?"

"I'm pretty sure you just ate that pig, so I'm safe."

Tomi spent the remainder of the midday sun coaching Ríona on what she dubbed "useful skills to have in the middle of nowhere when your van breaks down for no reason." Replacing parts, Tomi repeatedly warned, was a common issue with these vans. Luckily the parts are cheap and plentiful, but they can become costly if Ríona didn't take the time to learn to wrench the engine now and then.

They first went through the less common needs, primarily parts that although not worn from use would wear from disuse and age, such as the fuel pump and radiator hose. She took time to point out other key components known to wear out, such as the starter and alternator, both she said were good for now.

Next Tomi took her through changing the battery, which she explained she was replacing with a fancier sealed battery, one she ripped out of another one of her project cars. One small project after another the pair of women tackled. Tomi took care to ensure her charge fully understood the repairs they were doing, despite knowing one day her phone would be ringing with a panicked woman on the other end.

In a small, odd way, Ríona felt the time spent under and inside the engine bay brought her closer to Roan. Every nut she tightened, and every fluid she changed out, she slowly began to appreciate the bond Tomi developed with Mariam, and perhaps many other cars that have come and gone through this shop over the years she was unaware of its existence.

She imagined herself stranded on a dusty back road, for whatever reason she imagined the deserts of Nevada or New Mexico, the copper and iron sands rolling until crashing into plateaus and mesas. On that pebble laced road she'd be head first into the van when a driver would pass by and offer their assistance. Some middle-aged man with a beard and a truck no one believed he drove for work would stop and offer them help, Jordan popping out in her cut-off shorts and sleeveless loose tunic, sunnies the size of her face, to brag about Ríona's handiness.

That night she dreamt of all the adventures her and Jordan could have in Roan, travelling long stretches of forgotten highways and passing under palm tree lined coastal roads, pulling into quaint downtowns and empty Midwest ghost towns.

"Where to now," Jordan asks crawling into bed, her bleach blonde hair still tacky with moose and roots growing out.

"I was thinking Portland."

"Portland? It's always rainy there," her gruff voice complains.

"Wrong Portland. I read about this amazing doughnut place in Maine. They also have the best crab cakes."

"Ah, doughnuts. I forgot how much you love your sweets, Tiny."

"Hey Tiny, wake up," Tomi's voice called with a gentle rock. "You fell asleep on the couch."

Rubbing the sleep out of her eyes, Ríona propped herself up on the couch, a heavy blanket that wasn't there the night before weighing her down.

It had been a long day working on getting Roan ready, but ready she was Tomi proudly proclaimed before calling it a night. After killing the shop lights and locking the giant metal door, the two spent the night watching horrible movies Tomi professed a deep love for despite their utter campiness, a horror marathon of "classics" that Ríona barely watched.

After a pair of whiskey sours, the last thought she could remember was how warm Tomi felt as she curled up against the taller women, her protective arm wrapped around the tipsy girl while blondes destined for death screamed their lungs out at murderous men hidden behind masks of anonymity, an odd expression that the man stabbing you to death at the moment could be any man in your life.

"Sorry breakfast isn't ready. I thought you could use the sleep."

"Why didn't you wake me?"

"I tried. I sat you up only to watch you fall back over."

"Sounds like me... Anyway," she yawned deeply, letting out a small yelp at the end, "what's on the playlist today?"

"You get to drive Roan," Tomi said matter-of-factly before turning the coffee grinder on, drowning out any potential protests.

CHAPTER 13

"You're not giving it enough gas," Tomi explained again, her patience somewhat strained.

"But then you say I'm giving it too much gas." This was far more frustrating than the Celica. That one didn't feel as finicky as Roan, her clutch a tightrope of too much or too little. If she tried to not launch herself forward, the engine gulped its last breath and died. Or she revved it until the tachometer bounced past the red ticks with a terrified warning from Tomi about throwing a piston.

"Yes, you were. You need to relax a little and find the middle." Her reassuring hand felt nice, leaving her desiring a little more contact, the flannel cloth denying her that human touch.

What Ríona imagined to be a fairly short morning learning to drive stretched into the afternoon, both an effect of her struggling to grasp the nuances of the much older design, longer shifter throw, as well as learning to shift gears while on hills, while turning, and more importantly, how to properly downshift. Tomi made sure to teach her about "engine breaking" as well, a feature no one in Kansas or Nebraska has ever had a need for.

"How does she feel," Tomi quizzed loudly, relaxing into the passenger seat.

They cruised down the long highway devoid of all traffic on church Sunday. Unlike her truck, the eighty-five wasn't a max limit, but an unattainable goal in Roan. The engine was far too small to push her little van that fast. With the empty shell behind her, the engine echoed loudly, a powerful lawnmower perpetually chasing her.

With a giddy smile, "it feels nice. It's weird, honestly. It's like a taste of what's to come."

"That's good. There's still a lot of work to do, but if we keep at it, we should have her finished by the time you graduate."

Graduation... Thanks to Tomi keeping her busy all weekend, her mind escaped into a world where school no longer existed, finals no longer loomed over her, and life-altering decisions no longer broke over the horizon like an ominous black storm head roiling over the plains, a banshee of ill-fortune for someone whose luck had run as dry as the summer heat.

"Speaking of what needs to be done, we should head back and discuss what you plan to do. I also made a few calls during the week. A gal I met in basic did something similar, and looks like you're going to meet her next weekend. She texted me her blog. It's pretty detailed so we should be able to get a good start come next weekend."

Ríona had spent the week killing free time by browsing YouTube and Pinterest getting ideas for her van. It was a new world to her and surprisingly more vast than she had imagined. From the Tin Can conversions to million dollar motorhomes, to bare bone basic mattress in the back of a Volkswagen with skulls and flowers painted on the side with cheap spray paint.

Most of them she couldn't imagine herself living in. Rugs and tapestries dangling dangerously close to open candles while some leggings-for-pants-girl does yoga poses; strictly utilitarian carpet walls and plastic floors with removable cabinets and dirt bike tie downs; lavish exotic wood in a converted ambulance complete with electric lift Murphy Bed and stainless steel shower.

In her mind she imagined a simple decor with teal cabinets and rope net shelves, a simple bed with magnolia motifs embroidered on a dozen or more pillows. Strings of faerie lights ringing the van, a small

reclaimed wood table, and pinstriped box cushions—the more she imagined her van fully built out, the more she missed her mother.

It wasn't until she pictured herself sitting in her van over her tablet that
she realised what she was imagining was nothing more than a combination
of her mother's kitchen and her years long battle to decorate her bedroom
the way she wanted. In her flat, everything was temporary. A spare couch a
friend didn't need anymore, a broken futon with a cheap mattress; even the
plates were an inexpensive set bought from a big box store. With the sale of
the house, the new owner took possession of it fully furnished, a complete
working farm ready for a new owner to move in that day.

She was permitted only to take her own possession and her mother's
trinkets and a shoebox full of letters and important photos she had
collected from friends and relatives after the fire, which she now stored
underneath her bed.

"We also never discussed your budget...," Tomi blatantly hinted.

"Whatever it is, I'm sure it's fine. I can't imagine it's going to cost me
millions."

"No, but I don't want to suggest you buy a thousand dollar battery
only to find out that's your entire budget."

"First off, why the hell does a battery cost that much, and secondly,
you can add a zero to that."

After parking Roan behind the shop, Tomi suggested they take
showers since neither of them took one that morning. Ríona agreed,
joking that she wasn't *that* much of a hippie. Tomi tossed Ríona a towel,
offering to let her go first while she prepped what would become dinner.

Hot water poured against her sensitive skin, heightened by the
sudden flush of chilly air in the shower against her naked skin. Tilting
her head back, water soaked into her jet black hair, tendrils of warmth
caressing her scalp and her back sending shivers down her spine, and
triggering small contractions in her stomach as hints of liquid rushed
down the front of her pelvis.

Resting her forehead against the wall underneath the "rain" shower
head, she let her mind drift as the scent of Tomi teased specks of desire,
that cinnamon musk an invigorating stimulant. Between the heat grazing
her most sensitive parts and Tomi's musk teasing like her an appetiser

she couldn't taste, she found herself struggling to focus on the needs she came to satisfy, her massaging fingers itching to satisfy baser fantasies.

"Don't forget I need to shower as well, Tiny," Tomi's voice pierced her lustful daydream.

Secretly, she wanted to reply with a teasing invitation, an offer she deeply wished Tomi would take upon herself to fulfil. Those fantasies quickly faded as she let them play out in her head, the questions she feared on Tomi's lips rather than her own.

Resigned, she turned the water off, standing there letting the water slowly drip from her body, the chill welcoming her back to a reality she didn't want to return to. With a towel wrapped around her, and her clothes gathered, she waited by the door for an indication that Tomi was still in the kitchen. When the microwave dinged, she felt safe enough to make her escape.

In her blind rush she nearly collided into Tomi, who was not in the kitchen as the beeping microwave led her to believe, but was quickly rushing past to answer the summon. Ríona's face went tomato red with sudden embarrassment at being seen in her state of undress, her dirty clothes thrown hastily over her left arm.

"Fancy running into you here," Tomi teased with a hungry grin.

"Not funny," she replied in a disarmed panic. She was torn between bolting away and appearing aloof and prudish or staying to enjoy the gaze on her exposed moist collarbones, the skin dipping between the bones, collecting a mixture of sweat and passion.

"My other pick up line was: I can help you get dressed."

Tomi pulled a loose clump of wet hair from her brow, letting her hand run down the side of her face before setting the lock behind her, again causally letting her hand fall onto Ríona's drying skin, the dip on her collar bone now the focus of Tomi's sensual touch.

"Don't you have dinner to harass?"

"Maybe. But it's not nearly as cute."

"I'm not very cute when I'm hangry," she proclaimed before breaking away from the siren of Tomi's fingertips.

"Then I'm afraid to tell you: I still have to shower, so dinner will be postponed a little."

Ríona closed the door behind her, took a deep breath, "what are you doing," she asked herself.

Listening to Tomi take her shower on the other side of the wall, her toned body right there, offering itself to her... yet all she could think of was Jordan. This was the room the two of them shared when they visited. Some of her things still adorned the dresser, a small collection of cheap jewellery, a pair of her signature sunnies, and she imagined some of her clothes in the dresser as well.

What will Jordan say? Random scenarios of Jordan taking the news poorly flashed around, a funhouse of mirrors reflecting all her fears, all the hurtful words Jordan could say, much like her brother and her father. Not even about her being who she is, but about her being with her cousin of all people.

A knock on the door shocked her out of her spiralling thoughts, "you dressed yet in there? We need to get going if we're going to get there in time."

There? Tomi hadn't mentioned anything about going out again tonight, especially since she needed to drive home sometime that evening in order to finish her homework.

Pulling on her black combat boots, she opened the door a smidge, allowing Tomi the freedom to enter. "You're not going to terrorise me again, are you?"

"I would love to, but I had something else in mind. A sunset and a taste."

Pulling her other boot on and adding a double knot for safety, "a taste of what exactly?" All she could smell was the delicious musk of Tomi's freshly bathed skin, a painful tease adding to the imagery the word "taste" invoked after lingering on Tomi's sultry voice.

Tomi stepped forward, directed Ríona's face with those scrumptious fingers of hers, "this wine, of course," she playfully imitated Vanna White.

"Sunset and wine? What's next—"She stopped herself when she noticed Tomi's smile growing larger, the cheesiness oozing out of her with a sickly enthusiasm.

"I even have a basket. And I packed us a few blankets."

"Are we seriously going on a picnic date?"

"Hey, you're the one who's calling it a date."

"Ugh, you're impossible."

"And you're driving."

"Roan?"

"Of course. You're not going to learn by driving in circles around my barn. Plus... this will give you a taste of your future life. There's a lake not far from here we can hang out in Roan, have some wine, eat some spinach samosas, and you can play some fiddle for me."

"I think you've been watching too many Lifetime movies."

"But that smile tells me it's working."

"That's besides the point."

Outside of stalling twice, Ríona was finding herself getting used to shifting, in particular during turns at stop signs. Tomi, however, seemed to be making it a point to be as talkative and distracting as possible, making it nearly impossible for her to focus on anything the other woman was actually saying. It didn't help her use of the word "date" still haunted her.

Following the directions her backseat driver was giving her, they turned down a small grassy double track that looked to be seldom used, but the tall grasses maintained at some point, whether by machine or animal. Despite the annoyances the woman inflicted upon her during the drive, the view was worth it after all.

Tomi opened the side doors, swinging them wide open and beckoned Ríona to sit beside her on the thick blanket. The doors framed a picturesque view of the lake, a mirror broken only by the barren silhouette of thin trees piercing the water's surface surrounded by a handful of waterfowl enjoying dinner at sunset as well, their feisty dives for fish distorting the perfect reflection. Although they still had another fifteen or twenty minutes before the Earth fully obscured their view, the sky exploded with reds and deep oranges, a remnant of the dust blowing over the plains.

Slowly the hues painted the clouds, first the tops of the handful of fluffy cumulus clouds still lingering on the horizon, their bottoms reflecting brightly when they first arrived, but quickly fading as the sun continued its persistent, unchanging path through life. Reds continued to illuminate the strato-cumulus and cirrus clouds, a beautifully stark contrast against the still blue sky.

"Liking what your life will look like," Tomi asked before taking a large bite out of a samosa.

"I guess," she replied, taking a much smaller bite.

"You guess? Don't you have plans for where you want to go?"

The dreaded question everyone expected her to have an answer for. "Perhaps out west. I met some people the other day and now my interest is peaked. Sounds like a place I might fit in."

"You don't fit in around here, Miss Blue Jeans and Flannel? You and my cousin are practically poster children for the 'perfect Midwest wife'. How can you say you don't fit in?"

"I dunno. I've only ever lived here, really. I have some memories of Galway, looking over the bay, or dancing in the streets as my father played. But they're small... and fleeting. It's only images with no context, no real meaning.

"All the rest of them are here. Rural Nebraska. I'm just the farm girl with the funny Irish accent. You... you've seen far more of the world than I have, and then you came back. By choice."

"Not entirely by choice," Tomi finished by pouring herself another glass of wine, then topped off Ríona's with the last of the bottle.

"Right, sorry. Jordan warned me about not asking about your time in the Air Force. I've gathered there was some unpleasantness."

"That's a nice way of putting it. But yeah... not a fan of talking 'bout it."

"Maybe one day you'll be comfortable enough talking to me about it?"

"One day," Tomi smiled at her before pulling the smaller woman closer.

Ríona nuzzled her back under Tomi's arm, a safety blanket with a dark past.

"Your friends the other night—they're veterans too, right? I remember Brie talking about it."

"Yep," Tomi confirmed with a swig, finishing off her glass and returning to the small basket of food. "We served together. The others I met after my time in. Support groups, friends of friends, the usual. They're a good bunch, even if they do razz people a lot."

They silently watched as the sunlight faded over the horizon, leaving steaks of light shaped by clouds they couldn't see over the distance fields. As soon as the sun herself vanished, the night chill crept in slowly, a mark that the full moon would soon take over.

"Wouldn't it be gorgeous to watch this over an ocean? Not that the lake isn't divine, but the ocean! You could listen to the waves slapping the shore and the birds singing to each other. The smell! You've been to an ocean, right? You know the smell."

"Yeah. I do. It's salty."

"Wow, you're a true poet."

"I will tickle you."

"You wouldn't dare," Ríona loudly protested pulling away quickly, putting her right hand up defensively and hiding her left behind her back.

"I would. And I will. But not now. I want to know more about your hippie dreams."

"They're not hippie dreams. They're memories," she quietly explained, returning to her safety.

"How so? Were the hippies in flannel like you?"

"Cute. And no. Honestly, you sorta remind me of me pa. At least, the stories mum would tell me.

"When I was young, I would lie in the bay window in the kitchen and just stare at the sun as it set, crying my eyes out. To comfort me, mum would tell me stories of how her and my father met, how they would go to the bluffs sometimes and watch the sunset together, never saying a whole word to each other the entire time. Father would play his fiddle and mother would write her poetry."

"When did he pass?"

Ríona fell silent, watching the dying daylight transition fully into moonlight.

"I'm sorry, I didn't mean—"

"I was five."

"Oh god, Tiny, you were so young."

"Yeah... but at least I got to know him a little. I do have some memories of him, so that's something. They're all I have left of him actually, outside of my fiddle. It only survived the fire because he was quite forgetful, mum said. It's funny how she used to hate that about him but then after he died, it was the thing she remembered the most.

"Funny how that is. Mum said he was notorious for leaving his fiddle at the pub where him and the lads played, and would always seem to remember halfway home. Mum used to joke that she thought it was just an excuse to have another pint and a craic, but that night...

"We'll never know. That night he didn't go back for it. He forgot it like always but instead of turning around the moment he passed the bridge with the fiddle sign, he kept driving. And driving.

"When he was a mile or so out he saw the smoke. Mum greeted him in a panic because she didn't know where I was. I was still inside, trapped." Tears begun rolling down her face.

"Ríona, you don't have to continue if it's too painful." Tomi kissed the top of her head and gave her a squeeze.

"It's okay. I cry all the time anyway." She wiped the tears away with her sleeves, carefully pulling her left sleeve back down past her wrist. Unconsciously, she started scratching her arm, picking at it through the thick flannel.

"We'll never know why he didn't turn back, but it's why I lived. He ran in after me and managed to get me out of my room. He threw a chair through my window and helped me climb out, but the flames grew bigger and hotter with the rush of oxygen.

"Breaking the window saved my life... but it took his in return."

Tomi let her continue to cry hot tears. Not just for her father, but her mother. Never again would she be forced to listen to her stories, the same ones told over and over again until Ríona knew them better than her own mother.

Funny how that is.

"Is your arm okay?"

"Huh? My arm?"

"Yeah, did you hurt it working on the van? You're holding it like you hurt it and there's blood."

"Oh... no. It's just something I do. Don't worry about it."

"Ríona, honey, you're bleeding though. Let me take a look at it."

"I said it's fine," she defended herself with a little too much anger.

"I didn't realise it was such a sensitive topic. Are you ashamed you have chicken arms or something?"

No, but how do you tell someone? Only two people had ever seen her arm, outside of course the doctors. Jordan was the first to find out, barging in on her one day while she was still changing.

"Oh god, Rí, what happened," Jordan had exclaimed loud enough Mrs McGraw come upstairs to check out the commotion.

"Please, Jordan, don't tell anyone. Not even your mother, please," she pleaded just before the door opened, Mrs McGraw's normally cheerful disposition replaced with concern for her daughter, which thankfully allowed her to hide herself behind a towel.

"Sorry mom," Jordan glanced back at her, "I didn't mean to walk in on Ríona changing," she lied.

"Are you sure? It sounded like something was wrong."

"No, just me being silly."

Somehow her mother accepted the excuse and closed the door, leaving her to Jordan's incessant interrogation, a time before she understood the concept of hard boundaries, or how to enforce them.

Tomi cupped her face, "you don't have to tell me, I get it. I'm in no place to demand you tell me anything."

"I... I...," she sighed heavily, biting her thin lip, "I've never shown anyone, except Jordan." That was her own lie. Both to Tomi, and herself. Jordan was not the only girl to ever see her vulnerable. "I didn't just lose my dad in that fire.

"Remember I said I was trapped? It was my arm that got trapped. It melted most of the skin and damaged a lot of the muscle. I actually can't move my left arm as well as I can my right, but since you only really need your fingers to play fiddle, it works out and no one notices."

Tomi remained quiet, but focused, raptly engrossed in Ríona's story.

"I was in the hospital for months and months before they released me into therapy. Then not long after we came here."

"Can I see?"

"My arm?" She reflexively pulled back her arm, shielding its grotesque form.

"Yeah. I have a feeling you're ashamed of it," she cooed, placing the tips of her fingers on her collarbone, just underneath the edge of her flannel.

"It's not something I want people staring at, you know?"

"I understand. But sometimes there're things that makes us a little different and that's okay. Can I," Tomi asked, her fingers slipping further under her collar, the warmth of her hand sending shivers of desire down her chest, her breathing becoming increasingly difficult.

She took a deep breath, held onto it as if she was meditating on the request, then nodded, her chest falling as the air escaped her tight lungs. With her eyes closed, fearful of seeing Tomi's reaction mimic Jordan's, while in the back of her mind a small voice prayed she'd react like Jolene.

She did neither. Sitting there now in just her ribbed tank top, her aroused nipples clearly showing, Tomi said nothing. Instead, her fingers spoke to her, first slipping her top off, then exploring her soft pale flesh, starting at her shoulder and neck, her thumb tracing the outline of her clavicle.

When she no longer felt Tomi's curious fingers, she hesitantly opened her eyes, taking in Tomi's wide gaze of curiosity. In the darkness, only the flickering citronella candles dancing off her hair, the moonlight coming through the window casting heavy shadows, Ríona tried to decipher Tomi. All she managed was curiosity, a loving curiosity, not as a freak like how Jordan responded, not as a medical specimen like Jolene.

"You know, I can't actually feel that," she finally spoke with a tint of humour.

"That's a shame. I want you to feel me touching you," she whispered in her husky voice, her eyes locked with her own.

Then... warmth that stole her breath, a tiny gasp of air as Tomi's firm lips pressed against hers, forceful. Cinnamon. Her chest hurt, the tightness, the spasms in her abdomen...

Jolene stared at her, her face angry and red, puffy even, her eyes red after fighting back the tears.

"How dare you kiss me, you disgusting freak." Jolene shoved her away, then fled from her life.

Ríona violently pulled away from Tomi... *oh god I just want...*

Tomi pulled back slowly, licking her lips apologetically, "I'm sorry. Did I read you wrong? I thought..."

"Maybe... no... I—I..."

"I thought you were, you know..."

Ríona leaned forward; it hurt to kiss her; it hurt *not* to kiss her. It hurt more to not. She fell into Tomi, desperate to return her kiss, her arm furious with her as if an army of ants all bit her at once.

"I was just caught off guard. And I am. Or I do, depending on what your question was," she tried answering coherently as she scratched at her arm. "I just... I can't right now. I need my shirt back."

The drive back to her flat was torture. Two hours of solitude, a prisoner alone with her thoughts and regrets. Doubts attacked every action, every trivial word. She hated that she lied to Tomi, partially; using her arm as an excuse. It was half true, she silently pleaded to herself, desperate to justify her panic.

"I should go. I haven't done any of my homework due tomorrow."

"Why don't you bring it with you next weekend?"

She agreed, happy that Tomi still wanted her to come back.

"Before I go," the courage at the time now a marinating fear, leaned forward and gave Tomi a lingering kiss that still tasted salty on her lips.

CHAPTER 14

$\mathcal{M}$orning came too early. Her iPhone's alarm chirping at her hours before the sun rose. Desperate to shut the device up, she fumbled with it until finally it quieted. Only to once again start up again, this time a series of trumpets declaring the queen has arrived. Annoyed, she pulled her phone off the charger, opened the alarm app, and turned off the series of four alarms she had set, each spaced ten minutes apart.

"Fine you stupid phone, I'm up," she sneered at the inanimate object. "You're so annoying on Mondays."

It wasn't Siri's fault every week began with a seven a.m. class. She chose this class on her own volition, one of the final electives, a "fun class" as she called it. Although her major focused on performance, she decided a class on composition would be a way to take her mind off her other classes. Instead, it turned into her most dreaded class, not just because of the god awful start time, but because she felt she was absolute rubbish at it.

Fiddle wasn't a "read the notes and play like a monkey" instrument as one of the other fiddlers in town spit at her, disgusted that she would "sully herself" by learning to play for orchestras. Unlike him who only played for tips busking on the busy streets frequented by tourists, she wanted an actual career someday. That meant realising that she may end up teaching since Nebraska was far from the hotbed of professional musicians.

Her tiny shower stall with its low pressure and clogged shower head was a disappointing reminder that Tomi would not be in the other room preparing breakfast for her. Rather, the other room was filled the familiar scent of emptiness. No farm breeze, no cast-iron skillets filled with corn-bread, no cinnamon musk.

Unlike the weekend past, her breakfast was nothing more than a protein bar and a small bag of almonds to go. Campus was only a short fifteen-minute walk away, on the days Jordan didn't swing by on her way to offer her a ride. Jordan would never succumb to the temptations of an early morning class.

Today she walked with a perkier than usual step. Although she was the only person to notice her humming her composition as she mind-lessly followed sidewalk after sidewalk. She dodged other early morning classmates and those far more ambitious than her taking a run around the campus. The men shirtless, sweaty pecs and their unusually tiny shorts; the women a mixture of long yoga pants and sports bras, showing off their well-defined youthful abs whereas others displayed their defined legs but hid the rest of themselves behind loose sports tunics.

"Ríona," Mrs McGraw called out to her from an empty hallway, a back entrance to one of the engineering buildings seldom used. She wore one of her usual "business casual" deep blue sleeveless dresses, the kind that showed too much of her well-defined chest and left little of her legs to the imagination, all while hugging the curves her body shaper helped her keep despite having two children and growing into her fifties. For a much older woman, Ríona still appreciated the effort her friend's mother took on her appearance.

"What the—"

Without another word, Mrs McGraw turned and disappeared into the poorly lit hallway, more a result of the early sun blinding her as she walked towards class than the lack of lighting in the service hallway.

She watched the shapely figure disappear before scurrying to keep up, "why are you here?"

"Keep up and we'll talk. But not here," she stated, pressing the call button for the service elevator.

Desperate for answers, but knowing Mrs McGraw was serious about her silence, Ríona stood there, dancing back and forth on the heels of her feet. Quickly glancing at her phone, she had twenty minutes to make it to class and turn her assignment in. She had hoped to practise on one of the baby grand pianos first to give her stiff muscles time to wake up, and to experience the fullness a real piano produces versus the synthetic sounds her modest Casio could ever hope to reproduce. Even the weight of the keys just felt different; the strings producing a feedback a digital keyboard just couldn't.

On the fourth floor Mrs McGraw disappeared into a teacher's office, the name on the door belonging to a Doctor Julie Nunes. She followed, glancing suspiciously around the empty hallway, suddenly feeling like someone was watching her commit a crime; the grey areas good secret agents lived their lives. She felt like the opposite, desperate to shake off the feeling that she was doing something nefarious.

She had imagined the engineering department offices having more... engineering things. It looked no different from nearly every other department office on campus. Just an empty, wide hallway lined with doors and generic photographs featuring parts of the local geography long since bulldozed over for a strip mall and various fake trees in desperate need of dusting, the green leaves covered in a dull greyish layer. Inside the office, it was filled with books like every professor. A litany of required reading from the time the professor took a position at the school until when they retired, each subsequent book becoming a useless, expensive relic.

"Lock the door behind you."

"What's going on? Why all the secrecy?" Their game was beginning to spark a kindling of paranoia and fear in her. She'd always considered herself a fairly open person, at least, not the type of person needing to whisper in a stranger's offices about anything other than secret crushes and smuggled candies.

Mrs McGraw sat herself behind the desk, as if this was her office and she was in charge—she usually was. She motioned for Ríona to sit, the uncomfortable student's hard plastic chair her only option.

"You're like a daughter to our family, you know that right?"

Oh god... Did they know about Tomi kissing her? How could they know? Jordan was terrified of her parents finding out so unless her parents went through her phone. Would they do that?

"We need a favour. Zach," she emphasised his name, "needs a favour."

Zach? His name brought a wave of relief to wash away the worry that had been building in her since Mrs McGraw demanded she follow her into a creepy hallway.

"Did he wake up?"

"No. In a way that makes this a little easier. But, it means the focus is going to be on *you*."

"On me?" *At least it wasn't about Tomi.*

"We need you to pretend you're his girlfriend."

What? Me? Why? They hated each other. That was no secret. Jordan often intervened for them, calming her brother down by assuaging his ego in a way Ríona could never stomach.

"I've never even had a boyfriend though."

"That's why you'd be the perfect cover. No one has seen you date anyone; you've been so focused on your mother's health and graduating the top of your class—not to mention your regular performances during the week."

That's not why, she corrected in her head, repressing a laugh. She has dated while in college though, only her mother knew that secret.

"And there's no reason one of the boys around town wouldn't want you. Hell, if I was a dyke I'd want you."

That word made her cringe. It rang in her ears loudly, an angry bell shouting down at her from above, screaming its condemnation. There was something about the way she used it that made it feel slanderous, an accusation one hurled at those witches deemed worthy of the cleansing flames.

"Thanks... I think." She glanced at her phone again. Ten minutes until class started. Even if she left now, she doubted she would make it to class in time.

"Silly child, it's a compliment. You're family. Anyway, what I came to ask you."

Jordan kept her updated on her brother's condition throughout the weekend. Text after text of worry that Zach wouldn't wake, or worse the doctors warned, he may wake up with brain damage. The amount of narcotics found in his system shouldn't have been enough to cause him much harm under normal circumstances, but car crashes weren't normal.

The sheriff believed Zach's friend panicked, worried that Zach had overdosed and was unresponsive. According to those at the party, Zach and his friend Bryan were last seen leaving the house arguing about who would drive, Zach arguing Bryan "wasn't in his right mind."

Mrs McGraw checked her phone with a displeased look, before dropping it on the desk, turning her attention back to Ríona. "The police report is bullshit."

"I... I don't understand. What about it is... well, what you said."

She cursed like anyone else, but as Mrs McGraw said, they were family. The one time she cursed in front of her mother she cried for an hour, disappointed with herself and afraid her mother wouldn't speak to her again. She wasn't nine anymore but she still carried that fear of uttering even the mildest curses.

"Listen, we need you to pretend to be Zach's girlfriend. You two fought, he got mad and went off with some new friends and was taken in by them. He only got so messed up because his so-called friends pressured him into it. He was already drunk because of your fight, you told him you were breaking up with him, he ends up in the car with his friend who shouldn't be driving, and here we are.

"We're just thankful that, despite the horrors of drug abuse and worse, the peer-pressure drug addicts use to force outstanding students like Zach into their dark world, that in the end his drug abuse saved his life in the car crash."

"This is about Mr McGraw running for mayor, isn't it?"

"Yes, honey, of course it is. If word of this got out my husband's chances of winning are gone and that stupid councilwoman will win without a fight. It's already going to be a close race so we can't have *anything* negative come up."

"Are you going to tell me what really happened at least? What are they going to accuse Zach of?"

She cleared her throat, leaned forward over the random teacher's desk, her cleavage fully exposed by her low cut dress, "That Zach was driving."

"He what," she loudly exclaimed. This was the opposite of everything she had been told up until now. By Jordan, no less. "Does Jordan know?"

"He wasn't, of course. And no, I haven't told Jordan yet. She adores her brother unconditionally. I don't understand that child, but it's kinda cute. Sisterly love, huh?

"I'm going to tell her, don't worry, but first I needed to find you. They're going to be looking for you today." She sat back upright again, discarding the air of cloak and daggers and returning to her usual "I'm in charge" posture. "Jordan said you were down in Wichita with some friends drinking. I didn't even know you drank?"

"I don't, not really. She probably made it sound like I'm a sloppy drunk. But really I only had two drinks—just enough to get me to do karaoke," she rolled her eyes at herself, hoping the self-deprecation would stop Mrs McGraw from prying further.

"This is good. They can confirm you were there?"

"I guess. I don't know why they wouldn't."

"Good."

"So, how long have Zach and I've been dating?"

"I wouldn't know, you two hid it from us so well. My guess is years. All this time we thought you were coming to the house to visit Jordan. We were bad parents, trusting our daughter and the girl we saw as our other daughter, but really it was a cover for you and our son to see each other."

"Why did we hide it?"

"No clue. It's what kids your age do. Afraid we wouldn't approve, is my guess. Makes it sounds more romantic. Forbidden love. But now that we know, we fully approve."

"And how long do I have to pretend to be his girlfriend?"

"That's up to you. That should make it easy. You broke up with him, remember? That's why all this happened?"

"Wait, so it's my fault?"

"That's not what I'm saying, honey. You know what I mean. This will all blow over in a few weeks anyway after the election ends. Like five weeks from now."

"I have a feeling Jordan isn't going to approve."

At last Mrs McGraw's demeanour changed, relaxing a little from the stiff business woman to the awkwardly playful mother figure she knew her as.

"She would murder you if you really did date Zach. To be honest... I kinda thought you two would make a good pair, but you need a man with more drive. Our Zachary, I love that stupid boy, but his father coddled him too much."

A man... "He's tried. Painfully so."

"Has he? I think he's had a crush on you for years now actually. Jordan would always snap at him anytime he talked about you. That child loves you, you know that? You're the sister she wished she had."

"She means a lot to me too. I don't know what I would do without her in my life."

"Don't you worry, I'll explain to Jordan what's going on. She hasn't left her bothers side at the hospital."

"That's not good for her."

"I agree, it's not. Any chance you could use that adorable smile of yours to woo her away. She'll do anything you ask of her."

"Of course, Miss Delilah."

"I'd be much appreciated."

CHAPTER 15

"It's not good for you to stay here like this, ya know."

"I know... but I'm afraid he'll wake up all alone. My parents are too busy to sit by his side so I have to."

Zachary laid in his hospital bed, motionless except for the predictable rise and fall of his chest. The incessant beeping off to the side the only other reminder that he still lived. His normally rosy pale cheeks a ghostly white, no longer flush with testosterone driven aggression and horniness.

"You surround yourself with selfish people, you know that?"

"Says the girl dating my brother without telling me," Jordan replied coldly. Her accusation, she knew, wasn't intended to be venomous, but an acknowledgement. Even if the bite of her tone stung nonetheless.

"What? I thought your mother...," her words trailed off, feeling betrayed.

"Would tell me important family secrets? Are you kidding me, Rí?"

"Then how did you know?"

Jordan handed her phone. Forty-seven missed calls. Forty-eight now as the buzzing abruptly ended. Her phone wouldn't show the number of text messages, only that there were more than her notification screen was willing to admit.

"It's been like that all morning. Some not so pleasant ones too. I have a feeling there's some people who don't approve of my brother dating someone 'beneath him'."

She had always been careful about giving out her phone number. Only a handful of people had it. Mostly those who were close to her personally such as Jordan and now Tomi. Otherwise she gave people one of those forwarding phone numbers she could easily change, a holdover from her first experience being the popular kid's friend. Why Jordan never did so was beyond her.

"All the more reason to get you out."

Yes, Mrs McGraw was the one who made the suggestion, and also the one currently causing this whirlwind of harassment, but despite the origin of the request, she herself knew it wasn't healthy for Jordan. Even the nurses whispered to her as she walked past, pleading with her to rescue Jordan from her self-imposed vigil.

"Don't give me that look, Jordan. You know you can't stay here like this. The nurses will call you as soon as he wakes up."

Jordan looked at her, her face blank. "Am I to answer every single one of these calls? Most aren't even from people I know. A bunch of reporters are hounding me too, desperate for some sort of gossip about you and my brother in order to hurt my father's reputation."

"I'm sorry."

"Why? It's not your fault my mother decided to play media darling rather than tell everyone the truth."

It pained her to see Jordan like this, her usual annoying high-pitch twang replaced by a subtle, mature monotonous passive-aggressive anger. In the matter of a single weekend she aged from rambunctious teenager eager to take on the world to discontent social drunk who lingers at the bar too long hoping the barkeep will keep them company another drink longer. She had met one too many of those already.

"What truth?" She didn't want to know the answer, yet she was afraid the answer Jordan would give her wasn't the same truth Mrs McGraw told her. "That my brother is a drug addict and I had no clue how bad it was?"

Tears begun forming at the corner of Jordan's eyes, she tried hero-ically to hold them back, sniffling on occasion. Normally she'd be terrified to cry, afraid of ruining her Pinterest perfect makeup, but after days of social withdrawal she allowed the cracks in her mask to show. Only remnants of faded black eyeliner encircled her doe-like amber-brown eyes.

"Sunshine," she couldn't help herself anymore. Ever since Tomi called her that, Ríona felt a kinship with that name, as if it was hers to call Jordan all along.

Jordan collapsed into her arms, Ríona wrapping hers around Jordan protectively, Jordan's forehead buried into the nook of her neck. Warm tears fell onto her collarbone, a confusingly sensual feeling. Her sobs came fast, and painfully heartbreaking.

"It's okay, I'm here."

Jordan continued to shed her emotions, Ríona's heart aching for the poor girl in her arms, wishing she could take away the pain while knowing one day soon she was going to watch her friend split in two once the real truth was out.

"I feel like this is all my fault. That I pushed him away. If I hadn't, he'd have been there Friday, with us, instead of out there. And now I feel like my world is falling apart.

"My brother is in a coma, my father's campaign is in jeopardy, and my mother is blaming it on you. I don't know why? Why you? Why can't she pick someone else to blame? There must be a hundred other girls at school who'd happily pretend to be his girlfriend.

"All so people will think this was a one off episode? As if that's how any of this works."

Amidst Jordan's breakdown, she told herself over and over that all she had to do was lie. A simple lie, relatively harmless. Not for Zach and definitely not for Mr McGraws campaign.

"You know your bother and I didn't actually date, right?"

"Of course I know that, stupid. Y'all hate each other," she huffed while attempting to wipe away tears.

"And you would have murdered me a long time ago."

"Hell yes I would have," she laughed through the endless tears, loudly sniffling in a manner that would gross most people out yet held no sway on their bond. "You belong to me, Rí."

Her heart fluttered before shattering again as the tears returned in force, some unseen revelation ripping Jordan apart before her, too hidden for Ríona to stand up to, her fists balled as the senior girls picked on the twiggy freshman girl.

"I don't care if your parents are rich, you ugly brat," Sarah with an H shoved Jordan against the girls' locker room wall. "I saw who you were looking at, freak." Sarah shoved Jordan again.

"Leave her alone," Ríona demanded of the older, taller girl surrounded by her closest friends, all happily participating in verbally mocking Jordan.

"Oh, and who's this welp?" The girls laughed, one reaching out and playing with Ríona's black hair, marvelling at the depth of its inkiness. "And what's wrong with your voice? You sound like a stupid leprechaun."

The girl examining her hair took a fistful, violently whipping Ríona's head to the side before throwing her onto the ground. Without warning, the same girl dropped her weight onto her and started pounding at Ríona's face, blow after blow landing against her arms held up protectively, the girls laughing manically.

"She's mine," Jordan yelled hotly as she slammed her next to nothing body weight against the bulkier volleyballer before Ríona's world went black.

"I woke up. And he's going to wake up," Ríona whispered softly, more a plea than a statement of medical fact, a plea that was currently at odds with the looks the nurses and doctors secretly gave each other when the grieving parties weren't looking. Deep down Ríona knew she couldn't be the only one who saw their looks.

"Now," Ríona continued, "I'm going to take you back to my place and get you cleaned up."

Conveniently, as if the nurses had been spying on their intimate moment, Zach's nurse came zipping in, a cheerful song on her lips to assure them she would watch over the unconscious boy. Before they left, Ríona made sure to give the nurse her number, warning her that it was for her eyes only.

"Doesn't that feel better," Ríona asked as Jordan stepped out of the shower and into the waiting towel. Jordan only nodded her head in approval, her hair soaked and stuck to her face. Goosebumps ran up and down her arms despite Ríona's attempt to keep the small woman warm.

Jordan nodded, slowly agreeing that she felt more human now that she'd showered for the first time in several days. Ríona didn't actually know how long it had been since no one had been at the hospital to order her away, except the staff who Jordan easily ignored.

She smelled *significantly* better too.

"You hungry? You look like you haven't eaten anything," Ríona asked, pulling loose hairs off Jordan's still humid face.

"Yeah. I'd like to stay in tonight, if you don't mind," Jordan pleaded softly, a breakdown brewing underneath her calm resignation.

"No worries, Sunshine. I'll pop down and get us Chinese takeaway."

"Takeout."

"Takeout?"

"Yes. That's what the rest of us call it. Not 'takeaway'."

"Well, I call it 'an order of Kung po chicken with veggie fried rice and two spring rolls'," she stuck her tongue out as she held the phone up to her head, the number still in her recent calls.

CHAPTER 16

ordan rolled over, laying her arm across Ríona's rib cage. Ríona laid there, desperate to pee but afraid of waking Jordan up. Instead, she let her mind wander in and out of daydreams, various scenarios playing out in her head. All the imaginary arguments, the witty comebacks she'd never think of in the heat of the moment flowing from her gracefully, like a puppet show.

After her weekend with Tomi, those lips... those sweet, warm lip pressed firmly against her own. Her urge to relieve her bladder was quickly taking second seat to other growing needs. Jordan's warm body pressed against hers wasn't helping the cause.

After her weekend with Tomi, she decided she needed to tell Jordan at last. To tear down the one last secret she hid from her best friend; the person who considered her a sister. Yet, how could sisters keep such a personal secret from each other?

Jordan spent so many nights up passed curfew interrogating Ríona about boys before eventually giving up, resigned to the fact Ríona's taste in boys was altogether lacking, never questioning the reason why. Not that Jordan herself had the best tastes, she at least admitted a passing interest. Her dating history was littered with disposed boys, their partnerships always distant and "professional", a dance the popular rich kids practiced.

She ran imaginary conversations through her head. Ones where Jordan accepted it without issue, others, the ones she feared the most, Jordan reacted badly, leaving her alone buried in her own tears like that night in Omaha. One in particular... that one she refused to let herself entertain, that possibility too intoxicatingly delicious.

"You have to pee, don't you," Jordan interrupted her thoughts, squirming with a small yelp of a yawn.

"When don't I?"

Jordan removed her trap, freeing Ríona to take care of her bladder like she does every morning with a desperate urge.

"When you're done, make sure to come back," she instructed, snuggling with Jordan's pillows. "I'm not ready to wake up."

Tomi's lingering lips faded, replaced by a warmth deeper within her.

"Don't get too comfy. We have plans today," she announced as she retreated behind the bathroom door, shutting it with a lingering sigh.

Jordan greeted her outside her bathroom, which wasn't hard considering the size of her flat, but it still felt weird. "I thought you had class?" Jordan handed her a cup of coffee, her faded lipstick snuck onto the rim.

"No. I emailed my professors and explained I needed a day. Now go get yourself ready while I wipe your lipstick off my mug."

"Where are we going," Jordan pleaded as they slinked downstairs, Ríona watching for any potential stalkers desperate for a scrap of gossip from the town's only raging scandal.

"Out of town. Some place where no one really knows us."

Ríona shoved Jordan into the passenger seat, along with a small backpack full of clothes and their fiddles. Jordan continued to ask questions, to the point of demanding an answer or she wouldn't continue to play along. Ríona responded with force, giving a stern warning that she was making the decisions today and that there would be no discussions.

More importantly, there wouldn't be any talk about her brother's drug usage, or her parent's campaign, or even the annoying gossip mongers likely still hounding Jordan's disconnected phone.

"But you brought my fiddle?"

"Yeah, I did."

"Where are you taking me?"

"Have a little trust, Sunshine."

"It's not like you to be so forceful. And confident."

"Is that a bad thing now?"

"No," she sat reflecting, "it's kinda nice."

Hitting highway speeds, she continued the daydreams from earlier. Her truck faded away, Roan taking its place. Her and the blonde-haired country chick venturing out from home, free of the nets that acted more like shackles than the safety a tightrope walker trusted their lives with. Her passenger's long hair blowing in the wind, her arm wrapped over the door, chin resting effortlessly on her wrist.

"You haven't told me how things are going with you and Tomi," Jordan asked between bites. By the time they arrived in Omaha, the breakfast cafes were close to shutting their doors for the day, dashing the late breakfast Ríona hoped to be devouring. Instead they settled on a fast-casual chain.

Ríona choked on her minty Shamrock milkshake. *Did she already know?* "Tomi and me?"

"Are you correcting me? You know I hate that."

"No. Just... what do you mean Tomi and me?"

"You visited my cousin, didn't you? Unless there's another boyfriend you're hiding from me?"

"Ha, not likely." She sank in her seat, relishing the cold comfort of the sugar overload. "Things are well. We made progress on the van. She took me out to dinner and introduced me to her friends."

"Her friends? I'm sorry."

"Sorry? What for?"

"I've met her friends. They're different."

"Yeah, they are," she agreed, unsure what she was actually agreeing to, "but there's nothing wrong with that."

"Did you meet Brie? She's the wild one."

"Oh her, yeah, she's pretty intense. But she's sweet," she tried to deflect, burying her order of chips in a mountain of ketchup and mayonnaise mixed together, a habit that always elicited a grossed out look from Jordan who called herself a "french fry purist".

"Did you meet Julz? Her," Jordan dropped to a whisper, "her wife."

"Why are we whispering," her anxiety peaking while pretending to look around suspiciously with an impish smirk.

"I... you know why."

"Because they're both women?"

"Yeah... I mean no. Not entirely."

"Well that's going to be awkward then," she started. Before the words had a chance to lead into more words, she pulled herself back from the edge.

Jordan eyed her, waiting for Ríona to tell her something. Her brightness faded into a sullen expression.

Unsure of what triggered the change in Jordan's demeanour, she quickly shifted, "because we're playing at a benefit tonight."

Jordan slurped down the remainder of the milkshake loudly, an unhappy glower shooting daggers at Ríona. "We're playing tonight? Rí, love, I'm not in the mood to play. I just can't."

"You can, and you will."

Jordan sat the stolen milkshake glass down with a loud, angry thud, a pointed expression demanding her refusal be heard.

"It'll be good for you. Plus... I sorta already told them," she eked out, grabbing the milkshake and examining it with exaggerated disappointment.

"Serves you right. I should have ate the cherry too."

"I know I should have asked first, but you've been so distant."

"I know." She bit into a skinny chip, tearing the greasy potato apart with a despondent awareness. "Fine," she agreed bitterly, tossing the half-eaten chip at Ríona's face.

"Hey! Why would you waste good food like that?"

"Bite me." Quickly preempting Ríona's next comment, "don't you dare!"

Her mood was slowly changing. That morning Jordan moved slower than a sloth at the DMV; now she regained some of the cheerful banter Ríona loved about her. It wasn't much, but it was enough to give her hope that Jordan was finally coming out of her mood.

Walking into the coffee shop, Ríona was pleased to see that improvement remain. Jordan's flighty inspection of the drink menu brought a small half-smile to Ríona's lips, all the while knowing she would pick the same sugary drink she'd always pick no matter the cutesy name given to it.

Walking up to the barista, Jordan noticed the flyer hanging from the back of the nearly antique register, one of those machines where the teller needed to know the product codes rather than pressing a series of icons on a tablet.

"Tragic, isn't it," the barista said to Jordan, her voice filled with a sadness one would expect from a safe distance. "Her family won't claim her body so the local queer community is raising funds for a proper burial."

"Won't claim her body? That's messed up," Jordan absentmindedly acknowledged, somehow lost within her own thoughts. "Did you know her?"

"Not personally. I've seen her around, but I never had the courage to actually talk to her." The barista studied the pair, taking note of the fiddle case dangling from Jordan's hand. "You two here to play?"

"Yep," Ríona answered, pulling out cash and pushing Jordan's family credit card back into her hand. "Saw a flyer down in Lincoln so figured we'd come up and show our support."

"You're Ríona," she butchered her name with a knowing smile. "Yeah, y'all are pretty well known down in Lincoln. Cool. Sign-ups over there and your drinks will be a few. Take a seat, I'll bring them to you."

"My cousin's gotten to you, huh," Jordan said with a raised eye at the small flyer in her hand, studying the name of the victim before writing her and Ríona's name on the sign up list, one of the earlier spots but not so early to miss the larger crowds.

"I thought it would be nice to do something good. I only told them I was coming, so if you wanna back out," she let her sentence hang hoping that Jordan wouldn't accept the free pass.

Taking a seat closer to the small stage, Jordan fell into her chair with an exaggerated sigh. "No, I'll do it. My parents would kill me if they ever found out though. I'm surprised you're okay with it. Kinda why I'm shocked you and my cousin are getting along so well."

"What? Why? Your cousin is pretty cool."

"I dunno... I just got the sense that you don't like people like her. Like my parents," she said with a shade of embarrassment.

"Did you really think that?"

"Yeah—kinda. Most people around here do."

"What about you? Tomi says you're her favourite."

"Well, yeah, I'm the only one who didn't disown her."

"Then why do you seem so uncomfortable?"

"I worry about her—," the barista interrupted, setting their drinks down.

"If you two need anything, give me a holler, 'kay," she left with a smile directed at Jordan, whose eyes watched the girl quietly as she left.

"What if something," she continued, "like this happened to her? That sign would say the same thing. Her parents refusing to claim her body, my parents thanking god... it's too much." She buried her face in her hands, letting out a frustrated growl. "She's had such a rough life because of it."

"She seems pretty happy now. Her friends are awesome. She's doing something she loves for work."

"I dunno, Rí. I'm happy that you two are getting along well. I was really worried you'd freak out or something and turn down that van."

"Is this why you told me not to mention Tomi around your parents?"

"Yeah. They'd say she's going to corrupt you, turn you lesbian. They're barely okay with me hanging out with her still, which is why I just don't tell them. As far as they're concerned, I haven't seen Tomi in years."

"So you don't think your parents would accept me if, hypothetically, I came out?"

"You!? Gay? Ha! I'd think I'd know if your were gay, honey."

"I'm sure some think it though."

"Because you haven't dated?"

Mentally, she corrected Jordan. She had dated. Just once though. Jordan knew most everything about her life, but she wasn't there those months when nights became long and sleepless.

They had just returned from winter break. Her mother's illness was about to bring her back home. Jordan never knew who Jolene was, that tall twenty-year-old with the fake ID buying them drinks. A random encounter at one of the many pubs in Omaha.

Jordan and Jolene hit it off, chatting for hours while Ríona nicked small flir-

tatious smiles, Jolene's bare foot fighting its way up her trousers, tickling her hidden flesh. By the end of the night, Ríona was of the firm belief that Jolene had stolen more than one heart that night.

"I'm a little surprised to see you being such a bad girl," Ríona teased Jolene the night of their first date, safe from Jordan's prying ears.

Jolene was also stowing away from ever watchful overseers, "what my parents don't know can't hurt them."

This cat and mouse game of secretive visitations, both hiding the other from their life, continued for a few months, through the snow and into the threat of Spring. In a small way, the discretion heightened the fun surrounding their relationship, relying on back alleys and closed doors to consummate their affections, furtive touches and the warmth of a close body in the backseat of an Uber.

It was less than ideal, a long distance relationship without the distance. To Ríona, it was the best three months of her young life, now a wound full of salt which the softness of Tomi's lips slowly begun to wash clean.

"Yeah," she shrugged. "It's not like I haven't heard those things said about me."

"They say that about everyone they don't like."

"Do you say that about me," Ríona tried to ask as nonchalantly as she could, desperate to hide the eagerness bursting through her chest, her nerves barely containing themselves. This was nothing like the daydreams earlier.

Jordan looked like she choked on her sugary coffee, "me? What? Of course not. Trust me, I know you're not..." Her face went flush with embarrassment.

CHAPTER 17

"*I* thought I recognised you," some guy said, squeezing his way through the packed room. "You're the McGraw's daughter, Jordan, amirite?"

He dressed casually enough, unlike the normal business associates of Jordan's father's business. But he was way too old to be a college student. Trading questioning looks, neither of them recognised the man claiming to know Jordan or her parents.

"Do I know you," Jordan suspiciously checked the man out, something about his demeanour not fitting in. Everyone else had an ease about them, a weird body language that everyone could read but never quite articulate. He oozed that "you just know" vibe that you look for when meeting a stranger for a coffee meeting; an odd sense that they don't belong.

"Not yet. Name's Sam, miss," he held out his hand. Neither accepted, holding their fiddles as an excuse. "Ah, right. Loved your performance tonight. Shame you two didn't play longer." He focused his attention on her, never Jordan.

"It's an open mic," Ríona started, keeping her tone uninviting. "Standard is three songs. Gives everyone a chance to play."

"Ah, makes sense. Can't have you two beauties hogging the stage," he said with a wry smirk, the kind your friend's grandfather gave your classmate when she comes over to work on your group project. Even his city accent threw up red flags.

Ríona studied the man, suspicious of everyone now that Mrs McGraw instilled her brand of paranoia in her. His jeans fit nicely, not the skinny jeans popular amongst the hipsters and not the ridiculously baggy 90s jeans regaining popularity. They were professional looking jeans, the kind you expected a tech startup CEO to wear now after paying too much for them.

"I've seen you two before, but you were in a band. Do you two often play by yourselves?"

"Yeah," Jordan replied curtly.

Unsatisfied with the direct answer, Sam turned to Ríona expectingly.

"We've always played together, just the two of us. Playing with a band is pretty new."

"Wouldn't have guessed. All of you seem to really click on the stage. Like you're all best friends or something."

"Or professionals."

"That's good to hear. And that you two regularly play on your own. I hope you don't mind me saying, but I think you two sound better on your own. You two seem to have more fun when it's just you two. A real, um, chemistry between you two." He gave them a knowing smile.

When neither spoke, he continued, "I think it would be great to see you two performing around Omaha, don't you?" Neither replied. "Why don't you have a coffee with me? My treat, of course. I have a lot of connections around town I could introduce you to."

Jordan looked to her pleading, fear buried behind those doe eyes still coming down from the ecstasy of being on stage.

"Maybe another time. We have a lot going on in our lives. Finals are coming up soon."

"Ah, you need to get back to your boyfriends," he teased with another knowing wink. "Pretty girls like you must have boys lining up at the door."

"Are you one of those creepy old men who try to pick up twenty-year-olds," Jordan spat at the man, making no effort to disguise that she was over this conversation.

"Oh no no, I'm a happily married man." With a sudden realisation after taking a quick glance around, "to a woman. Of course."

"Then why do you want to know about our dating lives," Ríona asked, her contempt saccharine sweet.

"Oh, I didn't realise you were Irish," he ignored her question.

"I have an Irish name," she shrugged before turning to Jordan. "I figured it was obvious. Let's get going. I was hoping to stick around but not with this creep."

"No, you two stick around," the gruff open-mic host instructed as he forced his way between them and Sam. "Name's Dirt," he introduced himself with an overzealous calloused and deeply tanned handshake that caused Sam to wince. "You know these ladies?"

"I was just getting to," he said examining his hand, shaking the pain way. The tall, bald, but competitively bearded host paid no attention to the obvious show.

"So: no." He turned to them. "If I show him the curb, will you two stay?"

Ríona looked to Jordan who didn't seem to have an answer, only an uneasy glance towards Sam. Ríona did actually want to stay. At least, for another hour or two to listen to some of the other performances and enjoy the kinship they all shared as musicians. Open mics where more than a chance to perform for strangers, it was a place to see friends whose only commonality was music. It was her social hour, tonight in particular being a new venue and she hated the idea of missing it.

"Sam, let me introduce you to my husband, Bear. Bear's going to help you find the door."

As if the two practiced this routine, Bear stepped forward, his arms the size of their heads. A bit shorter than the already imposing Dirt, Bear looked like the bouncer you'd expect at a rowdy dance club full of drunken frat boys; his tight black spandex workout shirt highlighting the chiselled pectoral muscles and a smile itching to for an excuse. Sam took one long look at Bear before hesitantly turning around defeated.

"If that guy bothers you ladies again, just let us know."

Ríona handed him the microphone. "Thanks. Have you seen that bloke before?"

"Can't say I have. Looks too vanilla to be around here. Doesn't look like the normal kind of tourist we get."

Jordan eyed him suspiciously, "you get tourists here?"

He let out a hearty laugh, "tourist. You really don't know?"

Jordan shrugged.

"Straight people who come to watch all us qays like we're their own personal show. Anyway, you two go mingle. Bear will keep an eye out for that creep. Oh, and we'd love to have you two back anytime." He lowered his voice, "you two live up to your reputation."

CHAPTER 18

"*M*iss Kilbride," the professor called after dismissing class. An older Japanese man with greying black hair and a bald crown, his twiggy hair in a perpetual state of 'just woke up', his clothes a loose, casual pair of slacks and a button-up shirt, never fully tucked in and on more than one occasion, buttoned incorrectly.

She knew why he was calling her name. Over the course of her college career, she had maintained one of the highest grades in his class. While some of her compositions were less than emotionally moving, they were technically proficient. Fortunately for her, grades were based on academic precision, not whether you wrote a top ten hit.

"We need to talk," he stated the obvious.

After the night she had, she wanted to quip back, "well, duh" but restrained her tongue. Biting the head off her favourite professor, who coincidently taught most of her classes, a few weeks before finals was probably one of the poorer decisions she could make.

"About," she played along, feigning her innocence that neither of them believed.

"I know things have been... stressful the past few weeks. I had a visit from Mrs McGraw," he paused, letting the impact of his guest weigh on her, the implication of her visit needing no mention. "If you need to drop a few classes, I'm sure we can accommodate."

"Oh," this is what she meant by taking care of things. It was tempting... and an opportunity Zach would quickly jump on, and perhaps even Jordan if it was presented correctly. They were used to their parents buying influence, but it always came with a cost.

"No," she resisted, "I need to finish my classes on my own. I'm so close and it would feel like quitting."

"Hmmm," he pondered. "Honestly," he motioned for her to sit, his plump middle pushing the limits of the shirt buttons, "I would consider the offer if I was you. I get it, you have a lot on your plate. I can only imagine how you feel—losing so much."

He rested his hand on hers, squeezing it gently, attempting to comfort her. Only he made her exceedingly more uncomfortable, his dry, wrinkly skin easily enveloping her small, fragile fingers. Instinctively she wanted to pull away from the cold grip; instead she hid the grimace she desperately wanted to make before pulling away to her own personal space.

"I'm okay." She knew that wasn't enough to assuage his feigned concern, nor would she expect it to. It was nothing more than a customary response one gives when they would prefer to discuss other topics. A gentle lie, of sorts. Except, now it wasn't a gentle lie of her own accord, but an orchestrated ploy she was forced to play a part in.

"You sure? I understand the loss of a parent," he finally released her hand. "I wasn't as young as you, mind you. I had my own family, two teenage sons, a career here teaching, and plenty of other family around me to support me. You don't have any siblings?"

"I'm an only child," she answered, trying to recall if she ever mentioned that in any of his classes. Maybe it came up after her mother passed? The weeks shortly after were a haze.

"That must be rough."

"Eh," she shrugged, "I've never minded. It's nice sometimes." That wasn't a lie. "I've seen siblings in action."

Watching Zachary and Jordan grow up, their rivalries as fierce as any imagined in the movies. The shouting, the bickering, the conniving. Before they entered the early "official" adult years, they barely spoke to each other at times, their arguments an incessant battle the moment the two entered each other's spheres.

"Speaking of which, how is your boyfriend, Zachary?"

It pained her to not correct the older man. It pained her not to correct that weird man from the previous night.

"I imagine seeing him in the hospital is affecting your studies, no?"

She hadn't spent much, if any time at all since that time with Jordan, at the hospital visiting. Zach was the furthest thing from her mind, but she couldn't tell him that. Mrs McGraw somehow was corralling her small life to ensure she didn't stray from her script.

"I guess. I suppose I haven't been putting much heart into my work."

He nodded his head, acting like some wise sage, "I get it. This really isn't the kind of music you're interested in."

"I'm just happy to play," she quipped back halfheartedly, knowing somehow her answer was only vaguely true.

"Don't be a brown-noser," he stood up and walked back to his baby grand, the real ivory keys still warm from the student performers showing off their pieces.

His insult jabbed at her, drawing a sharp breath as she reeled her heartbeat back to normal. She watched Mr Chris, as he told everyone to call him, shuffle through the dozen or so scores sitting on top of the piano, before pulling the one she recognised as hers.

"You played it with exactly the kind of technical precision I expected. Frankly, you are one of my better students. Lucy plays with so much enthusiasm that she misses the downbeat too often and throws the listener off, or worse, her accompaniment. Tyler... that boy doesn't know a G-Major from a D-Minor. His idea of a chord progression is repeating the same five notes over and over until I just want to burn my ears." He turned to look at her, "you on the other hand... you have talent."

"But your talent isn't here. This," he held up her score, shaking the papers, "is, as you would say, is rubbish. Utter rubbish."

"The others enjoyed it, I thought," she meekly defended herself, still stinging from his poorly veiled insults.

"They also think 'Tay Tay' is a musical genius," he raised an eyebrow at her, glancing over his reading glasses. "She's an amazing performer, sure, but a genius she's not. She deserves her fame, don't misunderstand me. She knows the music business.

"But that's not you, is it? You're only in this class so you can play it safe. One day you'll be teaching students like yourself the basics they should have learned three years ago so they can pass my class. Or worse, you'll become me."

He turned back to the piano, arranging her score on the music rack. Starting with an unexpected forte in the key of G Minor then dropping to a mezzo pianissimo that inched its way through each chord, from Gm to an A7 for a subtle variation on a theme, Mr Chris rewarding her with an approving draw of the lips, before leaping into a frantic series of sixteenth notes running up and down the Bb and F chords, then returning to the clinical i-VI-III-VII.

Unlike her playing, he somehow managed to make the notes dance despite their boring existence, taking daring liberties with the whole notes, cutting some lives short, others lingering in the background before jumping into the next harmony.

He played it perfectly, never missing a single note or missing a down-beat, but it wasn't her sterile piece anymore. It had morphed into something she didn't recognise as her own work, her weeks of labour to craft the most acceptable piece possible, the one that would become her final assignment. It wasn't a piece she'd say she'd play for Jordan, but it was one that would send her walking across the stage, shaking hands of faculty she's only met in the school newspaper.

After mashing the final note, a punctuation mark dictating the terms of the breakup between the listener and the musician, he let it ring for what could only be described as an uncomfortable eternity—her sad it had finished, him waiting for Ríona to make some sort of self-discovery "aha" moment that despite his efforts was just elusive enough to taste, but never enough to savour.

"*That* is what I expected from you." He turned on the bench to face her directly, to make a point of his candour. "I've heard you play. And I don't mean in that band with the McGraw twins. I mean really play as if you're longing for something.

"I'm going to let you keep this—actually, I'm going to make you keep this. This will be the start of your final composition, but," he emphasised the word too forcibly, "I will give you the option to bow out now.

"No one says no to the McGraw's, so it is your choice. You can leave now, take the easy road, you pass this class, you graduate, and you pay whatever price you owe. Or," he drew out the word, letting it sink in, as he turned back to his piano, his fingers again playing joyfully on the keys, left hand a hammer, his right a ballerina.

"Or what," she asked, forever suspicious and afraid.

"Or you play for me like you played for that bleach blonde standing next to you on stage."

Mr Chris kept his back to her, the sounds of romanticism enveloping the room, a love song for the poets to revel in as Spring blossomed around them.

She sat there as if she had a front row ticket to a solo performance conducted just for her. A sonnet of notes and a symphony of emotion pounding her heart strings. His playing was entrancing. She closed her eyes and let herself be swallowed by passion and creativity flying through improvised progressions and runs, sprinkling the theme with licks here and there, but always finding its way back to her original piece, landing gracefully before once again taking off in a new direction, a new untapped emotion, some imaginative invocation her professor pulled from some recess of his mind.

"No, it's not me," Ríona said softly under the triumphant chorus before leaving Mr Chris to his wishful daydreams.

CHAPTER 19

"*W*oah, what is *that*," Ríona asked, shocked by the large white school bus parked behind Tomi's shop, only a few yards away from her covered Roan.

"That? That's Cam and her wife, Elle. Or as we call them, Tequila and White."

"I'm not even going to ask," she eyed Tomi.

The taller woman pulled her in close, "you'll find out soon enough. Oh, and they have two kids. Or bairns, right?"

"That's Scottish," she huffed, pulling away from the cinnamon musk, her arms folded against her chest protectively. "I'm insulted by that accusation, by the way."

"Ooooh, sorry," Tomi mocked. "What do you call them? Leprechauns?"

"Nah, leprechauns are quieter and you never see them. They're nothing alike, I promise."

"Really now? How many leprechauns do you have stuffed in the ol' truck of yours?"

Ríona put on her best worst Lucky the Leprechaun impersonation, "if I told ye that I'n ha' none o' me own."

"Whatch'y'all talkin' 'bout," the taller one of the pair asked, her messy curly crop crowning her head like an ironic tiara, her thick rural Texas accent making it nearly impossible for Ríona to understand without subtitles.

"Cam, meet Ríona. Ríona, meet Cam and Elle. Elle's the short one."

"I gathered that," Ríona quipped back falling back under Tomi's muscular arm.

The sun was quickly fading, the red hue of the sky painting the white bus in shades of pink. The windows, albeit heavily tinted, glowed softly with hints of a full kitchen and living room hiding inside.

Elle apologised for not shaking hands, citing a lack of being freshly washed after setting dinner out for the kids. Elle wore the same dark curly hair, only hers rested well past her shoulders. Her pleated calf length denim skirt and tucked in button up pastel baby blue an almost hilarious contrast to both Tomi and Cam's über practical jeans, cowboy boots, and plain tee shirt.

"I see you staring," Elle teased. "Wanna see inside as these two do their macho thing?"

"Um, yeah! I'd love to."

"Hey now," Cam interjected, "our 'macho thing' is called 'dinner'."

"Just don't burn it this time, okay, babe?"

"You hear that, Tomi? I'm still taking the blame for your catching that grill on fire." Cam turned and left Elle a wet peck on the lips before joining Tomi in a clamour of laughter and the retelling of stories both remember very differently.

"I apologise for 'em. They were once told to 'act like a lady' and they spent every waking moment since livin' up to the opposite." Her accent confused Ríona. One moment, she imagined Elle living in a swanky New York apartment sipping tea with a gaggle of ladies at an exclusive spa, the next her accent sounded like it was dug straight out of the Texas soil. Her freshly painted short finger nails and well trimmed short curly bob with manicured side bangs landed towards her first suspicion.

"So this is your home," Ríona asked in awe as she climbed the narrow bus stairwell, a recently distant memory of her early school years.

Unlike her school days, those three deep steps ushered her into a modern ocean front condo's living room instead of row after row of musty pleather seats best used as torture devices than devices to safely convey children.

It lacked no amenity. A full sized white porcelain apron sink with a stainless steel tap split a long live edge epoxied counter top filled with seashells of all shapes, colours, and sizes that much have taken a pair of children at least a whole weekend to collect. On the opposite wall was a small table covered in dirty dishes, a fallen bottle of ketchup, and various children's toys.

"This is fancier than my flat," Ríona said in awe, touching the seashell cabinet pulls, "not that my broken futon counts as fancy."

"Tomi said you were living in a van," Elle quizzed as she deftly cleared the table, dumping food scraps into a small bin on the counter. Loose toys found themselves dumped into one of the wicker baskets under the couch.

"Not yet. Still needs lots of work."

"Right. That's all Cam. She's the electrician."

Without warning, two small children burst through the front door, the older one complaining loudly and profusely that their younger pairing "won' l-leave me alone". While Elle attended to her parental duties of breaking up meaningless squabbles over how much of the tyre swing each could occupy, Ríona took to exploring the "public" spaces within the converted bus.

She imagined her future tiny home on wheels wouldn't be as roomy as this, but at least she wouldn't be sharing that space nonstop. Plus, she saw herself spending more times outside of the van than inside.

"Look," the younger one demanded from behind Ríona. He held up a small plastic terrarium with a small black and yellow striped lizard inside; its skin looked to be peeling off and discoloured.

"What is it," Ríona played along.

"I's-a d-dinosaur! Rawr," the kid imitated.

"You know what it's called, sweetie." Elle bent down to examine the child's specimen. "And it looks hungry. It just moulted its skin."

"A wace wunner," the little boy answered proudly.

"Yes, it is. We have these back home too, don't we?"

"Yeah. I caught 'em 'ere t-too," he struggled to get the words out, the hard consonants exceedingly difficult. It was cute, in a small way, how poorly the child spoke.

As if reading her mind, or likely her knowing smile, Elle answered with practiced eased of someone who's been asked the same question one too many times, "he's speech and language delayed. If he starts waving his hands at you, he's trying to sign to you. He likes to tell people 'no' a lot." Elle demonstrated signing "no", her pointer and middle fingers outstretched and clasping against the tip of her thumb, the other two fingers tucked away into her palm as if she was a three-fingered claw machine grasping at flies in the room.

"He's hearing, so don't let him pretend otherwise." She turned to the younger sibling sitting on the couch, minding her own business, her dress stained with splotches of red sauce. "And you, child, go'n wash up. I swear," she huffed.

Without taking her eyes off the toy occupying her attention, the younger child absently walked towards the back of the bus, somehow avoiding her brother's flurry to beat her to wherever the door at the back of the kitchen led to. Ríona wanted to ask, but it felt awkward asking to see someone's bedroom.

"To answer your question earlier though, we don't live in it full-time. We have a small homestead down in Texas."

"Ah. So it's more like an RV for you then?"

"You could say that. A lot of RV'ers also live in their rigs too."

"Why do I feel like I'm only recently learning about so much of the world," Ríona wondered out loud, mostly to herself than to Elle.

"Travel will do that to ya. Honestly the best decision we ever made. I'm guessing you haven't done much travelling?"

"Not unless you count moving here," she shrugged. "Me mum and I did take some summer trips, but not many. All fairly short since we had to come back to the farm."

"Ah. I hear that about farmers a lot. Can't exactly take a month off to backpack around Indonesia, can ya?"

"You could, but you'd come back to your neighbours hogtied and held hostage by the cows, and the goats wold have eaten all the linens. Best avoid the barnyard revolt." She smirked at Elle, hoping the woman understood enough about farm life and literature classics to get the joke.

"Ah, so basically it's the same as having kids. Only I'm forced to take mine with me."

"Ha! I guess you could say that. At least the cows don't tell you 'no'. The horses... they tell you 'no' with their hind legs. Ain't pretty. Friend of mine still has a hoof print on her forehead from when she got kicked as a kid."

Elle grimaced, "ouch. Worst we had growing up in the city was getting stabbed in the leg by your sister."

"Stabbed?" Again, someone reinforcing the idea that her growing up an only child was not a terrible arrangement.

"Yeah. I did something to piss my sister off, she had a pencil in her hand, so she stabbed me. She was like five or something."

"Brutal."

She brushed off her past with a gentle laugh. "Eh, it was fair payback for what I had put her through. I was the real terror in the family."

"How old were you?"

"I was seventeen. A high school senior, pissed off at the world, still buried deep in the closet. Somehow my little sister knew and I threatened to behead all her Barbies if she told anyone. She didn't believe me so I ripped a head off one," Elle emphasised with a roll of the shoulders. "So she stabbed me. We laugh about it now."

Behind the closed door, two children screamed out, the boy complaining about his sister invading his space. The girl resorted to crying, too young to form a coherent rebuttal for why she couldn't take a bath with her older brother.

"Motherly duties call. Why don't you go check up on the gals and make sure they haven't caught anything else on fire."

CHAPTER 20

*B*rie handed her a lowball glass with beautifully etched details —inside a handful of large ice cubes chilling the whiskey sour, a hint of grenadine floating towards the bottom.

"Thanks," Ríona said before leaning back in the uncomfortable picnic chair, a versatile metal chair perfect for weathering storms, but unduly uncomfortable on her sore body, still broken from the day's work wiring up Roan. After hashing out plans with Cam, Elle providing an occasional translation, they started the morning early to make the most of the short weekend visit.

The smell of roasting meats wafted through the air, the charred flesh tainting her enjoyment of the freshly made sour mix. At least the sauce smelled good, Ríona took comfort. Tomi made sure to grab some grill friendly vegetables just for Ríona. A variety of zucchini squashes, marinated cauliflower pieces, and her favourite, sliced aubergine and portabella caps. She may not get the appeal of eating animal flesh, but the very least should could participate in the meal. Mostly she wanted to try out this "famous" barbecue sauce of Cam's.

She called it her 'Texas Heat'. Something about a so-called secret blend of peppers she grew on her homestead that you couldn't find in any store. Tomi seemed pretty convinced it was indeed the best barbecue sauce she has ever had. Elle spent the day watching over the small pit Tomi built on the back patio while she kept her wife busy with questions about electricity.

Simple questions, it seemed, such as the differences between AC and DC currents. In her work helping a farmhand fix the occasional tractor malfunction, it was never a big concern about the "type" of electricity in the tractor. It just *was*. Grab a new part, rip the old one off, and replace it with the new one.

Roan was far from as simple. Mostly because it was a blank slate inside, aside from the custom electric pop-top the original owner had installed, it was basically empty. Cam was patient with her, carefully explaining what each component and wire did, always a dire warning of death or mayhem.

"Undersize a wire and next thing ya kno' yer van is on fire. Twelve volt won't kill ya, but the fire sure will," she cautioned until Ríona could repeat the phrase in her sleep.

Ríona had left the ordering up to Cam since this wasn't her first conversion. Their "skoolie" wasn't her first either. When her and Elle got together, she owned a much shorter bus that was perfect for a solo traveller fresh out of the Air Force. After a few years the couple decided to adopt, and Cam built a bigger, better bus.

She had been warned that the laying of wire through the van would take up most of the day. When Cam sent her what she needed to order, she thought Cam had made a mistake in the amount of wiring she needed. Her bus was less than twenty feet long, so how in the world could she use up close to five-hundred feet worth of expensive copper?

But they did. Almost ran out of it too, but Cam had planned well, her diagram of the bus accounted for nearly everything including her future faerie lights that needed something called a "transformer", but not those big giant ones she sees on the power poles along the interstate. Much smaller ones that could easily be tucked away behind her switch panel. Cam even planned for outside lighting. After seeing their skoolie lit up at night, it made complete sense.

Julz interrupted Cam and Ríona's exposition of the day, "so how are you affording all this?"

No one had outright asked her before. Tomi skirted the question as best she could, never once directly asking where her money was coming from. Only Jordan really knew, not that she would ask.

"Savings," was all she could muster for a lie.

None of the others seemed to notice Julz's question, except Brie who noticed everything her wife said or did.

"Savings, huh? What do you plan to do for work while you're out on the road?" There was a hint of bitterness to her question. It left Ríona wondering if Julz had some unknown dislike of her. The first time she met the woman, clearly at least a decade younger than Brie, and a touch more feminine than her hardcore butch partner, she was friendly enough despite being buried in her phone most of the night.

"Was hoping to do the same thing I'm doing now. Just, you know, not here."

Brie inserted herself into the conversation as others started quieting down to listen in, "you're a musician, right? Fiddle?"

"Yeah," she was pleased Brie remembered. Not just that she was a musician, but that it was the fiddle, not a violin. "I play at a few pubs in Lincoln, and sometimes I travel to competitions and country fairs and such. I've played at a couple of the Renn Fairs too—which are a ton of fun. I get to dress up like some faerie or pixie and walk around playing."

Ríona had convinced Jolene to go the Spring they were secretly seeing each other. Jolene's family wouldn't dare be seen at such an event, citing their belief in Jesus for their disgust of the event and any event like it. The girls showed too much cleavage and legs, Jolene's mother had complained. They had a laugh over the irony as Jolene recounted all the complaints her parents had about the events when they took over the RiverWest Park.

It was a beautiful backdrop for the boisterous event, complete with jesters and queens, mead and even knights jousting. During her breaks she'd take a peek at all the events, hand in hand with Jolene, both enjoying the sights Jolene's mothered disparaged.

"So," Julz rudely interrupted her solitary reminiscing, "you don't work. You just bum around?"

"Julz, what the hell," Tomi chastised her, accidentally slamming down her beer bottle at the same time.

"What? It's true," Julz tried to defend herself. Brie grabbed her hand

and squeezed before whispering at her, only the harsh tones audible over Tomi apologising to Ríona.

"She's a trust fund baby," Julz continued loudly. Brie's face paled. "She's off flaunting her money and travelling all over without a care in the world." She turned to Ríona with an icy glare, "must be nice."

Tomi leaped to her feet, "Julz, Jesus Christ woman. Shut it."

"She's half your age and has more money than all of us to just throw around on some shitty van."

"Honey, please," Brie pleaded, taking the drink out of Julz' hand and pouring it on the ground.

Ríona choked down a sob, the tears warming her eyelids. *Trust fund baby?* Her world suddenly felt as dark as the night's sky. A bleak weight crushing her, enveloping her. Try as she might, she couldn't hold back the tears anymore, the whimpering sobs turning into an angry torrent of salty warmth streaming down her cheeks.

"It's not a trust fund," Ríona finally said. Everyone turned to her—all but Julz had pity in their eyes. "It's me mother's life insurance. I'd much rather me mum be here. I wouldn't have to figure out what to do anymore, where to go—anything.

"I lost me only home. First... first I was ripped away from me home-land and all the family I woul' ever know—now the only home I know was sold without my consent. I didn't even know me mother had sold it until the lawyer showed up after me mother's funeral. She stood there with a pile of paperwork for me to sign—agreeing to leave everything that wasn't a 'personal item' behind in return for some fecking check.

"That's what they thought the 'fair market value' of me life was worth. Me world. Me *everything*. Once I graduate I have nothing. The lease on me flat is up. Me house is gone. And now the bloody McGraw's have drug me into their stupid political rubbish. I can't... I just can't."

She pulled out of Tomi's embrace, stumbling over the heavy metal chair as she tried to escape the moment tearing her heart apart. *Trust fund... if only.* Unlike home where she could hide in her bedroom, buried deep inside her too large for one person closet. It was comforting there, the lightless cosiness of solitude, untouched by anyone but her.

Behind her she heard Tomi's anger blistering across her words directed at Julz, some hints of a long unresolved dispute between them taking forefront once again. She wanted far away from it. Anywhere but here. Anywhere but this city, this state... this life.

With no where to go, her truck feeling too claustrophobic and a harsh reminder of why the title now displayed her name, she found herself standing in front of Roan, her beautiful escape. The escape she and Cam had spent a solid day working on, the one where Tomi and her shared a kiss, if only too brief a scandal.

She slid inside, the interior courtesy lights still disconnected, leaving her in a peaceful abyss free from outside judgement. So many weights stacked on top of her right now, she felt like her chest would collapse in on itself. For a brief moment she thought about how Giles Corey felt and laughed.

When she told her mother she was leaving, she couldn't answer why. She tried convincing her mother—in hindsight, she realised, she was trying to convince herself—that it had nothing to do with Jolene. The way Jolene turned on her so viciously and callously at that little Italian place in Omaha with the oversized booths and the almost red walls, not far from where her and Jordan just played actually.

It had taken all her resolve to convince herself to play there, telling herself that Jolene wouldn't be back ever again so it was safe despite the lingering memories. It was all hers now. And yet... she hated that like she hated that Lincoln was all hers now.

She pulled one of the blankets off the passenger seat Cam had used to protect the well-kept powder blue leather. The blanket was a little dirty, but right now Ríona didn't care if it was covered in filth. She desperately wanted to lay down, to press her hands against the bare metal walls, to feel the cool night air biting away at the leftover daytime heat. To feel connected to something that wasn't her past, that wasn't this hurt gnawing at her.

Outside she could hear the crunching of gravel under a heavy boot. It wasn't searching or wandering around aimlessly. It was meaningful.

Tomi gently knocked on the van door before carefully pulling it open and revealing her tall frame backlit by the stars and faint light of the fire pit, the moon hidden behind the Earth's shadow for another week. Her military build could be intimidating, but at the moment, as Ríona stared at her through blurry eyes, she was anything but.

"I'm sorry about her," Tomi started in her husky voice, a salve for the sting Julz' words still inflicted. "She's drunk... not that that's any excuse to treat you like that."

Ríona sat up, leaving space for Tomi to join her, if she wanted. Ríona hugged her legs to her chest and rested her cheek on knee caps. Tomi sat in the doorway, letting in a draft of fresh air.

"And I'm sorry about your mother. Jordan told me about her—and you of course—a lot over the years. She sounded like a wonderful woman and I'm sad I'll never get to meet her."

Ríona didn't comment. She was content to listen, just enjoying the presence of her voice while she sank further into the comfort of her imaginary closet littered with every stuffed animal a preteen could find at the various flea markets.

"I think I understand more now what Roan here means to you." She took a moment to marvel at the work her and Cam managed. Ríona knew she couldn't see much, but wasn't going to interrupt.

"It's what the Air Force meant to me. It was a new home when I felt like the home I had was pulled out from underneath me. One day every-thing is fine, you are where you feel like you should be, and the next..." She didn't need to say the words for Ríona to understand. She didn't know if Jordan had conveyed the fact Ríona knew her family disowned her. There was no need. That expression; those words; that sigh... it was a language she imagined few outside their hidden world would ever understand at a primal level, a hidden secret only people like them could see.

"I grew up around Wichita back in the eighties. It was a different world back then, back before the tech giants started moving in and all y'all younger millennials flooded in. I... I couldn't take it anymore so I left."

A stillness invaded the air between them. Tomi shifted uncomfort-ably, a secret itching to escape. She started to speak but hesitated.

"More like ran away," she admitted softly, her face turned towards the glimmering night sky.

She had never thought of it in that way. *Running away...* It had a ring to it. She wasn't running *towards* something. There was no destination in mind, no grandiose career path to chase after; nothing. Just a giant unknown world far from everything she knew and far, far away from all of *this*.

"Brie and Julz left, by the way. And Cam and Elle called it a night. Their kids wake up early. So why don't you come inside, take a shower, and get some sleep."

CHAPTER 21

*I*TRIED GETTING OUT OF IT, Ríona texted.

She stared at the phone, waiting for the little grey bubble with ellipses to appear. She shifted her weight hoping Tomi would reply before she was due in class. After a few impatient moments, she gave up waiting, put her phone in Airplane Mode, and shoved the phone into her back pocket.

Jordan called her midday Sunday while Cam and she were finishing installing the solar. Zach finally woke up and the doctors felt comfortable releasing him soon, saying in a few days' time he should be up and walking again. Luckily he suffered no broken bones despite the nasty cuts and even nastier bruising, but to expect some side effects from the coma. The doctor reassured them it would be nothing major, just irritability and some trouble walking, but otherwise he recovered remarkably well.

SEEMS SO SUDDEN, Riona texted.

I KNOW. THEY SAID THE SWELLING WENT DOWN QUICKLY. NO BRAIN DAMAGE.

I'M NOT SURE IF THAT'S A GOOD THING OR NOT. LOL.

HE'S BACK TO HIMSELF, THAT'S FOR SURE, Jordan had joked.

Not wanting to waste an opportune publicity stunt so close to the election, the McGraw's decided to hold a fundraiser dinner at their estate to celebrate their son's "miraculous recovery". Of course, Mrs McGraw pointed out with a mischievous grin, Ríona would need to be there for "appearances sake".

When you're done playing housewife with my asshole cousin, I would love the company, Tomi texted back after letting her linger in class suffering, itching to check her phone despite the professor's strict demands all phones remain hidden.

After quickly replying with a heart emoji, she found Jordan waiting for her outside the music hall. Her bleach blonde hair a beacon in the open-air mall as she pushed through rushing students eager to make it to their next class on time. The open field was filled with pickup frisbee players and young freshmen enjoying their first taste of freedom away from their parents' protective wing. Some simply relishing the fact they weren't expected to be somewhere every moment of the day while others sought romances and flings with someone outside their existing social circles.

"Shouldn't you be in class still," Ríona asked as she plopped down on the manicured grass next to Jordan.

Jordan watched the frisbee players run up and down a makeshift field lined with backpacks for a long moment before answering, her eyes trying to track the flying disc. "Yeah... I sorta snuck out early. Couldn't stomach being in there any longer."

"You feeling okay?"

"I guess. I dunno," she turned her attention to her fingernails as she picked at the imaginary dirt underneath them. "I know I need to focus more on school. Finals are, what, four weeks away? Four weeks, Rí, four! I'll be sent to whatever fancy law school my father can buy my way into. Which I'm sure is Harvard like him. And you'll be running off to do whatever. "

"What a way to word it," Ríona laughed at the absurdity. At any other point in their life, it would be absurd. Maybe it still was, her running away from home when she should be focusing on finding a partner to settle down with, building a family, doing all the things people her age were expected to do.

Ríona tried to shake those thoughts from her mind. "What's that test you have to take?"

"The LSAT? It's this summer. My dad's making me take this boot camp course beforehand, so it's not like I can even spend time with you to celebrate." Her tone turned from annoyed to sullen, "now that Zach won't be graduating this semester, its *all* on me. I'm the 'good twin' supposedly. I must carry on the family tradition or some bull." She rolled her eyes in disgust. Her usually bright face weighed down with worry. Even her chipper singsong voice drifted into adulthood, sounding more like a morose version of her mother. Minus the constant threat of sexual seduction.

She didn't know what magic words would comfort her friend. This wasn't something she had ever encountered, this pressure to be like someone else at all costs. Her own mother never had to push her to be like her father. Ever since she was little, she had always wanted to be just like him. To play music, to dance, to sing.

"So I won't be able to save you tonight," Jordan continued, somehow sensing the worry building up in her. "You're stuck with Zach. And you can't just shrug him off like normal either, sorry."

"Ugh," she complained out loud, letting herself fall back heavily on the soft grass springing back to life after the mild winter. "I hate my life." She buried her hands into her hair.

Jordan turned in defeat to rest her head on Ríona's stomach. Her thick hair tickling the exposed flesh between Ríona's raised flannel and her hip hugger jeans.

"Stop that," Ríona exclaimed, suddenly hyper-aware of Jordan's presence, her soft hair both a tease and a torture.

"Not my fault you're so ticklish. I'm comfy." Jordan didn't move. Ríona would be content if she never moved.

Ríona missed this. She *would* miss this. Only a few more weeks left and this would end. No longer would Jordan's parents let her get away with "girlish things" like laying on her best friend's stomach in public view. Soon she would be expected to wear dress slacks and fancy cocktail dresses at all times, and to carry business cards with her family's law firm embossed in gilded lettering like some pretentious Gatsby holdover from a hundred years ago.

Four weeks and she would be alone. No one would be dragging her to performances, no one would be greeting her in homeroom with a schedule she was expected to follow, no one would be gently knocking on her door when she was too tired and too heartbroken to welcome a new day.

Four bloody weeks.

CHAPTER 22

*D*inner wasn't until eight, but Ríona didn't want to arrive like a normal guest. She wasn't a normal guest. Her beat up Ford would certainly broadcast that to all the guests who'd show up in oversized blacked out SUVs and pickup trucks worth more than most families make in two years. Her hand-me-down that was older than her would be safely hidden out of sight behind one of the many buildings littering the McGraw's sprawling estate.

"Good day, ma'am," one of the staff greeted her with a tip of his hat. "You're good back here." He gave her a quick wink, knowing, like her, that the easiest way to slink out of the McGraw's estate wasn't down the main drive but out the service road that was a near straight shot to her home. Someone *else's* home now, actually.

"Thanks. Watch over her," she wanted to say his name, but she couldn't remember it. She wondered if she ever knew it. It was unusual for them to spend any time out by the large vats and thousands of glass bottles. Jordan's parents deemed her uncle's warehouses "unfit" for either of them to explore.

"Ya know I will, ma'am. You okay walking by yourself?"

"Yeah. Everyone will be busy schmoozing with all the rich folk they won't notice little ol' me sneaking out the back." She didn't know why she said that with a slight twang. It just felt right, and a little mischievous.

"That's what worries me. They bring their boys who thinkin' they can get away with damn near anything. Makes me worry about Miss Jordan and you. You two ain't like 'em."

"Don't worry, I'll get one of the staff to walk me back," she lied. Although she regretted he had a point, one she should probably listen to, but she couldn't risk someone noticing her sneaking out to visit Tomi.

"Good," he gave her a small smile. "I'm just gonna lock up is that's alright with you."

Walking the dusty gravel road towards the house, she missed the smell of hops lingering in the air. It was never a lovely smell, certainly not compared to the Yellowhorn trees, a smell her and Jordan enjoyed on their Spring rides around her mother's farm, but it held a nostalgia she yearned for right then.

At the back entrance to the kitchen, Mrs McGraw watched her from the window, disappearing only to open the door for her. Mrs McGraw was dressed provocatively yet just barely recognisable as classy to remain decent. In spite of being a renowned contracts lawyer, Mrs McGraw still intentionally relied on her curves and cleavage to sway opinions.

"They're upstairs," she announced nonchalantly as she gave her a once over. "I adore your dress." She pulled at the dress's lace sleeves, the sheer fabric underneath cleverly hiding her scars. "And just because he's your boyfriend now, doesn't mean you can slip into his room alone, ya know."

"Oh darn," Ríona replied flatly. There was no need for her to hide her dislike yet.

"Before you go up," Mrs McGraw spoke up before Ríona could make it through the door leading to the rear staircase. "Thanks for doing this."

Her respite alone with Jordan was a blip, her nerves and anxiety getting the better of her. She desperately wanted to focus all her attention solely on Jordan right now, but her mind kept wandering to her cousin, and the anticipation of spending a weekend alone with her.

"Shall we," Zach asked calmly from Jordan's door, leaning on a crutch. His face expertly stitched. Only short, thin red lines could still be seen. His left eye still puffy but no longer a horror show. Even the purple pooling underneath the skin appeared faded.

"We shall," Jordan regally replied. "You two lovebirds think you'll last the night?"

When she arrived an hour ago, the house was empty save for family and some catering staff popping in and out. Now, she felt like a sardine trapped in a nightmare she could never wake up from. Businessmen and CEOs filled the house, glasses of alcohol occupying a hand at all times while the other alternated between snacking on random bits of meat and shaking hands.

Mr McGraw brought his preferred guests to them, rather than letting Zach hobble about the house "like an invalid". One by one, a nonstop stream of men in suits all chatting vividly with Zach while only offering a cursory nod of acknowledgment towards her. She was just eye candy as far as they were concerned.

"We should eat," Zach finally interrupted his father's charade. "Ríona hasn't eaten since breakfast and I could use a drink if you're going to keep turning me into a pity party."

His father's face reddened as he tried to hold back his usual verbal lashing, drawn faster than a heroic cowboy. In all her years of being around this family, never once had Ríona heard Zachary speak to his father so flippantly. He was a golden boy who could do no wrong, but it meant his tongue was always bit.

"Listen here, boy. These men are the keys to the city and if you want any future of your own, you'd best learn some respect." He glanced at her for a moment, the same disgust unwarrantedly directed at her.

"Thanks." Ríona was relieved to no longer stand there idly tortured in silence as the only person she had any real connection to in the room fluttered around like a hostess seeing to everyone's liquor glasses.

"I'll be so glad when this is all over," Zach admitted with a loud sigh. It was uncharacteristic of him to be so... *normal.*

"Are you feeling okay? I mean, you did just survive a bad wreck. Heck, I'm surprised they even let you out so early."

"Yeah," he started off bitterly, "I'm not."

"Why is that," a man behind them asked nonchalantly munching on some bacon wrapped jalapeño poppers. He took a bite and exaggerated his approval. "Have you tried these," he asked with his mouth still full of unchewed food.

"I'm a vegetarian," Ríona replied coldly. "What are you doing here?"

"You two don't seem like much of a couple, you know that?" Sam shoved the rest of the popper in his mouth, then licked his fingers while staring at Zach, patiently waiting for an answer.

"Seriously, you two act more like disgruntled siblings than some lovebirds waiting for mommy and daddy to leave so you can get it on."

Ríona snapped back, "has anyone ever mentioned how disgusting you are?"

"Probably. But I'm here about you two. Not me. So anyway, what's up with you two?"

Zach took a small step in front of Ríona, placing himself between her and this weird, and gross, man. "If you hadn't heard, I was in a car accident. Barely survived—"

"Your friend died," Sam stated matter-of-factly, no longer attempting to overpower the slightly taller young man with his gaze. Instead, his eyes lusted after the sweeter snacks adorning his tiny plate. "And you lived. I heard. Tragic, really. You seem broken up about it." Sam paused before nibbling his sugary confection.

Zach didn't bite. "I barely knew him. He was a friend of a friend and, if I'm being honest, it was eye opening."

"Ah," he exaggerated before stuffing the rest of the pastry in, along with his fingers before pulling them out with a pop. "Now you've been set straight at last, instantly recovered from your drug addiction. It's a wonderful story, really. Like you're *driving* your own story now."

Sam turned to Ríona, "wouldn't want you to lose any other passengers, now would we? This one's too pretty to die, huh?"

Zach's anger flashed, the same kind he would let loose any time someone insulted his sister, or their hands got too curious. He grabbed Sam's shirt and yanked him towards himself, his weakened legs almost giving out before catching himself with the crutch. Sam noticed and chuckled.

"What's your deal?"

"So you forgive her for dumping you then," Sam teased, completely ignoring his predicament. It seemed he was actually enjoying his odd game of cat and mouse, despite the physical danger it posed. But he also knew Zach couldn't follow through with his threat without harming his father's campaign.

Zach released him with a shove that pained him more than it did Sam. "There's nothing to forgive. She was right to break up with me. She found out about my addiction, tried her best to convince me to give it up, and I didn't.

"So she dumped me. Can you blame her?"

Sam pondered his responses over another pastry, this one covered in icing sugar that quickly transferred to Sam's sticky digits. "Y'all tellin' me this has nothin' to do with your little girlfriend here leaving you for a woman?"

Zach looked at her, her heart pounding loudly in her chest, feeling as if it would burst any moment and leave her lying dead in the middle of the McGraw's house. When she didn't respond, he turned back to Sam, "excuse me? What in God's name are ya blabbering 'bout?"

"You heard me. You're 'girlfriend' here is a dyke. Even got the pictures to prove it."

Sam wiped his fingers on his jeans before pulling his phone out of its holster hanging awkwardly on his belt. With prepared ease, he immediately turned the phone towards Zach, showing him this 'proof' he had invested all his confidence in.

"So?" Zach glanced unfazed at the picture of Ríona standing in front of a giant Pride flag, her fiddle in hand, eyes closed, letting her ears see the world around her. "I'm sure you can find pictures of me and my sister in front of one too. Doesn't make us gay either."

"Her being at a gay bar with another woman isn't proof?" He shows Zach another picture.

Ríona recognised the bar. *That means this creep has been following me for weeks.*

"Yeah, that's my cousin. What of it?"

"They've been spending a lot of time together. Including the weekend you were, um, how did the sheriff word it after your momma had a chat with him? Oh, right, the 'unfortunate passenger' in a high-speed car accident that left one dead and one moderately injured but in a coma."

"She's helping me with a project," Ríona finally spoke up, angry and embarrassed. Angry at being stalked like some prey animal and embarrassed by Zach's sudden overbearing protectiveness over her.

"So y'all gonna be spending more time together, huh? Convenient, some would say...," he let the threat trail off.

"Yeah, we will," she angrily retorted, sickened by the incessant accusations both levied against her and against Zach. Yet, somewhere in the back of her head, she knew he was right. Not just about her, but about Zach. The way his mother and father acted, her being recruited to play his "girlfriend", and this creeper following her about. Despite all that, she felt a need to defend not only herself, but Zach. Not even for Jordan's sake, not for the cute little bleach blonde, but for the annoying brother who always tormented her, teased her about her accent, and clearly hated people like her.

She finished her lashing, "you don't restore cars overnight."

"Really now? That's not what I expected you two would be, um, working on together."

"Listen up asshole," Zach buried his anger, "I don't know what your deal is, but I'm done. *We're* done."

"Fine, fine. Tell me, what kind of car are you fixing up?"

"VW bus."

"Oh, one of those cute little vans with the air-cooled engines and four speed auto?"

"No. It's water cooled. And it's a five-speed manual. The weekend you took this picture of us hanging out we had just replaced the tyres, the fuel pump, all of the hoses and gaskets, changed all the fluids, and Tomi then took me out so I could get practice driving it."

Zach chimed in with a sudden realisation, "so you just happen, twice, to run into my girlfriend at *two* different gay bars? Since, clearly, you wouldn't stalk and harass a woman three times younger than you, and a family member of the McGraw's... we might need to talk to your wife and break the news to her, huh? Can you imagine that headline: McGraw's sue creepy pervert for stalking their adopted daughter.

"My father could even add that to his platform. Stalking and harassment is a big deal these days, isn't it, Sam?"

Sam tried to loudly drop the paper plate onto the table. Disappointed with his own display of anger, Sam warned Zach that he would find out what really happened that night before storming out of the house unnoticed by the other guests.

Ríona let Zach brood for a moment. "Are you going to tell me the truth at least?"

Zach didn't reply. He stared at the door Sam left through, something clearly on his mind.

"Zach," she batted his arm with the back of hand. "Are you still here?"

"Yeah, sorry. Was thinking about that night..." He dropped his weight heavily onto the plush velvet chair sitting nearby. "I can't stop seeing his face—all that blood; everywhere."

Ríona sat on the overly large armrest, practically a seat in itself. "I'm sorry." She ran her fingers through his hair, resting her hand on the back of his neck. "Before this is all over, promise me you'll tell me what really happened that night."

Again, he said nothing, preferring staring off into what seemed like nothingness. Instinctively, she checked her phone, both to see how late it was, and to see if Tomi had messaged her. She hadn't.

WHAT WAS THAT, Jordan texted.

DUNNO.

WAS THAT THE WEIRD DUDE FROM THAT BENEFIT?

YEAH. HEY, THINK YOU CAN COVER FOR ME?

YOU BAILING ON ME?

SORTA. SORRY.

TOMI ISN'T BOTHERING YOU, IS SHE?

WHAT? NO! SHE'S COOL.

NOT HITTING ON YOU TOO MUCH?

HA! JUST EXCITED TO WORK ON ROAN.

I CAN'T WAIT TO SEE THE WORK YOU'VE DONE. I'LL GO DISTRACT MY PARENTS.

K! ALSO... CAN YOU CHECK UP ON ZACH? I'M WORRIED ABOUT HIM. HE WON'T TALK TO ME.

CHAPTER 23

*A*fter texting Tomi, Ríona fired up the old pickup truck. Ideally she wanted to change before heading out, but after that encounter with Sam, she worried she was still being watched, despite no one being in sight. She hadn't noticed him before, she reminded herself, and getting caught changing behind the McGraw's hops shed wouldn't bode well.

Anxiously she sped down the service road, a mostly smooth dirt road intended for heavy trucks and tractors. At the gate, she glanced at her phone once more while waiting for the automatic opener to slowly, and loudly, creak open.

Just an address showed on her notification screen. She clicked on it, half expecting it to be the same bar they had gone to previously. Instead, the name of a karaoke bar popped up. She quickly glanced at the photos and the four-star rating before shoving the phone back into the console and letting Siri's ambiguous voice lead the way.

Just as the pictures advertised, Tomi had invited her to yet another dive. Giant neon letters blinked infrequently, broadcasting the one feature this pub had over all the defunct establishments. Beside it stood a deserted strip mall, a remnant of the boom and bust cycles all strip malls suffer made worse by the move to larger cities towards the coasts. The once bright blue facade washed out by a decade of blistering sun. All the doors replaced with plywood, broken glass, and caution tape.

Then there was the pub. A glowing beacon of life that buzzed in her ears as she stood outside while the bouncer checked her ID. The gruff butch woman with a flat top cut and baggy jeans eyed her suspiciously, as if she wasn't actually the age her card claimed she was.

Abruptly satisfied, the woman handed her ID back and wrapped a bright green band around her tiny wrist. Ríona slipped through the open door into a dark, hazy room filled with loud voices and an emcee who, surprisingly, could actually sing really well.

"There's your girl." Ríona recognised the voice as Elle's, but she didn't see her anywhere. Then a hand appeared from behind a short wall separating the pool tables from the lounge.

"Hot damn," Tomi announced like a thirsty coyote, her eyes eating her exposed legs up. "I didn't think you'd come still dressed up... not that I don't mind the sight."

"Ríona, you want anything," Cam asked after downing the last of her beer. Elle's wine glass was also empty.

"A whiskey sour." Tomi took her hand unexpectedly and pulled her closer.

"You two better be done making out when we get back, ya hear," Elle teased, giving Ríona a quick hug, the smell of Riesling lingering on her.

Did they think they were a couple? All they had shared was a brief kiss in Roan. It left her body on edge; but did it make them official?

Tomi seemed to sense her growing panic and squeezed her hand, "sorry 'bout her. She's a bit tipsy. And very much on team... um... you know, our names would make a terrible couple's name."

"Couple's name? I wasn't aware we needed one yet."

"How long have you two been dating," asked the tall brunette her and Jolene *met at an outdoor restaurant that only featured two long picnic tables for guests to share. An open concept meant to foster community, according to the hand-painted mission statement adorning the concrete block walls.*

Ríona didn't know what to say. How long had they been dating? Glancing at Jolene, it looked as if she was just as confused.

"Oh god," the shorter brunette who was still taller than Ríona exclaimed. Her ironic tee shirt saying lost on her. It asked 'What if Zelda was a girl'.

"This is so classic lesbian," she continued, pushing the wide-rimmed glasses back against her face.

The taller one joined in, "you two didn't even know you were dating?"

"No," Ríona protested, "I knew." She turned to Jolene, "we are, aren't we? I mean... we've... you know."

The other couple giggled in glee, excited to be witness to the birth of childlike realisation. They both watched, smiles plastered across their face, as Ríona and Jolene quietly debated if they were a couple or not. Finally, her cheeks flushed with embarrassment, Ríona admitted they weren't "dating" per se.

Dating meant exclusivity, Jolene went on to explain later than night, safely away from judgemental ears. At the time, Ríona didn't know what Jolene meant by the statement, or admittedly, she blocked out the possibilities Jolene alluded to, preferring to bask in the glow of what they had and the shiver her touch brought to her unclothed body.

Tomi moved her face close to hers, her cinnamon musk reminding her of the very real, and very present woman standing before her. "If I kiss you right now, will that make it official?"

Tomi leaned in slowly, her head tilted ever so slightly, her delicious lips only millimetres away.

"No," Ríona panicked, pulling back quickly and holding Tomi back safely, and respectably, at arms distance.

"Sorry," Ríona quickly tried to explain seeing the hurt in Tomi's eyes. "It's not that," she softly explained. "I want you to kiss me."

"But?"

She swallowed, unsure if she should just straight out tell Tomi, or come up with another excuse. "There's someone stalking me," she blurted out.

"What? Who?"

"Some creep named Sam. I think he's trying to find some sort of blackmail."

"Why would someone blackmail you," Cam asked suspiciously as she handed Ríona a beautiful whiskey sour.

"Because I'm... you know." She couldn't say it. Not out loud, and not with the threat of her weird shadow possibly lurking about.

Elle handed Ríona a pool cue, informing her they were stripes. "Is it because of the life insurance money? Were your parents not accepting of you coming out?"

"No." Seeing Elle's face suddenly sour, she quickly amended, "I mean, no, I don't think it's about money. Mum was the first person I came out to. Dad... he died long before I had any interest in anyone. But I'm sure he wouldn't care either. He was a peace and love type who lived through the horror of The Troubles."

"The Troubles," Elle asked as she watched Cam sink another solid.

"Civil strife in Ireland," Ríona started, falling back to grade school recitation of information. "A mixture of religious and nationalist fighting that was mostly just terrorism."

"I remember that," Cam said with a disappointed grunt as the blue two ball bounced off the corner pocket and mingled with the stripes. "I was in high school back then. Our international field trip was cancelled because of a series of car bombs."

Elle leaned over the pool table, her tongue sticking out. "Is that what the drink 'Irish Car Bomb' is named after?" She tapped the cue ball gently. It rolled slowly towards the mass of balls Cam interrupted and somehow knocked one of the striped balls into the pocket.

"Yeah. It's like naming a drink 'Twin Towers' and it's two tall shots lit on fire."

"Right," she nodded her understanding. "That probably wouldn't go over well."

Ríona distractedly watched Tomi play her round, her tall, muscular body on full display. Even her unobtrusive breasts seemed accented by her pose. "Where was your trip to, Cam?"

"Belfast."

"Ah, Ulster. Definitely not where you wanted to be back then."

"That's what the band director said."

Tomi balked, almost messing up her shot. "You were a band nerd?"

Elle sipped her wine. "Someone's sleeping alone tonight!"

Ríona stepped closer to Cam, grabbed her arm and proclaimed proudly, "we band nerds are offended by your accusation."

"Seriously?" Tomi leaned against her cue stick.

Elle giggled loudly, the wine fully taken over her senses, "looks like your girl is quite serious. Tiny, but feisty. You gotta watch out for the feisty ones, woman."

"If I give you hand massage, can we go back to you liking me best?"

"Sure...," she replied shyly, furtively glancing around. "But after we get back to your place. Don't know if my stalker is watching me."

"Or if someone is spying for him," Cam added, only heightening her paranoia.

"That too." She instinctively huddled in closer to Cam. "Haven't actually thought of that."

Tomi reminded her, "you never said why he's stalking you."

"I think he's after your cousin, Zach."

"Because of the car accident?"

"I think. I don't know. He only seems interested in proving that I'm not really Zach's girlfriend."

"Well, you're not." She leaned over the table, "eight ball, middle pocket." The black ball did as ordered.

Elle clapped before hopping down off the bar stool. "Next round, couple versus couple."

As a team, Ríona and Tomi did poorly. Mostly, Ríona admitted through the whiskey, she did poorly. Normally she avoided playing pool, knowing that her grasp of the game extended to only know that you hit the white ball towards the others and only aim for the black ball last.

"Alright ladies," Cam announced setting her cue stick back on the rack. "We should get going," she grabbed her smaller partner and pulled her close, planting a quick kiss on the top of her head.

"The kids don't care how tired we are," Elle added, "they still want to be fed. This is what we get for adopting children instead of kittens."

Cam laughed. "It's not too late, honey. We can trade them in."

"Oh stop, not like you're not the absolute worst at spoiling them."

Ríona was enjoying the free-spirited banter until a yawn overtook her and she realised just how tired she was as well. She was torn. If she stayed behind with Tomi, they could spend a little more time together. But if they were back at Tomi's place.. "I'm a wee bit knackered myself." Ríona turned to Tomi.

Tomi squeezed her hand. "You two head on. I'll ride back with Ríona."

Elle walked over to give them hugs and offering Ríona a bit of advice, "don't let her off so easy."

CHAPTER 24

*T*omi held the door open for Ríona, letting her slip into the dark house, only the glow of a small faux lantern illuminating the outlines of couches, end tables, and what she hoped was just a house plant cowering in the corner.

Tomi quickly followed behind to flip on the lights. The wall switch unusually placed in the hallway leading to the bedrooms. "Where's your fiddle," Tomi quizzed, noticing Ríona setting down her backpack.

"I left it back at my flat," she brushed off the answer, her body long past too tired to allow her mind to think anymore.

"Thought you didn't let it out of your sight?"

"I try not to, but didn't expect I'd get a chance to play."

"Hmmm, true. I can definitely help keep you from getting bored." She grinned mischievously as she brushed past, letting her hands run across Ríona's hips to close and lock the door behind them with a satisfying *thunk.*

Despite relishing the brief contact, Ríona rolled her eyes and headed towards the spare room, her new weekend home. Before she opened the door, Tomi caught Ríona's belt loop and pulled her away. A yelp escaped from Ríona as she fell back into Tomi.

"I owe you a hand massage, remember?" Tomi had a sparkle in her

140

eye as she looked down at Ríona who was too knackered to playfully fight back anymore. Slumber sung a sweet siren's song, but the electricity racing across her flesh at the thought of Tomi's hands all over her body hummed a louder tune.

"Trust me," she replied with a coy smile, resting her hands on Tomi's toned biceps. "I haven't forgotten you owe me." She bit her bottom lip remembering the tinge of ants biting at her arm. "I'm just gonna change real quick though."

"I can help you with that." Tomi spun Ríona around to face her, the heat of her body a palpable promise. "This," she held Ríona's scarred arm, "doesn't bother me. You know that, right? I like you. *All* of you."

"I know." She did, but a lifetime of hiding wasn't easy for her to overcome. "I also need to, um, take care of girl things."

"Why don't you use my bathroom then," Tomi quietly hinted.

"Yours? What's wrong with this one," Ríona pointed to the slightly ajar door.

Tomi shortened the distance between them. "Because mine is closer."

"Is this your way of asking me out?"

"Didn't take you for the traditional type."

"I'm not... I... I just had a bad experience is all."

Jolene gave the boy, about their age, a lingering kiss on the lips. She pulled away and flashed him her perfectly straight teeth, a courtesy of the years of braces painfully perfecting the smile Ríona still lingered over in nostalgia.

Ríona didn't know what to say. Should she go home and bury hear head in pillows? Maybe she misunderstood their kiss? Some siblings kiss on the lips. The tap he gave her butt when she turned was hard to mistake.

She glanced at her phone: 16:43. Still fifteen minutes until they were to meet for dinner. Those fifteen minutes, seventeen to be exact, dragged out like a child who'd discovered dragging the bow across violin strings could send their parents screaming. Multiple times she walked away from the restaurant, still hyperventilating, telling herself over and over again that she simply misunderstood what she saw. There must be an explanation.

There was, Jolene clarified. She was dating both of them, "but it's okay, he's just my cover. My dress."

"You're what?" Why would she need a cover—was she ashamed of them? Should she be ashamed of them?

141

"It's so my parents think I'm normal, ya know."

Normal... that word stuck with her. Her mother always made her feel normal, but the older she grew, the more she realised that was just what good parents do.

Ríona stared at Tomi trying to read her thoughts, determined to understand that wild internal dialogue. She seemed so different from Jolene. Tomi had introduced her to her friends. When asked if they were a couple, she didn't panic trying to find a believable excuse for their affections. She treated her like how she imagined a boy was supposed to treat a girl he just started dating.

"Ah. Then yes, we are Facebook official."

"Why can't you just ask me," Ríona teased, pushing against firm abs.

Tomi cocked her head, "why can't you ask me? It's the twenty-first century, after all."

"Fair point. Perhaps I like your kissing idea better."

"As you wish," Tomi whispered as she leaned in to place her lips against Ríona's hungry pair, already hot with anticipation.

Ríona leaned her weight into the kiss, letting herself sink into the Tomi's stern passion.

Pulling back gently, "thank you."

"For?"

"Humouring me."

"So... that massage; how about we make that a full body massage?"

CHAPTER 25

Sunday morning woke Ríona with the sounds of chattering voices outside the bedroom window. It sounded like Cam was excitedly showing off her handiwork while Elle chastised the wee ones to leave "her" alone. Whoever was out there, they seemed to be in high spirits.

She rolled over in a mess of heavy comforters, the stiff bed barely recognising her slight weight. Disappointed, she realised Tomi was no longer beside her. It surprised her a little that Tomi had let her sleep so late, judging by how bright the sun was shining through the curtains. *She needs heavier curtains,* she complained to herself, regretting that there would be no way she could fall back asleep now, no matter how late Tomi kept her up the previous night.

After a quick shower, she wandered into the kitchen, the scent of coffee still lingering over the cafetière forcing her feet to shuffle ever so slightly faster. Beside the press sat a homemade raspberry muffin, likely one of Elle's many scrumptious creations she had been forcing onto her all weekend.

Not that she minded. Everything Elle had baked that weekend had been divine, and the muffin was no different. Especially with a cold glass of fresh milk straight from the neighbours cow. Taking a bite of the milk-soaked muffin, she noticed Jordan's Jeep through the little kitchen window.

"What the—," she muttered to herself. Quickly, she checked her phone to see if there was a missed message she happened to skim over in their often long text chats. There wasn't.

Grabbing one of Tomi's many steel travel mugs, she hastily made poured her coffee, added more creamer than she normally would to hide the taste of someone's poor judgement in coffee quality, and popped outside to catch her friend as off guard as she was.

Her surprise attack was ruined when one of the tiny humans spotted her with a loud squeal of excitement, desperate to show off yet another hapless creature fearing for its life. This time it was a baby snake. One that looked like it would one day grow up to be a snake she desperately tried to avoid on the farm.

"Whatcha got," she played along yet again.

"Momma c-calls it a 'd-danger 'oodle'."

"Hmmm. Looks like a baby danger noodle. Hopefully momma noodle wasn't nearby watching you."

"She wasn't."

"Maybe she was invisible?

"I can see—isible."

"Is that why you can see me?"

He whipped his head up to stare at her, the serious concentration paining his face as he tried fruitlessly to determine is she was lying. The chance that he might believe her amused her to no end.

"Hey Rí," Jordan called, breaking the spell over the wee lad who now gave her the stink eye.

He turned and hid the terrarium from her before running off after his sister, who upon seeing the snake sitting in the little plastic prison screamed like a banshee.

"I didn't know you were paying us a visit."

Jordan collided with Ríona, wrapping her arms tightly around and squeezing hard, holding onto her for a short eternity. Her soft hair felt decadent against her sunburned skin. She would love for this hug to last forever, but people were watching. Jordan felt their eyes too.

"Sorta last minute, sorry. Hope I don't slow down your progress today."

"Oh no, no. Cam and I got a lot done yesterday, and Tomi got my floors and walls in. You'd love what we did. We stuffed the van with sheep peels!"

"What in the world are sheep peels?" Jordan looked at her as if she had lost her last marble.

Tomi waltzed over, standing beside Ríona. "Insulation. She wanted something more 'natural' so I called a guy I know who imports that stuff from New Zealand. Smells like a petting zoo in there right now," she laughed.

"You're kidding!"

"Nope," Ríona assured her. "It'll go away... I hope."

"Why don't you go show her?" Tomi put her hand on the small of her back. Ordinarily that would elicit feelings she would seek to calm in private, but with Jordan standing arms distance away, her hands still holding onto hers, it caused her heart to panic. "I'm gonna go help Cam get ready to leave."

"They're leaving already?"

"Yeah. They'll be back soon though—promise."

"Make sure they don't leave without saying goodbye. I need to thank Elle for the muffin."

"Don't worry, hun, I'll make sure they don't sneak off. Now," she pinched her side, "go show my cousin your van."

Jordan watched their display with fascination. "You two seem to get along well," a hint of suspicion tinging her voice.

"She's fun. And of course Cam and Elle are amazing."

Ríona pulled Roan's side doors wide open. Jordan peeked her head in, her amazement at the transformation the empty shell she saw a few weeks ago had taken impossible to disguise.

"Tell me, what's going where? I'm sure you have some Pinterest board stashed away with every little detail."

"Oh hush you." She wasn't wrong.

"You've always wanted full reign to decorate your own place."

"Decorate. This is a lot more than decorate."

Ríona hopped inside behind Jordan and shut the door so she could get a better sense of the space. And so she could smell the fragrant aroma of wool.

"Oh god, it does smell like a petting zoo," Jordan exclaimed in a bout of giggles. "Remember that petting zoo we went to?"

She, unfortunately, still remembered that day. It was an unseasonably hot Spring and all their adult chaperones whined about it the whole time. Her classmates didn't care. They got to pet "exotic" animals while poking fun at the city kids who'd never milked a cow before squirmed incessantly as the farm hand showed them how to grab an udder.

She had other memories. "The one where the goat pulled my skirt down in front of everyone?"

"Yeah... right, forgot about that part."

"Like you didn't enjoy the sight," she teased playfully. She didn't expect Jordan's cheeks to go that shade of red in response. "What's with the embarrassment?"

"What? I'm not embarrassed." Her tone was defensive.

"Don't be weird," she teased, flicking Jordan on the forehead. "This is Roan." She swept her arms wide, careful not to hit the walls or Jordan in the tight quarters. The air still smelled of sheep, but also of the wood freshly installed the night before after a marathon sprint of stringing twine across empty cavities to hold the fluffy fibre fill into place and installing anchor points for the shiplapped planks running the length of the van.

"I'm guessing that's gonna be your bed, huh?" Jordan motioned towards the back where the floor was decidedly raised due to the engine and wheel well.

"Nowhere else to put it. Just makes sense, ya know. This front part will be storage." She laid down on the wooden platform and sprawled out.

Jordan came over to join her. "Hmmm. You need a skylight."

"I kinda have one. The whole roof lifts up and there's windows all around."

"What? No way!"

"Yeah, it's kinda cool. Means I can actually stand up to do things like cook or getting dressed. I can show you in a little bit when we start painting."

Jordan rolled her head to face Ríona, "I distinctly heard the word 'we' in there."

"Ya did. It's what you get for showing up unannounced." She sat up, resting against her elbows. "Come, can't sit around all day."

"You're serious?"

A sudden loud knock on the van caused both girls to jump; Jordan letting a small scream out. Outside, Tomi laughed hysterically, proud of her antics.

"Told ya I could make 'em scream," Tomi proudly boasted to someone, likely Cam who from her boisterous laughter enjoyed playing these kinds of pranks too. Elle must have the patience of a Goddess to not have murdered her spouse.

"Is your cousin always like that?"

"Figured you'd have found that out by now with how much time you two are spending together anymore. I feel like you see her more than you do me."

"Oh that's not true." The sudden guilt rushing through her body believed said otherwise.

"Cam and Elle are heading out."

CHAPTER 26

"Where's Jordan," Tomi quizzed with some concern as she brought the first cabinet to the van, the beginning on her galley counter. This would be the only one she could actually store cooking utensils and food in. The other two were destined to house a small chest refrigerator and the other two small jerry cans for her fresh and grey water supplies.

Tomi warned her that she wouldn't have much, maybe only a few days' worth. It had never occurred to her just how much water she went through on a daily basis, or how reliant she was on hot water. When she voiced this concern, Tomi told her about a "solar shower" they could install on the roof rack alongside the solar panels, but she'd be saving that for when she's some place private unless she wanted to give the world a free show.

"She's inside laying down. I think the paint fumes were giving her a headache."

"She's a frail one. Why don't you help me get this into place, then you can go check on her while I get them fastened in."

Ríona knocked gently on the spare bedroom door before quietly entering. Inside she found Jordan, motionless, laying on her back staring at the ceiling fan that just spun round and round, a slight rock in its motion causing the draw chain to *clink* every so often. It was almost hypnotic, if you paid it any heed. Otherwise it just blended into the background noise of crickets and katydids at night, the only time when people actually used the empty room.

"You okay, sweetie," Ríona cooed as she sat gingerly next to Jordan. Petting her hair, she asked if she was feeling alright. Jordan's face looked a little paler than normal, and a worried complexion marred her near perfect face.

"The bed is made." She said it so matter of factly Ríona wasn't sure if Jordan had even said it.

"Huh?"

"I know you, Rí. You *never* make the bed."

"So? Tomi always makes the bed. I'm surprised she hasn't given up on me, to be honest. You did."

"Yeah, I did. You'd just make a mess of it again the moment you came back into the room."

Jordan went quiet for a moment, letting Ríona run her tiny fingers through her hair some more.

"Where's your stuff?"

"What stuff? I don't actually live here ya know."

"Your bag... I don't see your bag. Or your fiddle."

"I left my fiddle back at my flat. I didn't feel safe leaving it in the truck and I wasn't going to have a chance to play. I've either been working on Roan or chasing down children. They're terrible at hide 'n' seek," she laughed. "I mean *terrible*. Cute, but terrible."

Jordan sat up and folded her legs underneath her. "Ríona Kilbride, you didn't sleep in this bed last night, did you?"

Ríona didn't answer. Instead, her heart started racing and droplets of sweat started beading her guilt. She pulled her hand away from Jordan's comfortingly soft hair and picked at the button on her sleeve instead.

"Whose bed did you sleep in?" She swatted Ríona's hand, forcing her to stop picking at her clothes, a reason most of her shirts no longer had functioning cuffs. "I thought you were staying here all weekend. Your van doesn't have a bed yet." She paused, running through a mental list of possibilities. "Do... do you have a boyfriend?"

"Me?" That wasn't the question she feared Jordan would ask her.

"Hmmm. I don't understand, Rí. If you *did* have a boyfriend it would explain why you've been acting different lately."

"Different, how?"

"Don't give me that. You've been different. Distracted, yet somehow a little happier. You don't seem to zone out at much, but you're never freakin' around on the weekends anymore. At first I thought it was because of Zach's accident, that perhaps you did have feelings for him or something. But the more I thought about it, the more I knew something was up with you *before* he screwed up everything."

"I assure you—I don't have feelings for your brother. Never have, never will."

"I know. Ugh, I dunno, Rí, I can't figure you out right now. Why won't you tell me? Did you sleep in their bus last night? Is that what you're afraid to tell me? I'd get it, if you did. You're about to make a huge leap and you wanted to have a little taste of what it felt like or something. I dunno."

Jordan stared her directly in the eyes with a sheen of wetness on hers. *What do I tell her,* she kept asking herself over and over, desperate for an answer that would satisfy her... yet she desperately wanted to confess, to just lay it all out before her best friend, to tell her those little words she knew would change everything between them.

Jordan jumped out of bed and rushed out of the room leaving the door creaking its own discomfort behind her.

"Jordan?"

She heard Tomi's bedroom door open. Panicked, Ríona rushed into the master bedroom. In the corner, hanging off the back of the small reading chair, her dress laid uncomfortably. Her fancy boots tucked underneath the hem. Her bag sat on the dresser, the contents spilling out like a gutted animal.

"Oh god... Rí, my cousin? You and my cousin," she couldn't finish the sentence.

"I'm sorry, I wanted to tell you. I *tried* to tell you. But with everything going on with your brother and finals, I just couldn't bring myself to."

"Who asked who?"

"Huh, why does that matter?"

"Did she convince you to do this?"

"Convince me? You're making it sound like she tricked me into this or something. I didn't need convincing. I wanted her to ask me out."

Jordan studied her. She wanted to say something; it was written plain as day all over her heartbroken face. "Are you gay?"

Ríona paused, afraid to answer that simple question with a single simple word. *Yes,* was all she had to say, all she wanted to say. Somehow that single word and the admission that lies behind it were too much still.

"Rí, yes or no?"

"Yes," she forced it out of her lungs, small wells of water building in her eyes. For the first time she was able to admit it to Jordan. "I'm gay. Lesbian. Whatever you want to call it. I... I like women. And only women."

"When did you know?"

"When I was twelve. I had a crush on my music teacher and it crushed me when she left. I didn't understand it then. I thought maybe it would pass, that I just so wanted to be her that I thought I liked her.

"Then I met a girl in school. She liked me too, but then her parents found out and pulled her from school. One of the teachers saw us kiss and called our parents 'concerned about our sinful behaviour'."

"I remember this. Oh god... she's the one we met at that bar a few years ago. What's her name?"

"Jolene."

"You've known this whole time, and you never told me?"

Ríona didn't answer.

"You let me kiss you, Rí."

"I know."

Jordan stormed out of the room and through the front door. Ríona stood there, frozen by the shock of Jordan so abruptly rejecting her. A faint engine rumbled to life. Still, she stood unable to force herself to follow after, to do anything but let the sound of tyres over gravel fade into a long distance.

CHAPTER 27

"*H*ow's dinner at six," Mrs McGraw's scandalous voice casually asked on the other end.

"With the whole family?"

"Did you want some alone time with Zach?"

Ríona stammered her words, never sure if Mrs McGraw was being serious or not. Or worse, testing her.

"It's okay, honey, it'll be just the four of us. Jordan's in a mood. Says she needs some time out to study."

"Oh, yeah, she's cramming for her finals. Her case law professor is seriously insane."

"Jacobs?"

"I think that's his name. He's an adjunct."

"I know him. He's like that in real life too."

"Jordan would be thrilled to know that... Anyway, I gotta go. Class is starting."

"Okay, we'll pick you up from your apartment. Dress nice."

When Mrs McGraw's name appeared on her phone, her gut reaction was that Jordan told her parents about her. Told them the only secret she kept from Jordan. One so big she couldn't imagine Jordan being able to contain it to just herself.

She questioned why she'd assume Jordan would tell them. In a small self-loathing way, she hoped Jordan would confess her sins. That would put her out of her misery of pretending to be Zach's date to whatever fancy restaurant they picked out so they could all be seen together, a happy little family with their future daughter-in-law trophy. Proof everything in their family was as the white picket fence advertised. Except Jordan, who hasn't answered her texts or calls since she walked out.

Tomi came in shortly after Jordan left her alone to languish; Ríona sat on the edge of her bed. "Why'd she take off? Something happen?"

She couldn't come up with an immediate excuse to brush it off. If she told her Jordan got her period, she'd be lying, and that wouldn't be enough of a reason to run like that. Jordan kept a change of clothes in the spare dresser and both Tomi and her kept products on hand. She needed a better reason, something that even she could believe.

"Did you two have a fight?" Tomi was careful with her words and her tone.

That could work. They kind of did fight. More like Jordan gutted Ríona while she laid herself bare, free to be torn down to nothing by the single most important person in her life.

"I think. I'm not sure. I came in to check on her and... I don't know. I don't think she's going to talk to me again."

Tomi sat down on the bed's edge and wrapped an arm around her. "Oh baby girl, I know my cousin. I know how much she loves you. Whatever it was about, I know she'll forgive you."

"Will she? I think I broke our friendship."

Tomi intertwined her fingers into Ríona's. "Did you fight about us?"

"Us? No, it wasn't about us."

She regretted that lie. It felt like a lie, even if it wasn't. It wasn't about them; it was about her and the truth's she refused to confront.

She slammed her laptop shut and dropped her head onto her folded arms. Moon was slow, as it normally was mid-afternoon Monday. She enjoyed the break between classes when she could escape from the chaos of campus and focus on notating her score.

Her heavy over ear headphones drowned out most of the bustle and energetic punk music barely squeezing out of the ceiling speakers, but for some reason she found Moon's chaotic atmosphere allowed her to focus more intently. There were no distractions here, except perhaps the owner who kept casually flirting with her.

"What's wrong, honey," Ashleigh asked when Ríona's blasé tone barely registered she was still mentally in this world.

"Huh?"

"You, honey, you seem... out of it." She handed the drink she had already prepared. Ríona noticed the heart topping the 'i' in her name. "And you're here without blondie. You two on the outs?"

She wanted to reply with the truth. That yes, they were on the "outs" but the more she imagined herself confessing her secrets to the barista, the more she recoiled. "Finals are killing me. I have to write this score and I need, like, ten more weeks to finish it."

"When's it due," she asked, resting her hand on Ríona's.

"Three weeks." Three short, bloody long weeks. She wasn't going to finish in time, not if the McGraw's keep dragging her to dinner parties and fancy restaurants. Behind Ashleigh a clock ticked down the remaining hour and half before she paraded the facade of her life before men who cared nothing of her.

"Oof. Already finals again? How I don't miss 'em."

"Yeah. Didn't you graduate from here?" The random alum trinkets could easily be explained as up sales for visiting parents, but the scarlet and cream paint job felt painfully purposeful.

Ashleigh laughed, removing her warm hand from hers. The human contact was nice, the fact it came from a beautiful woman made a little more exciting, but she felt like it should have elicited more butterflies, like it had nearly every time Ashleigh "accidentally" brushed her fingers before this trauma between her and Jordan.

"Yeah, got my business degree there. Worst decision of my life."

Ríona's small smile faded.

"Oh honey, I ain't saying you shouldn't, just that it wasn't for me. I spent five years there struggling my way through, no idea what I was doing or what I wanted."

"Why a coffee shop then? Doesn't seem like a place someone goes to business school to open."

"Whatcha mean?" Ashleigh's poker face told her nothing.

"I didn't mean it as a bad thing," Ríona pleaded, honestly terrified she hurt the woman's pride.

She smirked. "I know, but I'm curious to hear what you think."

"I just picture people who go to business school come out wearing suits and sitting behind desks in stuffy skyscrapers. Like they're completely removed from the real world, making decisions that don't effect them, never producing something they can touch, or hear," she flicked her nail against the coffee cup, "or taste."

"You ain't wrong, honey. That's why I left. Spent a year in that corporate hell working in a real estate business office. I didn't build houses. Didn't design neighbourhoods. Never even saw a single homeowner. All I got were headaches and paychecks."

"I can't imagine you all gussied up in a blouse and sleek pencil skirts." She did imagine her dolled up in rockabilly to match her bright makeup and her perfect wavy curls.

"With these tats? Ha! When I quit, first thing I did was go down to Timmy's and had him do this." She pointed to the large butterfly tattoo on her right forearm. A bright indigo blue and black butterfly emerging from a burning cocoon.

"Can't get an office job with this beauty."

"It's pretty. I just can't imagine doing something like that to myself."

"Why," she quietly teased, taking Ríona's hand, then tracing outlines of invisible artwork under her flannel sleeve. "Don't you ever get hot always wearing long sleeves?"

"Eh, not really. I'm used to it." She pulled away her arm, grabbing the coffee cup and taking a sip to poorly disguise her recoil.

"Sorry, didn't mean anything by it."

"No, it's okay. It's just a thing. You still haven't told me how you came to open a coffee shop in the middle of Nebraska."

"After I got this, I packed a backpack and rode the trains all o'er Europe. Booked a cheap flight to Lithuania, stayed at a hostel, freaked out because there I was, twenty-seven, never been away from home, never even been out of Nebraska, sleeping in a room with four other girls I had only met when I walked into that smelly room.

"It was just terrifying. But I lived. They were doing the same thing. One chick, Safira, was a pro. She'd been all over the world and just came from France. She spent a month on a vineyard learning to make wine and paying her room by picking grapes, mopping floors, and watching the owner's children."

"Sounds like a dream. But I don't think I'm that brave anymore. I'm not even sure I want to leave Lincoln anymore. Just the thought of leaving everything behind; leaving everyone behind. It's scary."

"I was there too. But it was less scary than staying. Thinking about my future, married to a man I never had any interest in, destined to work a desk job. *That* was terrifying. Looking back now I can't imagine that's who I was. I had never done anything that was just for *me* until I bought that ticket. One way. Signed the divorce documents. Hopped on a plane and that's that."

"Why do you still wear your wedding ring?"

"'Cause I'm married, nosey. I only flirt with you because you're so much fun. It makes your girlfriend so flustered but she never says anything. It's kinda adorable. But you'd like my wife. She's one of the girls I met that first night in Lithuania."

Ríona noted the pronoun. She didn't know why that shocked her. It was normal for Ashleigh to playfully tease her, but she figured it was just Ashleigh being Ashleigh, or at least teasing her because she enjoyed making Ríona blush. Not that she possibly had any real interest in her.

"Have I met her?"

"Anastasija? Ya have, plenty of times."

"Ana?"

"You sound surprised," she laughed. "You didn't know, did you?"

"No! Never even crossed my mind."

"Jesus child, your gaydar ain't good, is it?"

"I guess not."

The store phone rang loudly drawing Ashleigh away with a quick apology. Again checking the time, Ríona seated herself at her abandoned table amongst the sea of empty tables. With a heavy sigh, she opened her laptop to be greeted by a bright screen filled with half-finished sheet music. She donned her headphones and sat her MIDI keyboard back in her lap.

She stared blankly at the track marker, it waiting for her to return to the here and now. *Is that my problem? Am I just afraid?* The cursor blinked. Ríona lost herself into her thoughts, her fingers sitting casually on the warm plastic keys as if the notes were on the verge of flowing freely.

"*Mo wee páiste,*" *her mother cooed, weeks after they moved into their new home. The strange walls, the strange furniture, the strange yard. Everything was foreign to her, no longer the familiar world she was so happy in, the one where she could dance and sing loudly, basking in loving praise.*

"Why don' ye pop out for a spell?"

She remembered crying when her mother practically forced her through the door, locking it behind her. A young Ríona sat there on the porch with salty streaks running down her face, vacantly surveying the new, unfamiliar world of brown fields and forever blue skies. Even though everything inside was just as foreign, it reeked of a safe familiarity, a distant taste of her world before the fire, one that she had a dictatorial reign over.

Out there, on the open porch, the warm dusty Summer air blowing through the wheat stalks, she was prey animal diving through broken barn walls. Inside she could dance freely, eyes closed, chasing away the world—out here people could sneer and smirk, despite literally not a soul haunting her for miles. After an uneventful hour passed, she slowly ventured down the steps for the first time by herself, touching her tiny foot onto the loose gravel.

The wooden chair in front of her squealed as the hard feet rubbed against the concrete floor ripping her out of her nostalgia. Bryce was sitting across from her, concern distorting his face. He wore his ordinary black slacks and a blue polo shirt with his company's logo too large to blend in gracefully.

She took her headphone off.

"Where were you just now?"

She closed her laptop once again, resigning to abandoning her score for the night. "Was just thinking about things."

"Whatever you were thinking about, it must have been pretty intense."

"It's this piece I'm working on for class. It just has me thinking a lot."

"That emotional?"

"Gods no. Anything but."

"Then what?"

"Just thinking... am I making a huge mistake with my life?"

"Ríona, I know you have a lot going on. Hell, that's why I came here looking for you."

Although he didn't say it, she knew he was referring to her ignoring his, and everyone's for the matter, messages asking how she was, where she's at, if she wanted to go out for drinks or even just coffee.

"Sor—."

"Don't apologise. I get it. It's been rough for you. But Jesus, giving up music? What brought this on?"

"Just thinking about what I'm doing after I graduate. Whether I should leave, stay, or what. For so long I was dead set on leaving, but now I don't know anymore."

Bryce watched her for a moment, contemplating what he wanted to say next. The longer he waited to say something, the more pressure she felt to say *something*.

"I dunno, Bryce. I feel like I have to decide my *entire* future right now, that whatever I pick will stick with me forever, or I'll have spent four years getting my music degree just to work as a cashier at Leon's."

"You know what you do today doesn't have to live with you forever. Even marriages don't have to last forever."

"Are you two getting a divorce?" She didn't know much about the inner dynamics of their marriage, aside from the occasional complaints he made about not having his "freedom" anymore.

"Us? Oh no, we have a good thing going, but we both know if things aren't working out, we don't have to force it to work. People change." He shrugged. "And who knows, maybe in ten years you'll still love the same things and the same people, but you'll never know that today. I'm definitely not where I pictured myself when I graduated high school, but I'm happy. And no, I see that look on your face, I ain't telling you."

"Oh, why not? I'm imaging young Bryce wanting to grow up to be a hunky fire fighter posing for all the calendars."

This was nice. She rarely got to talk to Bryce one on one, and when the other two boys were around, he was always hounded by the younger two who looked to Bryce as some macho role model.

"Speaking of which, that's what I came to talk to you about."

"About hot firefighters?"

"You're a hot mess. But no, Joey from the club called me and wanted to know when we could get back to playing."

"Seriously? With everything going on?"

"You mean with you and Zach dating?"

She folded her arms and fell against the back of the chair.

"Don't worry, I know you two ain't a thing." She relaxed a little, her initial feeling to defend herself melted away. "You're a good friend for doing that. Just want you to know. I'm sure Jordan ain't taken that well. Heard she's been MIA lately."

"Yeah... you could say that."

"So what do you think? About gigging," he quickly added.

"I'd love to, but with finals and everything I don't think I can. I'm struggling like crazy with this score and it literally decides if I graduate or not."

"Want me to take a look at it?"

"Ha! You don't want to. It's boring. I want nothing to do with it."

"Then why are you still working on it? Here's an idea: we *all* work on it together. As a band, we add your Irish flair that everyone loves us for, you dress it up in Finale and boom. You're a music school graduate."

"I hate that you're the rational one here. You're supposed to be Mr Cool Guy who does lines of coke or something."

"You're welcome. Now... one small favour though."

"Why is there always a catch?"

"It's not bad. It's just I haven't really gotten to talk to Zach much. I kinda brought up us getting up on stage again to him, but that dude is like a whole new person. Which I get—he watched his friend die, so I'm not trying to push him. But it would be good for him, and for you, to get back up there and do what we love."

"And Jordan?"

"Eh, she'll come around. Just give it some time. Time heals all wounds or some nonsense like that." She glared at him. "I'm just saying, I get why she might be upset. I just don't think *you* know why she's upset."

"I'll talk to him tonight." She checked her phone.

CHAPTER 28

*R*íona struggled into the lifted limousine black pickup truck that Mr McGraw loved to show off. It was the most impractical and grandstanding truck a person could own. Complete with undercarriage lighting and mud tyres that have only seen mud from a safe asphalt distance.

Inside was just as over the top. Recently treated leather, inlaid wooden accents, and a sound system Mrs McGraw wouldn't dare let him put to full use while she was within earshot, let alone physically inside the behemoth of opulence.

"You look nice," Zach greeted her with a dashing yet sad smile, holding a hand out to help her in. Her dress, a simply black and lace piece with long sleeves and a short, flared skirt didn't offer her much flexibility without also giving Zach a quick peek.

"Thanks." Both for his hand, but the somewhat genuine, if not practiced, simple compliment. "Should have worn some mountain climbing clothes."

Zach chuckled. Mrs McGraw called out from up front, telling her that she looked fabulous and would fit in "splendidly" at the club. Mr McGraw merely offered her a gruff hello before going back to his normally sullen self while Mrs McGraw cheerfully grilled her about her life and school.

"What are your plans after you graduate," she inquired. She knew there was a hidden message in there, a silent offering that this family would find a way to weasel her into. Ríona had no clear answer to give her, so she steered the conversation away as best she could towards how Zach was fairing catching up on his classes.

They pulled up to a tall, grey building near the edge of the downtown core. Overall, the building was nondescript, something she had never paid attention to other than noting its archaic forbidding appearance of reflective glass and concrete lines stretching upwards with no clear end.

She imagined this being the place where Ashleigh felt trapped in a hellscape of suits and cubicles, not where someone dressed up for a formal dinner ball. Yet, they were there, walking across a pedestrian bridge that reeked of stale mould and into the world of corporate drudgery and conformity.

Mrs McGraw tapped her long manicured fingernail on the electronic directory, not too subtlety pointing out this is where their law office had a branch. Mostly staffers and paralegals doing the grunt work "real" lawyers couldn't be bothered with.

Upstairs they walked what she imagined was to some a beautifully curated dining hall with an expansive view of downtown Lincoln. It was actually quite a marvellous view of the shimmering city, and of the state capital building standing stoic and proud over the city core with a hazy red backdrop accenting the century old Art Deco concrete. On the opposite side you could watch the sun lazily set behind the horizon of grey roof tops.

Much like their dinner party, the small restaurant was filled with men in stuffy suits and a few wives in the background enjoying their dinner over animated and often loud "shop talk". All that was missing was the unbearable haze and skunk of cigar smoke and a low-key piano singing in the background.

"Right this way," the host directed them without questioning them. She had gone to dinner with the McGraw's hundreds of times throughout the years, but always to more typical family styled restaurants with cheesy "themes" and menus with actual prices on them.

Zach pulled the chair out for her. She wanted to chastise him, remind him that he can be his normal annoying self around her, but she bit her tongue. This wasn't about her—even Zach knew to play along.

"Isn't this nice," Mrs McGraw cooed. "A girl could get used to this, ya know. Especially if you two make it official," she winked at her son, her voice carrying over the curious crowd.

"Mom, stop it," Zach growled, desperate to keep people from staring. "Please, don't be making a scene of it."

"Don't you talk to your mother like that," his father snapped back, also trying to keep his words out of the ears of eavesdroppers. "After I win this election, you can go back to being your useless self."

"Honey, be nice," Mrs McGraw swatted his arm, a smile still plastered on her face. It pained Ríona to watch the charade.

"Sorry about that," she told Ríona as sweet as ever, "he's just stressed about the election."

Ríona had kept away from the news regarding the mayoral race, but no matter, somehow the news always managed to filter back to her. Mr McGraw was assumed to be the loser this election. His opponent, a well known liberal councilwoman, was already dubbed by many as the handpicked successor to the current mayor. While the current mayor could run again for a fourth term, he had decided it was time to retire to private life away from all the annoying showmanship she was currently enveloped in.

Dinner passed much the same way it started. Husband and wife quietly bickered over fake smiles and chipper tones, everyone who considered themselves a somebody paid a visit to their table to wish Mr McGraw luck on the election, stating empathically they were voting for him. Always accompanied about some rhetoric about what they felt held them back personally that only a man of their political persuasion could fix.

None escaped without first making a comment that made Ríona winch at its blatant sexism towards his contender. Since none acknowledged her existence outside their obligatory greetings, it was doubtful any noticed her displeased looks. Except, of all people, Zach, who on one particularly egregious slur grabbed her hand to give her a reassuring squeeze.

After dinner, wanting desperately to escape the hawkish gaze of his parents, Zach told his mother, uncharacteristically loud that him and Ríona were going to go for a walk. He made sure those around could hear forcing his parents to agree despite clearly not wanting to. His father merely glared at him while his mother, after seeing Zach hold her hand, proclaimed it was a fabulous idea. That the two "love birds" should spend some time alone and "talk about what their future holds for them."

"Sorry 'bout them," he finally exhaled a safe distance from the men in suits. "They piss me off so much sometimes."

Zach had never talked about his parents in such a manner. If anything, she always felt he was far more like his father than he ever realised, but now... something was different. Something was eating at him that she never noticed was there before. A parasitic bitterness that he had kept securely tucked away, waiting patiently until it could lash out with teeth gnashed and claws bared.

Curiosity bit at her. After he woke up from his induced coma, he'd been subtly different. Just little subtleties here and there, but she couldn't find the words to articulate them. That, and since then, she'd been so distant herself, no longer playing, spending her weekends at Tomi's rather than with Jordan. It wasn't her place to ask, she felt, having abandoned the little world she had wrapped herself in.

They slowly strolled down empty streets only broken up by the occasional passing car, their headlights a blinding glare as they slowly streaked by. Most of the buildings laid empty, quieted down after a day's work, while many of the storefronts sat unused. Giant "for rent" signs decorated the windows. Inside, it looked as if someone had simply abandoned their shelves and registers long ago to thick layers of steely dust. Many of these empty shells had been empty for nearly a decade after the recession hit pretty hard, and many more had shuttered as well over the past few years. The lights they walked towards, glowing casually over the tops of short three or four-story buildings and their grey parking garages, told a different story.

"I talked to Bryce," she started.

"He got to you too?" He laughed. He finally started to relax his posture and become the slacker Ríona remembered.

"I'm not opposed to the idea," she meekly stated her case. "If you don't think—"

"No," he quickly chastised her. "Look, you're doing enough for me, alright?"

They walked the wide sidewalk in silence the remainder of the block. A red hand shone brilliantly from the opposing pole.

"What do *you* want, Ríona? I was there because my sister drug me there. But you, you actually wanted it. I'm pretty sure it's what you live for."

When she didn't respond, still lost in her thoughts and assumptions, "is it Jordan?"

"Jordan?"

"Yeah... I know you two are fighting about something. Hell, we *all* know you're fighting about something. I've never seen her this upset."

With a loud beep, the hand signal ahead turned green. Around her the cool night air hugged her body forcing goosebumps down her thinly covered arms. Her bare legs and short black dress were a wonderfully sexy combination when paired with the warmth of a dinner party, but utterly useless when faced with the reality of the world outside.

Seeing her shiver, Zach wordlessly removed his dinner jacket and wrapped it around her small shoulders. It felt heavy on her, like a burden, but the residual body heat quickly fought off most of the chills.

"Don't worry, she hasn't told me, whatever it is. Which, honestly, kinda surprises me. I get that I'm the asshole brother. I deserve that title, but it's not like her to not tell me."

It struck her as odd that he was being incredibly introspective. In all their years growing up, he never once cared that others disliked him. Or that he was simply disliked for always being the contrarian seeking out trouble. He always seemed to thrive off it.

"But she's my twin. There's just this sixth sense about us, ya know?"

"Yeah, I suppose."

"I'll do it."

"What? You'll perform?"

"Yeah."

"You're not just saying that?"

"No. I'm not. And no, I'm not going to run off and do something stupid."

"Does this mean..." She wanted to ask. It wasn't her place to ask, but in that moment she felt like they had actually made a genuine connection, one they hadn't experienced since Zach's teenage hormones kicked in and he sought companionship amongst the boys at school instead of his sister and her friend.

"I've been clean, yeah."

"That makes me happy."

He chuckled. "Somehow I knew you'd say something cheesy like that." He wrapped his arm around her, pulling her in for a comfortable embrace as they continued down the last quarter block before turning onto the busier stretch of downtown.

"Who knew? You two really are a couple." She immediately recognised the Sam's voice, his face hidden behind a camera.

"Dude, what gives?" Zach immediately went defensive, returning to the angry young man she knew and loathed.

Sam dropped the camera to his side, "just getting a photo. No harm in that, right?"

"What do you want?"

"From you, nothing. Your friends at the party though, they had plenty I wanted. So Miss Irish, has your boyfriend told you the truth yet? Are you a part of this coverup too or are you the one using our prized son here to hide your own secrets?"

"I have no clue what you want or what's going on. We're just out for a walk, that's it."

"Funny how you two keep so many secrets from each other. Tell me, Zachary, what were you and Dustin arguing about? You seemed pretty upset when you stormed out of the house."

"I've already told the police what happened. Why don't you check the police report, bro." Zach glared at the older man, his eyes burning a hole straight through his sole and into the afterlife.

"I did. The sheriff is a good friend of your mother, ain't he?"

"I don't keep track of her friends."

"Perhaps you should. They're handy when you need a favour. For

165

instance, making sure a police report doesn't reflect who was actually driving."

Zach grabbed Ríona's hand and pulled her along as he hurried away from Sam. Behind them, he trailed them for a bit silently before hopping into a car conveniently parked near where he ambushed them. *Was it mere coincidence or had he been following them?*

"Is what he says true, Zach?"

"Don't listen to him, Ríona. He's some hack reporter that's just bitter he got fired from The Star."

She fretted over what Sam said. He somehow knew about her, even if he was just guessing. What if he published a story and outed her to everyone? It would destroy her if that got out to everyone, whether she knew them or not. Her face plastered on the front page next to Zach who was being accused of some hideous crime she was clueless about.

Not that she didn't entirely believe Sam. She hated admitting it to herself, but the things Sam said made sense.

"Can I ask what really happened?"

"I don't want to talk about it right now, okay?"

CHAPTER 29

"How much longer do you think we have left to work on Roan," Ríona asked taking shelter under the back porch. Around them a freak rain storm poured down with a thunderous roar. Large drops collided loudly with the tin roof over their heads practically deafening her.

Looking out at Roan, she watched the puddles pool rapidly around the wheels and bead off the freshly waxed paint. They had managed to get a lot more work done on the cabinets. Tomi got the slides into place, a time-consuming process Ríona didn't anticipate. Having only bought cabinets from the store when her mother redid her kitchen, she assumed it would be like last time where all you did was install a few screws and everything magically lined up.

"Why? Are you getting impatient to leave," Tomi teased, wrapping her arm around the smaller woman.

"Just follow the instructions, child," her mother snapped, even her legendary patience growing thin at the young teen anxious to skip ahead.

"I am!" Ríona hadn't entirely. Instead she skipped ahead a few times, bored with the pages tediously explaining which screws went in which holes, and how to line up the track guides. In her impatience to get on to more exciting endeavours, she had installed all the drawer slides backwards.

When her mother told her they were remodelling, her initial excitement drove her mum crazy. Every magazine her mother brought home for inspiration was torn apart by young fingers and taped to a leftover poster board still decorated in her previous school project. For Ríona, the thought of the remodel was all the excitement she needed.

But soon the days drug out. Gutting the kitchen was far more work than she imagined. Ripping out old cabinets, replacing rusted cast-iron pipes ripe with decades of rotting decay, and her worse nemesis of the entire project: the white floral wallpaper that her grandmother adored, even when everyone else could stand the yellowed colours any longer.

"Mum, are we done yet," Ríona would whine when the days turned into weeks. Her mother smiled sweetly at her, sweat beading on her forehead. That Summer was exceptionally warm, she was told by nearly every adult, a trend that continued the years afterwards marking new records each time the weatherman came on the television.

"Patience, mo cailín. It's hard now, but when it's all over, it will be wonderful. But things won't be wonderful unless you have a little patience."

Ríona laughed to herself before stealing the drink out of Tomi's hand.

"What's so funny?" Tomi watched as Ríona guzzled half her whiskey sour.

"Just remembering things. I can't help myself sometimes, you know," she paused to finish the glass, "I still think about her a lot."

"Your mom?"

"Yeah. Probably doesn't help I'm always getting lost in my head anyway."

Tomi took her empty glass back. "Do I need to refill this?"

"It couldn't hurt. I don't think we're going to get any more done today by the looks of it."

"We're getting close. I'm thinking another couple of weekends and she'll be perfect."

"That soon?"

"Yep. She's close to being done."

Ríona eyed the empty glass. Tomi took note of her wandering eyes and popped off to make another. Ríona continued to watch the heavy rain from the dry comfort of the porch. In only a few weeks Roan would be complete and she would be free.

For a moment Jordan crossed her thoughts. She still hadn't responded to any of her messages, nor had she been at any of their usual spots. When she left class on Friday she wasn't waiting for her, despite all of Ríona's bleak hopes. Even Zach doubted she would show for dinner.

He was right. Mr McGraw made no effort to hide his fury at his daughter. As far as Jordan's mother could tell, Jordan had packed a small bag while they were all gone and found a friend to stay with. She made a few calls to the school to check on her. According to all her professors, Jordan hadn't missed a single class. They were concerned about her performance, commenting she seemed overly distracted, but none expressed any worry she would have issues with the coming finals.

Tomi returned with two drinks this time. Ríona took hers with a wry smile, noting that hers was the usual citrusy colour with a hint of grenadine tainting the bottom red. Tomi's was much darker, almost thicker looking with few ice cubes bobbing about lazily. It had a creamy caramel colour that looked like unadulterated whiskey.

"Are you trying to get me drunk," Ríona teased. It felt wonderful to so openly flirt, to not hold herself back or worry what someone around her might think. Even better, to know that person she was batting her lashes at smiled back because they had desire in their eyes. Desire for her, not a larger tip, but a carnal lust for her body.

"I prefer 'loosen up' myself," Tomi's eyes glinted with mischief. "But mostly I actually wanted to have some. Some sexy little brat keeps stealing mine."

Ríona frowned. "But it always tastes so much better when you steal it from someone else."

Ríona eyed Tomi's glass, then her own. Noticing that Tomi's was a little more full than her own, she grabbed Tomi's and gave her hers. Tomi smirked.

Ríona took a sip of her freshly stolen drink and nearly spat it out, "what the hell's in here?"

Tomi burst out laughing.

"How can you drink this? Give me mine back!"

"No no, you said things taste better when you steal them." Tomi leaned over and stole a kiss.

Ríona instantly froze as the euphoria of Tomi's whiskey scented lips touched hers. Ripples of pleasure ran down her chest and into her midsection, causing the muscles to flutter uncontrollably.

Ríona pulled away slightly, "was I right?" Tomi's cinnamon musk intoxicated her more than the whiskey could ever hope to.

"Hmmm. I'm not sure," she whispered in her husky voice before pressing her lips against Ríona's.

The wave that washed over her body wasn't as intense as the first. Although, not that she could tell since her body still glowed in the euphoria of Tomi's first kiss.

"I think you might be right," Tomi teased, pulling back, her right hand resting on Ríona's hip.

Ríona could feel Tomi's warm fingertips teasing the flesh just above her belt line. They felt like branding irons against cool flesh, covered in goosebumps still from the chilly evening air. With her free arm, Ríona cupped Tomi's rugged face and admired her handsome looks.

Without thought, Ríona gave into her own desire and pulled Tomi back down to her face. Tomi didn't resist as Ríona forced her own body against the muscular woman. Tomi's warmth against her own lit a desire deep inside that she wanted desperately to quench.

As if reading her thoughts, Tomi's fingers cautiously explored the smooth skin hidden just beneath her jeans. Then, slowly, masked by a flurry of passionate open mouth kisses, those fingers found their way to the small of her hipbone. That little spot that was both exceptionally ticklish, forcing a giggle out of Ríona despite her best efforts, and highly erotic.

Right then she wanted more than just Tomi's fingers touching that delicate flesh always protected from the world. Her touch was a siren song for unfed desires raging between her legs.

"Tomi?"

"Yes?"

"I think we should finish our drinks and go inside."

Tomi's fingers paused. But the borderline painful contractions inside her did not. If Tomi didn't keep going, she feared she would burst just at the thought of what could have been.

"And why would we do that, Tiny?" Tomi's hot breath on her ear sent shivers down her neck.

"Because..." She couldn't finish her thought. Tomi's teeth nibbling on her delicate nape chased away the words Ríona sought.

Tomi pulled back, letting a rush of chilly air sober her up. *Not fair*, she muttered to herself. Her body ached. Places she hadn't felt desire on her body in years suddenly woke up demanding her full attention. Her breasts felt heavy, her breath felt light.

"I'm enjoying the rain," Tomi teased before taking a long swig of her drink.

Ríona turned to once again stare out at the cool rain with hints of a fading sun streaking through creating bright splatters of sunshine. She took a sip of her own, much sweeter, whiskey, relishing the coolness.

She could feel Tomi's presence behind her, even though the taller woman didn't touch her, Ríona felt the electricity ripple through her spine. With a gasp, Ríona reacted to the sudden icy touch on her neck mixed with a sweetly warm breath. The ice cube shocked her sun kissed skin, melting into tendrils of Tomi's sensual touch, reaching places Tomi's fingers could not.

Ríona took another sip before tilting her neck, inviting Tomi to tease her hot flesh. Tomi obliged her request, wrapping her lips around the thin outstretched muscles, then biting. *Hard.*

"Ouch," Ríona complained coyly, pulling away playfully. Tomi quickly grabbed her belt and pulled her back, rewarding the bite mark with a long, gentle kiss.

Tomi wrapped her arm around Ríona's waist, settling her hand on her belt buckle. Thinking about where her hand was leading, Ríona melted further into Tomi, pressing her electrified back against Tomi's strong embrace. Tomi's smallish breasts brushed against her, a simple yet wildly welcomed reminder that despite Tomi's rugged butch appearance, that underneath it all she was still a woman.

The mere thought was too much. Ríona bit her lips, the pain teasing that she may draw her own blood, in a vain attempt to stop herself from exploding right then, before Tomi could have her fun. The yearning tearing at her raging libido wanted to give itself entirely to Tomi's control, to her touch, to her command.

Sensing her surrender, Tomi sat her drink down and used both hands to teasingly loosen Ríona's leather belt, first tightening it far beyond what was needed. It took her breath away, feeling the sudden controlling constriction wrapping itself around her before quickly releasing its careful dominating embrace.

Tomi slowly pulled the belt off, loop by belt loop, then unceremoniously dropping it to the ground. Around her the blaring sound of rain on tin drowned out the world, leaving her alone with her eyes closed to a black world of nothing other than Tomi's maddening touches.

"Still want to go inside?" Tomi unfastened the button holding the jeans snug to Ríona's slender hips.

"Only if you promise to not stop." Ríona was surprised by how husky—how desperate—her own voice was. If her body hadn't broadcasted how badly she desired Tomi, her voice trumpeted it.

"Hmmm. I'm having so much fun here though."

Ríona opened her eyes. She remembered where they were, the world of touch relinquishing her to the real world where she stood on Tomi's porch, exposed to the world. Out here there were no walls to safely steal kisses behind, and no closets to hide her unbridled desire for the woman pressed up against her, her fingers now slowly, and obviously, unbuttoning her flannel. One button, pause, a second button brushing against her navel, then a third lingering touch teasing her flat stomach, a fourth testing the base of her ribcage, a reminder that the next button was all that kept her flannel from falling away.

Ríona grabbed Tomi's hands before she could pull her flannel apart, leaving only the thin fitted tank top keeping her clothed.

"It's not like anyone's around," Tomi hissed into her ear.

"Still...," she pleaded halfheartedly. Even though she didn't want to admit it, the thought of being exposed like this ignited a desire between her legs she hardly expected. Something about the potential to be caught in the embrace of another woman took the air out of her lungs.

Tomi pulled the pink flannel off Ríona's shoulders. Before it could fall to the ground, Ríona downed the rest of her whiskey with two large gulps. Tomi gently rescued the empty low ball from Ríona's shaky grip, then without another word, pulled the offending overshirt off at last.

Chills ran across her shoulders and down her naked arms. Her first instinct was to pull away from Tomi, put some distance between the object of her unquenchable desire and her exposed arm, the scar still visible even in the gloomy filtered light. Ridges and valleys, the little reminders that her life was once at the mercy of a raging fire lapping up all the surrounding oxygen, suffocating her in a cloud of black, lung burning smoke.

"Honey," Tomi cooed, closing the divide Ríona made between them, "you don't have to hide from me."

Tomi rested her hands on Ríona's shoulders. Slowly Tomi's hands crept down her goosebump covered arms that still reeled from their nakedness, inching sweetly down Ríona's biceps, then elbows. Ríona inhaled sharply, again biting her lips painfully, as Tomi's hands ventured further.

If Tomi had a reaction to the mangled skin, she hid it well. Ríona watched Tomi's left hand slide over her arm, an invisible sensation only one of them could feel.

"Doesn't that feel nice?"

Hesitantly, Ríona agreed. It was freeing, in its own little way, to not have to hide her arm around Tomi. Even though that feeling between her legs calmed, replaced by the overwhelming feeling of gratitude, the thought of Tomi looking at her with only hunger in her eyes brought her that much closer to the edge.

Tomi slid her hands quickly back up her arms and down around her waist. With practiced ease, she unzipped Ríona's jeans, giving her more access to let her fingers tenderly explore. Slowly, tenderly, her finger tips poked underneath the band of her cotton panties. Ríona pressed her back against Tomi, throwing her head back into Tomi's shoulder. Seeing her wish, Tomi answered the begging lips waiting for her.

Ríona opened her mouth, beckoning Tomi to explore the inside of her mouth while her fingers explored the inside of *her*. She absolutely melted at her touch. She felt exposed beyond her imagination, standing on someone's porch, embraced by another woman so openly, while she brought her to the verge of climax.

She pulled away from Tomi's kiss and found the soft flesh at the base of her jaw and bit. Tomi reacted with a small squirm, but rewarded her by thrusting her fingers harder and faster into her sending her over that erotic precipice at last. Waves of contractions rippled through her body, her chest felt airless, she bit harder, telling her partner that she was enjoying her orgasm.

Coming down from her high, she felt weak. If Tomi wasn't grasping onto her, an arm around her hips, she would be afraid of collapsing to the ground in a panting mess.

"Did you enjoy yourself?"

Ríona giggled uncontrollably. Unable to contain herself, Tomi laughed along. With a deep breath, Ríona was finally able to ask, "I hope I didn't hurt you."

She looked up at where she instinctively bit her lover. It was red, but not bruised.

"The gals are gonna get a kick out of that." Tomi tested the bite mark, checking to make sure nothing was broken.

"Oh god, please, no." Ríona suddenly felt a huge crushing wave of embarrassment at the thought of others knowing. She was never one to discourage others from enjoying their adult life, but the people knowing about her... that was different.

"Whether I tell them or not they're gonna know you're a biter. Now, you had said something about going inside."

"Really," Ríona asked with a flirty smile on her voice.

"It's only fair we take turns."

CHAPTER 30

*R*iona waited at their usual spot. It was a chilly Monday morning, far colder than the past few had been. The weather, thanks to the jet streams, took an unseasonably cold turn. Most of the students took note and kept inside, making the campus feel eerily empty so close to finals.

Since their first day at university she has come to this spot to wait for Jordan. Depending on their schedules, it would sometimes be first thing in the morning, or even as late as sundown. Their early freshmen years was like that, cramming as many classes as they could into as few days so they could skip out on their off days.

It didn't take them long to grow tired of that as they spent most of their time inside their dorm room huddled over a stack of books and papers, desperately trying to decipher which class they were writing their next paper for. That first year was the only year they ever had a matching schedule, let alone matching classes.

Now in their final two weeks, she couldn't stand the notion that it wasn't their schedules that kept them apart. It was Jordan. Or really, her, for having hid that secret from her for so long.

She checked her phone again, knowing that there would be no reply yet hoping that just maybe Jordan had replied. Nothing. Just several messages she had sent, begging Jordan to talk to her. Her latest simply read, "I'll be in our spot if you're willing to talk." Jordan wouldn't have to say anything. She could just listen while Ríona poured her secrets out, letting Jordan pick through them while she sat there vulnerable and afraid. She'd happily subject herself to that scrutiny, so long as it meant that Jordan was there.

CHAPTER 31

"What are you doing here?"

Zach sat down in the chair next to her. Around them the campus food court was bustling with activity. To the world around them, Zach and her sitting alone at the table likely seemed normal. Just another normal day in a boring part of the universe.

But it wasn't normal. Zach sat where Jordan normally would with a baggie full of carrots and celery on the table, her laptop glowing menacingly in front of her. They didn't need to say much, both enjoying the simple joy of the other's presence. There was no one else Ríona felt that connection with, save perhaps her mum.

Zach's presence demanded attention, no matter the context. If he was there, her muscles tensed in anticipation that he wanted something, or he was simply there to stir up trouble. This time felt... different. There was an aura of calmness about him today.

At first Zach said nothing. He just sat there, frazzled. It was as if he just came back from an invisible war and he was still processing all the horrors haunting him. Even his face turned a ghostly white, his untamed stubble making him look far more rugged than he really was. He looked more like a man than a child.

It made Ríona uncomfortable to contemplate. He was getting older, as was she. They were no longer young teenagers roaming the back roads looking for the slightest excuse to expunge their boredom. Somehow they had grown, sometimes in the smallest ways, and sometimes, from the hallowed look on Zach's face, in bigger ways.

"Thinking about the accident," Ríona probed carefully.

His facial expressions didn't change. While he didn't answer, she knew he was. She imagined there must be times when random triggers would send him spiralling into the darker recesses of his mind, weighing him down with the squealing tyres as they left the road.

"Sorry." He shook his head. "Yeah," he rubbed his hands across his face bringing some colour back, "someone said his name and it... you know."

"If you ever need someone to talk to, you know you can talk to me, right?"

"Thanks."

"I know I'm not Jordan or anything. You twins have that weird magic bond and all that."

"Funny that. She won't tell me what's bothering her. I know I'm prying, but what happened between you two? I thought for sure the only person who she loved more than me was you."

She wanted to tell him. It sat there, desperately banging on her chest, begging to escape. If she could ease that burden paining him right then, she would. But she thought back to all the times he's called Jordan and her "gay" as an insult, or used slurs to refer to others he thought was like her.

Their hair was too short, or they're too ugly to get a boyfriend, or any number of things that she would never remember that she had to endure silently. No, she couldn't tell him. If Jordan's reaction was any indication...

"Anyway," he blurted out with a loud exasperation. "Tonight?"

"Yeah, of course."

"Bryce says he has some new music he wants us to look over. When's your last class over?"

"Four fifteen."

"Is it cool if we all come crash at your place until we play?"

"Sure."

Her flat wasn't much, just a simple studio above some downtown offices sitting off the main roads. It was quiet enough. It could be a little too quiet at night, her being only one of a handful of people living along this street.

When she originally agreed to rent the place from a friend of her mother, it was the perfect space she could imagine. Which at the time wasn't much as the tears still came easily and the thought of living alone crushed her. After she regained her composure and she began to explore its limits, it ended up being the ideal place to practise her fiddle. No neighbours meant no need to worry about playing until well after midnight.

Or if her band mates wanted to practise, her flat—although tiny— was perfect. Only thing she hated was the fact Zach and Paul would sit on her bed. She didn't think it occurred to them that they were sitting where she slept. For that matter, she doubted they even know what a futon was, both coming from the luxuries of wealthier families.

"Here," Bryce announced while handing out actual sheets of music. "This is something I've been working on." He looked at her with an apologetic look.

Skimming over the notes, she recognised the piece as hers. It was different in subtle ways, a few chord progression changes and a new harmony. Singing it in her head, it sounded like what she had *wanted* but couldn't find the energy to transcribe it.

The others skimmed over it as well. She looked to where Jordan would sit. It was empty still. It wasn't like she was going to suddenly appear, hair and makeup freshly done. She wasn't coming.

"Not bad, man," Paul said as he noodled about on his banjo, running through a few of the runs and testing the transitions.

Not wanting to make a scene out of it, she teased out a few notes herself. She had never played it on her fiddle and quickly realised she should have been all along. The melody never sang to her the way it did now, even without the changes Bryce made, it was just better played on the instrument she knew best. It connected with her body as she swayed losing herself in the melody, naturally picking up many of the nuances Bryce had included in his version.

"Wow, Ríona, you picked that up pretty quick," Paul praised.

"This is your final, isn't it," Zach added with a smirk.

Ríona stopped playing. She dropped her bow and fiddle to her lap and looked up at him apologetically. Suddenly waves of guilt washed over her, as if she was using her friends without telling them.

"Yeah," was all she could muster.

"I saw her struggling to work on it," Bryce tried to clarify.

"Girl, you coulda told us." Paul laughed, then studied the piece some more. "I think I can get the hang of it enough to play tonight."

"Zach," Bryce questioned.

"Why not? The beat isn't difficult and we have," he pulled out his phone, "three hours."

Ríona caught the hint of disappointment in his face and the hesitation in locking his phone. She wanted to ask him what he read, to know if perhaps it was a text from Jordan. If it was, by the expression he gave, it was worse than her not coming out later.

She had wanted to text Jordan as well to let her know they were playing, and that she would love to have her there, even if it was just to listen. She typed out the message only to stare at it for a few minutes, locked her phone, reopened it, stared some more before ultimately deleting it.

If Jordan hadn't responded to any of her other messages, she wasn't going to respond to this one. By now it must sound like she was desperate. As much as she didn't want to admit it, she was. *Why won't she text me back?* It was fruitless.

CHAPTER 32

*I*t was a packed night. She wanted to attribute the shoulder to shoulder crowd with the fact they were the ones up on stage playing. It would be nice, she thought, if that really was the reason. They did come for the music, she knew, but it rarely mattered who was playing.

They came for the drinks and the atmosphere, to flirt with the barkeeps and each other. They came because it reminded them they weren't living their lives anymore. To the people filling the room she was background noise, a decoration they only noticed when it was missing.

Joey, the owner, took the microphone on stage. On cue, the lighting technician, who also doubled as the sound technician, and also tripled as the "everything technician", dimmed the house lighting and brought up the hot, blaring stage lights that made it impossible to see the crowd before you. The stage was bare except for the electric drum kit that all the bands used and a handful of amps and microphone stands, as well as a sea of snaking cables and taped set lists leftover from the previous night's band.

"Hey everybody," he yelled into the microphone with a glaringly bad Scottish accent. *It's an* Irish *pub you fecking eejit,* she thought ruefully. The crowd returned a halfhearted cheer, oblivious to her pained reaction. "I'm sure you guys are ready for finals to be over, huh?"

A few yelps and cheers erupted from college students. The others simply quieted down, pausing their conversations until the loud man stopped drowning out their words. Joey went through his standard pleasantries, thanking everyone for coming out, telling them they're "gonna love the acts tonight" as if everyone didn't already know the music.

"I may not be Irish," he continued with his bad accent, "but our lovely Ríona Kilbride is." He looked at her as she stood at the edge of the stage, fiddle in hand, waiting to come up. "Come on, don't be shy," he called, his accent nearly lost.

"Here she is everyone. The reason most of you even know what Irish music sounds like." He put his hand on her back like she was a child being shown off by a proud parent. "As some of you probably know, she's a senior here at our wonderful college. Which means," he paused for effect, "she's leaving us soon."

Silence fell over the large pub. Only the sound of barkeeps cleaning and stacking glasses echoed in the large open void. "So, before she goes, I want everyone to show their appreciation for her fine talent and show her some love."

It stunned her how enthusiastically the crowd clapped and cheered for her. For a brief moment before the extreme embarrassment set in, she felt like a rockstar. A few "we'll miss you"'s could be heard tossed out over the applause by voices she didn't recognise.

Joey waved at the busty barkeep Zach always tried to flirt with. She quickly darted over with a pair of drinks. With a wink, she handed Ríona a glass, then Joey. Sniffing it she understood the wink. It was just carbonated apple juice, her usual before performances. It was enough to fool most into thinking she at least drank ciders.

Joey held up his glass and waited for the crowd to do the same. He turned to Ríona, exclaimed "sláinte" and clinked his mug against hers.

"Who's ready for me to stop yammering and for these guys to start playing?" A boisterous cheer went up around the pub.

Behind her, the rest of the band walked onto stage. Zach quickly took the opportunity to test the drumheads. When the monitors immediately kicked back his beats, a smile spread across his face. He had spent the past few hours diligently practicing their new song on voiceless drumheads.

Not wanting to drag out their introduction any longer, Bryce took the microphone and introduced their first song, a classic pub song that always got a few early drunks singing along. Which she always found a little ironic and was certain Bryce picked it as their opening song most nights for that very reason.

Even with his deep, nearly bass voice, his vocals were still limber enough to belt out, "what would you do with a drunken sailor" in rapid eighth and sixteenth notes before drawing out "early in the morning". That part would always elicit a yelp or cheer for the prematurely intoxicated amongst the crowd. Even when they'd perform at festivals or fairs there would always be that one person, no matter how early in the day they started, who would find themselves in those lyrics.

One time, when it was just her and Jolene wandering around a Scottish festival where everyone who wasn't remotely Scottish donned their best Braveheart impersonation, oblivious to the fact their kilts were as authentic as a Disney movie, when a man stopped her. He recognised her as "the chick with the violin" from earlier in the day. Her job was simply to wander the fairgrounds playing random Celtic sounding tunes, and this drunkard of a man wanted her to keep playing.

"You know," she translated through his slurry of words, "that song about whiskey."

She knew which one he referred to. Everyone in the world had a cover of that song, even if most Americans thought it was a Metallica original. Only the punk kids knew it wasn't, instead preferring the Dropkick Murphy's version. Or at least Thin Lizzy's "original".

She played a few bars, purposely picking a completely different song about a love duet of sorts between a man bringing the whiskey, and the moon bringing the light. The man drunkenly started dancing to it, oblivious to her deceit.

After humouring the stranger for a minute, she dropped her fiddle to her side and told the man she needed to go. Ignoring her, the man insisted she keep playing, claiming "I'm not done yet." She laughed nervously. The man closed the distance between them, his rotten stench evident even amongst the crowded smell of dirt, sweat, and fried meats.

"I want to hear another," he demanded through a slurred threat, his eyes never leaving hers except to appreciate her exposed cleavage.

"Sorry, I have to go." She tried to duck away but he sidestepped in an attempt to get in her way. She feared for her fiddle foremost, holding it protectively away from the larger man. Although it wasn't her father's fiddle—she'd never risk it at such a chaotic event like this—it was still her first and only concern.

"Where are you in such a hurry," he asked with more in his eyes than liquor. *"I was just getting to like you."*

"Babe," Jolene said loudly like a megaphone blasting in his ears, *"we're going to be late to your next show."* She grabbed her hand and gently pulled.

"Babe?" He huffed. He eyed her up and down, taking in her more period accurate tartan and plaid with the long-sleeved léine underneath, all provided by the events manager.

"Yes, babe," Jolene interjected his vulgar glances. *"She's mine, and we have to go."*

"Can't believe they let a dyke around children," he muttered to himself. *"Eh, whatever. You're too ugly for me."*

Jolene's face turned even redder than the summer sun had already painted it. This time it was Ríona who had to pull Jolene away. *"Stop, you'll make a scene."*

"What? You're serious?"

Ríona quietly pleaded with her. She wanted away from the drunken man who looked on the verge of unleashing his anger on them. Around them the crowds merely floated past, whether uncaring or simply distracted by their own lives, they were left to face this man who was close to twice her size and his injured pride.

"Yes, please," she remembered pleading. It took Jolene a moment to think over Ríona's begging. Eventually, Jolene huffed and walked off, letting go of Ríona's hand.

Bryce encouraged the rowdy drunks some more, cheering them on as he introduced "their new song" as he called it. "I want y'all to go gentle on us here."

The pub quieted down for a moment, surprising her with their attention. Despite the glare of the lights blinding her to anything behind the edge of the stage, she could make out the shadows of patrons mingling around the high tops watching them play.

Behind them Zach counted off and Ríona delved into the melody with a long draw of her bow. To everyone else, it seemed a simple enough action, a sweet, mellow note verging on the edge of tears weeping along slowly, but for her, this was perhaps one of the more difficult notes she could play tonight.

Bryce either wanted to torture her or had far more faith than the skills she showed at practice would indicate. A quick quarter note was a flick of the wrist. Tied whole notes took a master's touch to tease them out without sounding like her first days as a wee child deftly torturing her adult captors.

Holding her breath the whole time, she finally softly exhaled when Bryce snapped the first bass note on his upright signalling the start of a feisty tirade of boot stomping melody, a complete turn from the heart wrenching hollowness that she had tried so hard to instil in the piece but could never find the right way to express it.

That sadness and heartbreak, the feeling that everything was a long, drawn out metaphor for despair. Death, and heartbreak, and betrayal. Paul joined in a call and return with her. They took turns dancing in 9/8 time, the crowd now clapping along to the beat. Although no one knew the words Bryce was singing it felt familiar enough, Irish enough, to hum.

Bryce's voice while smooth belied the words he sang, words she herself hadn't written. Somehow Bryce had taken her piece and found a way to weave his own lyrics into the piece, while as she listened earlier at practice, managed to catch the nuances in the heartbreak she felt.

Zach silenced their heart, their pounding rhythm that told the world they were alive, only the ring of a high hat still ringing quietly in the chaos. Ríona was alone again, her voice strung across four thin lines of catgut singing their warm, mellow tones to a silent audience.

This was the score she had been trying in vain to write these past few weeks. To put down the secrets haunting her heart buried underneath her flirtatious smiles and singsong conversations. Between frantic bursts of glee laid troughs of unforgiving sadness, of mistakes, of women who stole her heart, of bitter slurs used to stab her back, and the bitter pain of scars that would live with her for the rest of her life.

Quietly, as if life was being breathed back into her, into her score, into

185

the audience, Bryce and Zach revived their heartbeat, a steady and strong pulse reminding the listener that through the storm there was an end.

Applause snapped her out of her post performance meditative high, a comedown akin to her weekend at Tomi's after each explored the other's body to the fullest. When she opened her eyes to take in the crowd roaring with approval, her eyes quickly caught the figure standing closest to the stage.

CHAPTER 33

"What are you doing here," Ríona quietly asked while looking around making sure no one was watching them.

"It occurred to me I had never seen you play before."

It was true, she hadn't. Even the times she had taken her fiddle with her to visit Tomi, she had never once played for her. They were either too busy working on the van trying to beat the rush her deadline forced them to compete with, or they were out with Tomi's friends. With a flush of passion on her lips, she remembered why she never played for Tomi the night they watched the sunset from Roan.

"And I haven't seen you in your element. I'm always dragging you to my hangouts."

"I don't mind." Secretly, she had been enjoying that aspect of their relationship. Lincoln was safe, but she knew it intimately. There was nothing special here, nothing new aside from that pop-up event she randomly drove past, it was always the same here.

"Still, I wanted to see you play. And damn Tiny, I've missed out."

She blushed.

"Don't be embarrassed." Tomi grabbed her hand that cupped a mug of sparkling cider. "Did you write that song you guys played there at the middle?"

"You were here for all of that?"

"Got here just after you started playing. Was a bit crowded, so I grabbed a beer and hung back with Brie for a bit."

Ríona's blood went cold. It had been a few weeks since Julz' comments about her finances, but her words still stung. From Tomi's look of knowing concern, her poker face was failing to hide her hurt.

"Don't worry, she hasn't been drinking. Matter of fact," Tomi announced as Brie and Julz joined them, pushing Tomi close enough she could wrap her arm around her small shoulders.

Frantically, her thoughts went straight to her band mates. *They should already be at the diner,* she assured herself. She turned her focus onto Julz while the anxiety of their communal silence ate at her.

Brie nudged her wife. "Fine," Julz spit out coldly. With a loud sigh of defeat, "I'm sorry."

"For," Brie softly tried to tease out the rest of the apology.

"She knows what for."

Brie glared at her.

Ríona stayed quiet, not wanting to get caught between those silent daggers. In a small way, she wanted to hear Julz say what she was apologising for. It would give a validity for the hurt she felt so acutely that night. Another part wanted her to just forget it occurred, let that sleeping dog lie peacefully in its forgotten slumber.

"I'm sorry for calling you a trust fund baby." It was quick, and from the look Julz gave saying it, agonising.

Brie laughed. A wave of relief washed over her, even if Brie's amusement of the situation confused her.

"Julz has been wanting to apologise," Tomi explained, "but she absolutely sucks at it. She's the *literal* worst."

"She is sorry," Brie added, "and I hope you forgive her. I miss ribbing you. The group isn't the same without our little baby dyke."

Internally Ríona cringed hard at that word. It still ate at her no matter how much she knew Brie used it in an approving manner. The situation reminded her of her first year English professor.

Somehow she had enrolled in an "jazz oriented English course studying the power and meaning of the jazz counter culture". On a whim she chose Miles Davis as her topic, knowing nothing of what she was getting herself into.

It was when her professor asked her to read, aloud, the passage that most struck her as odd, the same one she had been writing her paper about and knew that she had no hope of switching out a less... profane scene.

Standing at the podium, her entire class of thirty other freshmen with their Midwest innocence still intact, she found herself fumbling for words. Her professor encouraged her along, assuring her that anything she said would be understood not to be her words, but the words of a man who died over a decade before she was born. A product of his time, as it were.

Skimming ahead, reminding herself of the vicious language, the vulgarity and utter disregard for the female anatomy, she couldn't muster the strength. Like a lost child in the untamed wood she stumbled until the professor told her she could use the overhead camera.

As the words shone dimly on the white Smartboard, her classmates read the words silently. Some giggled, mostly the guys, while others expressed their uncomfortableness with Davis' brutal vulgarity using words to describe both female anatomy and words with such horrible history that she could never bring herself to even use the word in quotation.

It horrified her to be the person who made those words appear before class, even if she herself never wrote those words, or in the entirety of her life brought herself to utter anything that was written on that page.

"Why won't you read them," her professor finally asked.

To her, the answer was obvious. Those words had meaning and history, and one in particular, was a word used for centuries to persecute and demean other humans for no reason other than a meaningless variation in skin pigment. That single word represented the antithesis of everything her mother raised her to be.

He turned to the class, "there's power in words. You can either let them define you, to shackle you, to oppress you. Ríona isn't wrong for not saying that word. Why?"

The class was silent. They were in just as much shock as Ríona was at the depth and detail of Davis' vulgarity and justifiable anger towards the police harassing the jazz club Davis played at, a night that went down in infamy for its violence and animal-like brutality against people just enjoying the brilliant horn now regarded as a masterpiece.

"What does Davis get out of reclaiming those words; the same ones used to enslave him into a society of systemic and blatant racism?"

The professor paced, pointing to random students who either shrugged

189

because they didn't know the right answer, or they were too afraid to attempt one.

"He gets to define their meaning," the only black kid in class quietly answered.

Baby dyke, Ríona repeated in her head. Those words still stung, yet she couldn't articulate why.

"Apology accepted," Ríona distracted herself, forcing her mind elsewhere in the crowded pub.

"Good," Brie announced boisterously as she slammed her mug down on the table and drawing only a moment of amused glances from around them. Her outburst wouldn't be the most unusual drunken proclamation these patrons would hear.

Julz perked up. "How come you've never played for Tomi? Or us?" It was as if the tension between them had never happened.

"Been too busy."

Brie smirked, "that's our Tomi for you."

"What does that mean?" Tomi feigned a shocked face. "I am the epitome of a gentlewoman."

"You're a modern day Anne Lister is what you are," Brie shot back before downing the rest of her beer.

Tomi leaned in, "don't listen to her. She just likes to get me in trouble."

It never occurred to her to ask about Tomi's love life. What was it like, she wondered, imagining the woman wooing all the Air Force cadets, rushing them away in Mariam to some distant locale? She would have to ask her about that later.

"Who's Anne Lister?"

"Oh god," Julz started, "don't ever say that in front of Brie. Not unless you want to suffer through one of her history lessons. Even her students know better than to ask."

"You only hate it because you've heard it before."

"Only because you won't stop telling me about it every chance you get."

"You two." Tomi shook her head with a small laugh.

Brie looked longingly at her empty mug. "Another round and then we're calling it a night. You college kids and your crack ass of dawn classes are killing me."

Their final round didn't last long. Brie and Julz excused themselves, again complaining about how early she had to start teaching. Tomi claimed she had no such rush to get home, but Ríona knew she was only saying that for her sake. It was late, and if anything, she needed to get home herself. Brie wasn't the only one who had to wake up too early.

"Hey, Ríona," a girl called out from a line of people filtering out the pub across the street, another popular midweek destination for those seeking a different flavour of nightlife.

Her plus two other girls from her composition class ran up to her full of giggles and one clearly full of too much liquor.

"Saw you play tonight. You're like a whole other person up on stage," the girl who called out to her started. Ríona wanted to say her name, but in the heat of the moment couldn't pick out the correct one. Her intoxicated friend was Jackie, an otherwise fantastic pianist, but right now Ríona doubted she could manage the coordination required. Not when she needed her friends to keep her from tipping over forward and busting her nose on the brick street.

Jackie tried adding to... *ugh, what is her name*'s compliment, but all she managed was a slurry of garbled words. From the tone, she seemed quite pleased with Ríona's performance as well.

"You in Kaley's class too?"

That's her name! "Yeah, Kaley and I've been in a few classes together now. You sorta know everyone in the music program."

"Cool, cool," the other friend nonchalantly replied. Ríona couldn't tell if she was just that aloof, or insanely disinterested in what was going on around her.

"Who's this," Kaley asked pointing to Tomi.

It was then that Ríona realised she was still holding Tomi's hand. Hoping Kaley wouldn't notice, she quickly pulled her hand away feeling the sudden nip of cold night air eating away at the warmth Tomi's hand provided. Hoping no one noticed, she used the same hand to emphasise her answer. "This is Tomi."

"Hi," Tomi greeted them curtly with a small wave.

Kaley eyed Tomi with a small smirk. "I haven't seen you around before."

"Don't come up this way much." Tomi shrugged. "Only came up to see Rí play tonight."

"Aww," the unnamed friend cooed, "that's sweet. I wish my boyfriend would do something like that. Where're you from?"

"Just north of Wichita." Tomi's answer was short and to the point. It felt like she was avoiding all conversation even though a moment ago she was as lively as always.

"Oh, a Kansas girl, huh?"

"I guess. It's where I was born. Didn't go to college there."

"Good," Jackie blurted out. "Sorry. That was loud."

"Went straight into the Air Force from high school. Now I'm back."

Kaley gave Ríona an approving smile. "A woman in uniform, hmmm. I won't keep you two. See you in class tomorrow, Ríona."

"Bye," she waved at them as they faded into the crowded sidewalk.

"What was that about?" Tomi stood back, a mixture of anger and hurt in her eyes.

"Sorry... I," she stammered trying to buy herself time to find an answer. *What do I say?*

"This isn't Kuwait where they'll drag you out of your house and beat you simply for existing before locking you away, Rí. Lincoln isn't like that. Hell, this whole country isn't even like that. At least not anymore."

"I guess not," she meekly stammered, her cheeks flush with embarrassment, wondering if there was more to her statement. She knew history wasn't always in their favour... *our* favour. Even her mother expressed concerns, in particular after that June in Florida. "I just..."

"Just what?" Tomi sounded defensive, if not a little hurt. In their weekend sojourns she had never seen Tomi mad, let alone hurt. Not emotionally hurt, at least.

"Are you afraid of what your classmates would think?"

"Maybe. It's not something I discuss with them."

"I get that. Not their business. You don't have to introduce me as your girlfriend, but you pulled your hand away as if it embarrassed you to be seen with me. It makes me think—" she stretched her cheek out with her hand, "are you not out?"

Ríona didn't have an answer. She'd now only come out to three people in her life. One was dead, the other turned on her calling her a freak in the middle of dinner, and the other still hadn't spoken to her.

"That's why Jordan isn't talking to me." It felt good to confess that to Tomi, a weight she could finally offload onto the stronger woman's broad shoulders.

"Jordan? You mean the day she left suddenly? That's what that was about?"

It stung, recalling the look of betrayal in Jordan's eyes. "She figured out we were together. And then realised I'm... you know."

"You can't even say it? Seriously!" Tomi stormed away.

For a moment, Ríona hesitated, standing there on the sidewalk dumb-founded and suddenly alone. Tomi wasn't stopping, nor looking back. No gallantly walking her back to her flat in the late night darkness, no lingering goodbye kiss with promises of more to come.

"Tomi," she caught herself calling after the woman she knew she hurt. She didn't fully understand how she had hurt her, or why pulling away her hand was causing so much tension between them.

"Tomi, please, wait!"

Tomi paused her escape, but didn't turn back to face Ríona. Instead she jogged over to the hurt woman and pleaded fruitlessly for Tomi to face her. When Ríona tried to get a look at Tomi's face, Tomi would turn her own.

"Tomi, look at me, please," Ríona begged.

"I can't do this. Not again, Rí."

"I don't understand. Can't do what again? I'm sorry I pulled my hand away, I'm new to this."

"I like you, Ríona. I really do. I like you more than I've liked anyone in a long while. You're gorgeous, you're smart, and seeing you play tonight there's no denying you're insanely talented." She sighed, her whole body sinking. "I just can't do it again."

Tomi left.

Ríona watched as the woman she had been sharing such a fantastic few months full of weekends with left her stranded on the sidewalk, her heart breaking into millions of little pieces. Worse, her mother wouldn't be there to console her this time, and Jordan... Jordan wouldn't want to hear how her cousin broke her best friend's heart.

CHAPTER 34

$\mathcal{T}$he first rodeo she had gone to was with Jordan and her mother, almost a decade ago. There was never a desire to be a "horse girl" lurking somewhere inside her. An early morning ride along the trails, perhaps—a weekend activity she missed. Not for the horses, or the smell of hay and manure permeating the barn with its dusty windows. She missed the act of simply riding alongside Jordan.

Mrs McGraw would often accompany them, along with her own mum, referring to it as their "family time". The pair would show up to their front porch an hour before Fall's sunrise, crisp air threatening yet another cold Winter of snow and the occasional ice.

Rodeos were another matter. They were loud, crowded and so dusty you weren't sure if you were in a sandstorm or not. Really, she just didn't understand them. Before she went to university, it was an amazing adventure, wandering off to the Lancaster Event Center. Aside from the white plastic rail fencing and the overabundance of four wheelers and lifted pickup trucks, it looked nothing more than a fancy warehouse filled with dirt and the stench of farm animals and sweaty testosterone.

"I'm surprised you wanted to come," Zach commented.

"I've come every year." Ríona shrugged, her mind still wandering elsewhere.

"I know. It's just, you know, with all that's going on." He looked sheepish as he tried to pitifully explain away his concern.

"It's not like I could have said no." The McGraw's made it clear over dinner that this would be her last time needing to be Zach's girlfriend. But until then, they needed to put on a good show for everyone.

Mrs McGraw had gone through her own clothes to pick out an outfit for Ríona to wear. A plunging neckline to show off what cleavage she had and to accentuate her youthful frame, one Mrs McGraw remarked she would miss having once she was older and had a few kids.

"You and Jordan would make wonderful mothers," she had wistfully teased, not so much a direct statement but a moment lost in future thoughts that they both knew were nothing more than wishful dreams.

"True. I am glad you refused to wear what my mom picked out. I don't understand why she thinks everyone wants to be like her."

"Mood."

He burst out laughing. "Yeah... Don't get me wrong, you looked good, but that's so not you."

"Don't wanna marry a girl just like your mother?"

"God no. Unless you're offering?" He chuckled at this own comment before looking at her. She gave him a blank stare rife with displeasure.

They continued making their rounds through the small section of vendors selling small horse related crafts to the more serious artisans selling leads and saddles. She stopped and nudged Zach when she found the one she never could pass up.

"Seriously? You're just going to get it all over you."

"So?" Ríona ignored his warning and stood in line behind the half dozen teens eager to spend their parents' money on fried sugar topped with even more sugar. It was the only pleasant smell to be found and the single best part of any fair or festival.

"Maybe we could come back later and get you one?" He tried walking away, pulling on her hand. If he wanted, he would have no problem dragging her away. But he didn't. Instead, he turned to her, a small look of worry on his face.

"I always get funnel cake when I'm here. It's half the reason I come out to these things." The other half was Jordan. Without her, there wasn't any real reason to come, except of course, "appearances".

"We haven't even seen any of the competitions. Won't this make you sugar crash?"

"Huh? I mean, of course I'm going to have a sugar crash, but then I'll just get a coffee or something."

She didn't understand why he was being so insistent that she not enjoy the one simple pleasure to be had. It wasn't like him to be so concerned over something so trivial, in particular for a bloke who would normally jump at the chance to bring her a treat.

Zach pulled out the event flyer from his back pocket and unfolded it, skimming over it looking for something. Satisfied he found what he was looking for, he glanced at his smart watch. "Barrel racing starts in fifteen minutes. We should probably go grab our seats."

"I thought we had seats up front already?"

"We do, but it's good to be seen."

Annoyed, she pulled her hand out of his. "Welp, you go save us our seats, and if anyone asks, you can tell them your girlfriend is treating herself to a funnel cake."

She didn't understand what his issue was suddenly. The man who ran the small food stand, alongside his two daughters, happily served each customer before her with an enthusiastic flair. There was no real secret to funnel cake, just sweet batter poured into hot oil, then coated in icing sugar. The first time her mother tried one, at this same rodeo, she nearly gagged at the incredible sweetness.

Even to Ríona's American tuned taste buds this was an overabundance of sweetness, one she had no fantasy that she could finish on her own, no matter how many times she would try. It was at the least, an act of normalcy that was predictable, that was there, that was answering their texts, and would never ignore her.

"Hi," she said. The man and the two girls didn't say "hi" back.

"How many?" His tone was devoid of the excitement he greeted the teenagers before her. The girls, both in their early teens, hair pulled back in tight pony tails and wearing loose grey tee shirts, refused to acknowledge her existence. Instead they sullenly focused on keeping the confections from burning.

"Just one," was all she could say. She didn't understand his dislike of her. In the years past, she was just another customer in the sea of hyper young adults that filled the food stands. Jordan never failed to blush at the man's casually flirtatious behaviour towards all the pretty girls, which she rewarded him with a few dollars stuffed in the tip jug humorously labelled "sugar daddy fund".

"Your other half doesn't want one," he asked with a snark to his voice. There was anger in his eyes.

"No, she's not here…"

"She?" The anger softened in his look. "You're not with that boy then?"

"Zach? No, no. I'm just his date." She added air quotes around "date" for emphasis that she was *not* happy with the arrangement, more so right now.

"Good. Stick with the girl, she's safer for you." One of the daughters handed her a funnel cake. It smelled divine, yet somehow tainted by the odd conversation happening.

"I will."

Ríona found Zach waiting for her down near the floor. A small section reserved for donors and VIPs demarcated by obnoxious yellow tape as if warning "normal" people that those inside will suck them dry of their money to maintain their social status.

"See, plenty of time left."

"Ríona," Zach started, "this is Mr Harkness. A client of my father."

Feeling suddenly out of place with a bite full of cake in her mouth, she tried to say hello, but for fear of embarrassing herself, she gave the man a small wave.

He chuckled. "It's okay, my daughter loves those things too. You into rodeos as well?"

Finally managing to swallow the still hot piece, she answered after what felt like an inappropriately long pause. "Yes!" Her answer was louder than she planned, making her feel even more childlike around all these men in suits. "I mean, yeah, been coming to them ever since we moved here."

"From the looks of it, you must ride?"

"Used to. I haven't gotten much riding in since going to university."

"Understandable. Sometimes our future plans get in the way of the things we want to do today. Are you one of the lucky ones graduating in two weeks?"

"She is," Zach answered for her. "But she doesn't need any luck."

"Shoulda known Barry's son wouldn't pick himself a slacker. If she's able to ace college, you know she's going to make a great housewife." He slapped Zach on the shoulder.

Housewife? We're not even dating. Silently, she rolled her eyes at the old man. Part of her desperately wanted to correct him, remind him that she's not Zach's possession to show off, nor was she one of those girls who went to college to land themselves a husband.

"And a great musician. She's an amazing fiddle player. Maybe my father can arrange for her to play at one of the company retreats."

"That would be nice." He inspected her, slowly, from head to toe then back to her head. "We could use a lovelier distraction at those god awfully boring retreats your father loves."

CHAPTER 35

"*I* don't blame you for leaving like that," Zach told her after a long pause. He didn't say anything else, nor did she respond. The two sat there leaning against the back of a horse stall far removed from the crowds and the chaos of the rodeo.

Without Jordan at her side, the magic of the event was shattered, leaving her disillusioned and aching for her company. It also made Tomi's words haunt her more. "I can't do this." Then, she was gone.

Those were the same words she snapped at Zach before storming out of the stadium leaving him and his father's associates confused and angry. She left them with the same abrupt ending Tomi left her with. No resolution, no explanation; nothing. Inside her own head, she understood the turmoil, those raging emotions eating away at her. Thinking back on it, Tomi must have felt the same way.

"You don't?" She felt a tinge of guilt knowing she did blame Tomi—and Jordan.

"No. My family threw you into this without asking your permission and without telling you the truth. You got nothing out of it, yet you did it anyway. And then to have him harass you like that... you didn't deserve that."

"You could have said something."

199

"I should have. It was kinda nice pretending we were a couple. I just —you know? Ugh. Who am I kidding, I know you hate me. I still don't understand why you even agreed to all of this."

"Well, you may be an ass, but I don't hate you."

"I'm Jordan's brother. Don't go soft on me."

"I do think of you as a friend though. That's why I did it. But him being a creep wasn't the issue."

He went silent. Picking up a few small clay pebbles, he started tossing them towards the opposing wall. They hit and exploded into little puffs of dust before being dragged away by the soft breeze.

"I know."

Somehow, without him even explaining, she knew what he was referring to. *Does that mean Jordan told him?*

"I know why Jordan is upset with you, why she hasn't talked to you in weeks."

"She told you?"

He mulled over his next few words. Throwing his last clump of sticky dirt, he turned to her. "I suspected you were. When I heard you and Jordan weren't talking, I just *knew*. Then I saw you and Tomi."

Her blood ran cold. She knew it was risky letting Tomi take the lead like she did, letting her hold her hand in public in her own city. Wichita was safe. There, even though it was still so close, it felt like a different world where she could be free, free of the judgement she felt would follow her home here.

"We didn't go to dinner. Bryce had to go home, and Paul... well, he was being Paul. So I wandered around a bit and saw you two holding hands." His tone mellowed. "I realised how much of an ass I had been to you. The things I've said, ugh!" He slammed his head back against the wooden wall.

She knew the words. Zach and his father used them often to demean people, to insult women who weren't pretty enough, or to make fun of guys who weren't "manly" enough in their desperate need to validate their own masculinity. They were words tossed around regularly without provocation or consideration to those ears whom they fell onto.

"I'm sorry. I'm sorry to you. And I'm sorry to my own sister. I wish I could tell her that in person right now.

"I thought I knew everything about her, ya know. We're twins. We know everything about each other. *Everything*. But she couldn't tell me *that*. Man, I can only imagine how she must have felt all these years."

"Tell you what? That I'm…"

"Come on, don't act like you don't know." When she didn't reply, he gave her a look of shock, then shook his head. "You'll figure it out—why she's avoiding you."

They watched as rodeo hands shuffled past, pushing carts full of large wooden barrels the next competition would be using. It was Jordan's favourite event to watch. They didn't fully understand the point, running literal circles around barrels as close as possible without touching, but it was primarily a woman's event so they rooted until their voices gave out on them.

"Zach?"

"Yes, Ríona?"

"Can I ask what happened the night of your accident? When I got my funnel cake, they almost didn't give it to me because they thought you and I were together. Is that why were you were trying to drag me away?"

"Yeah. He's Dustin's uncle."

"Dustin? Is that who was driving?"

"No. He wasn't."

"Who is he then?"

"He was the passenger. *I* was driving. I'm the one who lost control and caused the wreck."

Ríona went silent. The shock of his revelation still hadn't registered. Was this why the McGraw's asked her to pretend be to his girlfriend? To cover for him. Thinking back to the day in the hospital, to the comment Mrs McGraw made… She knew. They *all* knew. Everyone but her.

"Does Jordan know?"

"I told her the other week. The week she stopped talking to you. She came to me crying saying you broke her heart. She said you had lied to her about who you are. At first I thought she was being dramatic—you know how she can get."

Ríona chuckled, recalling the many times Jordan could have won an

Oscar for her performances. It was just a facet of their friendship Ríona came to accept as normal life.

"Hearing her heartbreak like that... I had to tell her the truth. Our parents didn't want me to. They wanted her to be as clueless as you so if anyone asked, neither of you could slip up.

"By the time I woke up, it was too late for me to say anything so I played along. I didn't have a choice, Ríona. I'm sorry."

"I want to say it's okay... I do. You're like family, ya know?"

"I do."

"So what happened?"

"That weekend I blew you guys off, I went to a kegger at a friend's place way outta town. Dustin drove us out there. Said he needed to get away from his parents and let loose. He was the one hooking me up with my stash, so I went along. I didn't want to be here hounded by my father so I went and the two of you were rightly pissed at me.

"I took a few hits with this hot chick I met at the party. She was fun, if you know what I mean."

"I don't need the details." Ríona shot him a disgusted look.

"She also had a friend who was just as hot as her and I knew Dustin and his girlfriend had broken up, so I tried to get him to hook up with her.

"He brushed it off, but I kept insisting. Like why man? You're single, you're good lookin', she's smoking hot. For some reason, I just couldn't let it go. I hounded him and hounded him but he told me he wasn't interested. He was seeing someone.

"Which was news to me. I hadn't seen him with any of the girls there, only his friend Thomas. That's when he broke down laughing at me. Then it dawned on me.

"I couldn't believe it at first, but he insisted that yes, him and Thomas were together. Had been for months. He wasn't gay. How could he be gay? He had a girlfriend!"

"Some people like both, ya know."

"That's what he said too. But I couldn't wrap my head around it, and being as trashed as I was, I got pissed instead. I called him all sorts of names. Ugh! Names that I've called so many people without ever thinking about it. Without ever wondering who exactly I was hurting, or if they were right there next to me silently feeling like I was stabbing them in the back."

He glanced at her. Guilt riddled his misty eyes. She sat her hand on his knee and let him continue.

"I stormed out. Man, what a scene I caused. Threw my beer through a window, hopped in his car and started to leave, but he jumped into the passenger seat. He begged me to give him the keys, saying I was too wasted to drive. That we could talk it out.

"Instead... instead I gunned it. Just slammed the pedal into the floor as hard as I could and took off down the road. Dustin kept begging me to stop and I yelled at him; called him a faggot. Said he lied to me.

"I couldn't shake the thought of all the times we shared a shower during gym class with all the guys. That he had been watching me. To be honest, it creeped me out big time.

"He confessed that when we first met he did think I was cute, but after a while, he only saw me as a friend. That's when it happened. I turned to tell him how disgusted I was, how betrayed I felt...

"Then there were bright lights and then—then I found myself waking up in the hospital with my mom watching me. She told me I was lucky to survive. That thankfully I wore my seatbelt.

"When I asked about Dustin, she told me that he hadn't been wearing his and died instantly. And then she told me how he had been driving me home because I was drunk. When I went to correct her, that I had been the one driving, that I had stopped paying attention, she told me to shut up and listen. That my injuries would make me forget things and that her and my father had taken care of everything."

"I'm sorry, Zach."

"Don't be. Seriously... I'm the one who should be sorry. Sorry to Dustin for saying those things to him. Sorry for killing him."

"You didn't kill him. It was an accident. I saw the dash cam footage, Zach. I saw the other car slide into your lane. Anyone would have swerved."

"I was the one who freaked out and got in the car. If I hadn't been such a complete asshole we wouldn't have been on the road. We were there because it freaked me out he once had a crush on me. And I can't stop hating myself for that. I've spent so much time hating my father, hating who he is, only to become just like him.

"I'm sorry to you too, Rí. I can't believe the way I acted around you and Jordan, never realising what I was saying would hurt the both of you so much."

"Yeah... honestly, it really hurt. But it wasn't only you, you know. Everyone but my mum was like that. The first girl I dated, Jolene, did that to me. Twice." She laughed realising how bad that made her sound.

"What about Tomi?"

"She broke up with me."

"What? No way! Why? She's not who I'd pick for you, but still."

"Oh really? Who you'd pick for me? And just who that might be?"

"No no, I know a trap when I see one."

"Awww, you're no fun."

"What happened with Tomi though?"

"I don't know. We ran into some of my classmates and I sorta freaked out and pulled my hand away. Afterwards she told me she couldn't 'do this again'. But I have no idea what she's talking about. She hasn't responded to my texts. I'm torn between giving her space and just driving up to her house this weekend."

"She never told you why she came back, did she?" Ríona could only shake her head. "She got kicked out for being gay."

"You're coddin'?"

"No. They used to do worse but then they made 'Don't Ask, Don't Tell' and basically so long as you didn't tell anyone, they wouldn't hunt you down anymore. I don't know all the details, just that she got caught in another woman's bunk and she came back home. Never had the courage to ask her and she's never freely talked to me about it.

"As you can imagine, my family wanted nothing to do with her anymore. They don't even know Jordan still visits her. My dad would probably disown her too if he ever found out."

"I can only imagine how bad they're going to freak out when they find out about me. They're never going to let me see Jordan again, are they?"

"I don't know. That's probably going to be the least of my parents' worry."

"What does that mean?"

"Just... I couldn't take the guilt anymore. I honestly don't know how you've managed to deal with your own for so long.

"Which also means you don't need to worry about that Sam asshole anymore. I showed him the footage, how my parents were involved, how the sheriff knew. It was bad enough knowing what I had done, but to see you and my sister be dragged into it—it was too much."

"What's going to happen to you? How did his family react?"

"Better than I expected. I told them everything. I think the worst part for them was finding out their son had been hiding such a big part of their life. Even Sam agreed to leave out the part about Dustin being bi saying his family suffered enough. Seems he was more interested in finding something to use against my father than what really happened.

"As far as me... rich, white dude, remember? I'll be fine. My father won't be winning the election."

"That's gonna sting a bit." She chuckled. They all knew he wasn't going to win, but it remained unspoken amongst them, as if by never saying it aloud they could make it vanish.

"Thanks for telling me."

"I'm sorry you and Tomi broke up. Guess that means you're still leaving us?"

"Yeah. I guess."

CHAPTER 36

*Y*OU CAN PICK UP ROAN ANYTIME, Tomi's text started. It was a lengthy text. When her name first popped up on her notification screen, Ríona got excited, hoping that Tomi had finally come around and would let Ríona apologise.

She imagined ways she could explain to Tomi that it was a one-off incident, that she panicked. Try as she might to rationalise her apology, she knew it was more than just her pulling her hand away. It was that she had never told Jordan until that Sunday. After all those years of friendship, or her restless fondness for that Sunshine.

DON'T WE STILL NEED TO WORK ON HER?

Half a day passed before Tomi responded. Ríona completed yet another final. It didn't take much imagination to assume the professors praise meant anything other than a passing grade.

NO. THERE WASN'T MUCH WORK LEFT TO DO.

That was a lie. It had to be. Last time Ríona and her worked on Roan, Tomi said they had at least a few more weeks left, that it wouldn't be ready until after she walked.

Ríona typed out a new message, rewording it over and over in hopes of figuring out the right combination of words. How do you ask for forgiveness when you're not even sure what you're trying to apologise for?

She *knew* what happened. She watched Tomi walk away with her own heart pounding in her chest. All she did was pull her hand away. *Why did I do that?*

Unsatisfied with the message, she deleted the whole thing and started over again.

Can I see you?

The grey ellipsis appeared. They bounced back and forth, over and over, dragging out time painfully while Ríona anticipated Tomi's response, hoping that somewhere in the agony of waiting she was saying "yes".

No. Short, simple, and a blow to her already tight chest.

Ríona fought her urge to argue, to plead and beg for a chance to discuss what happened. Like she had with Jordan—who still hadn't responded. Ríona had already come to the conclusion that Jordan wasn't going to respond, that their friendship was over for good. When she finally revealed her one secret, she ruined their relationship while with Tomi, by hiding their secret, it ruined their relationship.

I'll pick her up Saturday morning.

Okay. Don't forget the title for the pickup.

Saturday morning carried a weird dread to it. Morning started with a heavy fog over the fields, thick and heavy. The type of fog as a kid that both scared her, worried that buried in there was a monster or perhaps an alien invasion, and gave her the exciting possibility of getting lost in the rows of corn where she could imagine she was back home in County Galway where a similar fog was known to smother the county on particularly cold sunrises.

Ríona waited until the sun burned off most of the fog. She told herself it was for her own safety. If she waited long enough, Tomi would have woken up and found an excuse to leave the house for the morning. Or who knows, maybe she never even came home after a night out with the gals?

Her house felt lifeless when she pulled in. Only the sound of moaning gravel gave the place a feeling of any life. The workshop was still closed up. Her front door was closed. But in the driveway a beautiful baby powder blue van awaited her arrival. It glistened in the sun from a fresh wash and waxing.

Of course she went all out, she laughed to herself. *Some leave roses, she leaves cars.*

She walked around Roan, running her hand along the silky skin. It felt a little surreal. Her new home was so tangible, so real. So hers.

Seeing the van was unlocked, she opened the driver's door and slid in. The feel of the baby powder blue leather felt cool and familiar. She ran her hand over the steering wheel and rested her hand on the shifter knob as if she was already on the road.

Beside her sat a plain white envelope with her name written on it.

Ríona,

I'm sorry I left the way I did. It was wrong of me to leave you there alone like that, but I couldn't stay. You asked about my time in the Air Force once, but I never told you what happened.

I think telling you is the only way I can explain why I had to leave.

I like you, Ríona. I really do. I wish things would have worked out differently between us because I think we could have been good together.

I was like you once. Still in the closet and scared to come out. I'm not mad at you for that, and I don't fault you. I get it, I really do.

When I first started questioning my sexuality was when Matthew Shepard was murdered. Seeing that nonstop on the news scared me for years. I was still in high school; I had been asked to prom by a boy and being scared anyone would find out, I said yes.

It was horrible. He tried to hook up with me afterwards and seeing him naked. I knew right then I was gay.

I had no plans after high school so I joined the Air Force on a lark. I wanted to be a fighter pilot. It was a tall order considering the number of female fighter pilots was zero. They told me it would be nearly impossible, that I would need to apply myself like I've never done before.

At first I was so busy I had no time for anything else. When I wasn't training, I was working on my degree. When I wasn't working on my degree, I was studying for my pilot's exams.

I had forgotten all about having to come to terms with being gay. I had just passed my exam and was shipped off overseas. When I got there, I met the most amazing woman and fell in love almost instantly.

All those feelings I had repressed came flooding back. We started seeing each other in secret, hiding everything about our lives from everyone. No one could know. That was my life, and was going to be my life for the next ten years at least. Always paranoid someone was going to walk around the corner, or someone would see through your window and report you to the C.O..

It ate at me so much. It was worse than the first time I hid who I was. At least then I wasn't in love and the only thing at stake was my high school reputation. On base, I faced time in the stockades and losing the only thing I wanted.

After a few years, I couldn't do it anymore. I broke. I couldn't take hiding who I was, always kissing the woman I loved in secret, never holding hands, not even hugging each other.

I asked her if she wanted to come out with me, to tell everyone we're gay, accept the consequences, and then start a life together. She said yes.

When I came forward to my C.O. and told him I was gay, that I had been seeing another officer on base, I found myself alone. She had chickened out, preferring to stay in the closet so she could continue to serve.

It crushed me but there was no taking it back. At the time, being gay in the military meant a dishonourable discharge. I accepted my fate and returned home, bought this property and vowed to never again live in the closet.

That's why I can't do this again. I am proud of who I am and I won't live in the shadows anymore. Coming out cost me everything, but I wouldn't change it for the world.

I'm not going to force you to come out. I'm not going to ask you to put yourself in the position I was. Especially not for me. You need to find yourself and learn who you are. I'm sorry.

Tomi

ANOTHER LETTER INSIDE THE ENVELOPE EXPLAINED WHAT SHE NEEDED TO DO in order to finish transferring the title of Roan into her name. Sign a few pieces of paper, go to the DMV, pay whatever fees they assess and Roan will officially be hers.

Ríona couldn't help herself anymore. She had broken Tomi's heart and hurt her in ways she couldn't have fathomed, but Tomi still finished Roan for her. She was beautiful, and detailed in ways Ríona never would have figured out on her own. Drawers that hid a small cutting board, and the little bench seat that hid a small toilet, even the curtains fit snug over the windows making the inside of Roan dark as a deep cave.

It was a little weird knowing this was now hers, that she would be sleeping in that bed every night now surrounded by a world that changed every sunrise. Her tiny microcosm would always stay the same, always hers, always laid out the way she left it; messy and dishevelled and uniquely hers.

All that was left to do was finish packing up her apartment, donate anything she couldn't take with her, and start her new journey.

CHAPTER 37

"It's happening," a girl squealed to her friends before group hugging. More excited cheers could be heard over the murmur of the large crowd of students—former students—lining up to receive their caps and gowns.

In a few hours, they will all walk down some cheesy red carpet and onto a stage where they will briskly rush past department heads, popular professors, and the president on the university. Most of them would have no clue who the excited young adult was, nor did they really care. It was just a traditional dance everyone performed.

"Your mother would be so proud of you," Mrs McGraw said, a reassuring hand on her back.

"I know." She'd never admit it, but she fought back tears all morning. Only once did she lose and collapse onto her bed sobbing, longing for the comforting embrace only her mother could provide.

Her tears came hot and fast, as did the roiling emotions gnawing at her. Roan had kept her distracted on the weekends, and between her gigs and desperately trying to complete her final project, she never let herself have a moment for the weight of her moment to sink in.

When her mother first admitted she was sick, Ríona swore she would never leave. She would live in that house until the day her mother died, which Ríona threatened would be decades away. Not the handful it really was.

"She would have given anything to see you here today. She always worried you'd never leave because of her."

"When I told her I was leaving after college, I always imagined she would be there waiting for me to come back in a few years."

"Her cancer took us all by surprise. I had looked forward to the two of us watching our girls graduate together."

Ríona turned away from Jordan's mother and glanced over the line forming outside the back entrance of the stadium. Jordan had to be out there, somewhere. It surprised her a little that even now Jordan was avoiding her, the day the two of them had waited for so eagerly together. Always together. *Is she going to skip walking?*

"Don't worry, Ríona, she'll be here."

"You think so?"

"I do. You mean far more to Jordan than you realise."

"I thought I did, but I'm pretty sure I royally messed up. I shouldn't have…" She wanted to finish her thought, to say it out loud as if she was simply confessing eating the last slice of cheesecake she didn't know was being saved for someone else. She turned to the older woman, someone she knew had experienced her own heartache and lived through it. Someone who at some point stood where she did, even if that woman could never understand *why.*

"We all make mistakes, hun. I've made my fair share of 'em, that's for sure."

"But what if that mistake makes your best friend hate everything about you? Something you can never change no matter how hard you try?"

"I'd say, make sure you know what your mistake was. You might be surprised. I know my daughter, and I know she doesn't hate you. She's just… hurt.

"Anyway. Looks like y'all are finally getting to line up. We'll meet up with you afterwards and you can show us this van you built."

Inside was packed shoulder to shoulder and buzzed with more excitement than she cared for at the moment. She mourned the fact she couldn't feel their nervous joy. It was a noisy, hot mess of bodies desperately trying to squeeze through a series of doors while donning their rented cap and gown.

The stadium wasn't much better, just bigger. It was a far cry from the picturesque romances of Hollywood graduations out in open fields under perfect sunny days. Hot lamps shone down on them; bad speakers piped out vaguely familiar popular-a-decade-ago radio hits that only the parents waiting in the stands would appreciate.

A handful of "notable figures" stood up to speak, including the newly elected Lincoln mayor. She spoke of bright futures ahead, of the strength and dedication it took to earn their place walking across the stage. She spoke all the right words without any of the obligation of greatness.

They were merely empty words as empty as she felt.

CHAPTER 38

"*Hi*," she whispered with a small wave and a smaller smile. She stood there like a forgotten goddess leaning against Roan, hiding in the cool shade the Volkswagen provided on the sea of blacktop. Her bleach blonde hair, noticeably fresh and flowing down to her shoulders in wavy ringlets, framed her handsome face.

Ríona was speechless. There were too many confessions and apologies eager to flood the gulf between them... *where do I even begin?*

"I'm sorry," Jordan started. "I promised you I'd be there to walk across the stage with you."

"I never meant to hurt you, Jordan, I swear. I... I..."

"Didn't want to ruin our friendship," she finished for Ríona. "Somehow I did that instead."

"What? No you didn't! I should never have dated your cousin. That was my mistake."

"It wasn't a mistake, Rí. You had every right. I mean... how were you supposed to know? I shouldn't have freaked out like I did, but it just hurt so much knowing you were dating her."

"I'm sorry."

"Stop apologising! You didn't do anything wrong." Jordan watched her, silently seeking resolutions to answers Ríona could only imagine. "Do you love her?"

That was not one of them. "Love? Tomi? No, I wouldn't call it love. Fun, sure. It was definitely nice feeling wanted. She liked me even though I'm... I'm gay."

"I think that's *why* she likes you, hun. Kinda how it works, ya know?"

They shared a laugh. It felt good to laugh again and to hear Jordan's annoyingly chipper giggles. Was her smile always joined by those tiny lines radiating out into her flawless face?

"When I kissed you that night in our dorm room, why did you freak out?"

"I don't know. I think about it often. I remember being so afraid that you'd figure me out. That somehow you could tell me letting you kiss me wasn't some silly school girl thing we used to do.

"I was so afraid to come back to the dorm and you'd be gone. That you would know I wasn't *normal*. I was afraid that you'd figure out I've only ever liked girls."

Jordan's face sank. "When you didn't come back, I was certain you didn't. So anyway, I tried to peek inside, but I couldn't see through all those girly curtains of yours. Are you ever going to show me your new home?"

Ríona fished her keys off her belt loop and turned the lock, freeing the side door. There was something weirdly satisfying about unlocking her "front door"; unlike nearly every car she's ridden in with their keyless entry or remote locks. This felt purposeful, like she *owned* the place.

She had intentionally parked along the edge of the surface lot so she could open up Roan to wait out the rush of traffic to get in, and the rush of traffic to get out. Jordan climbed in and quickly found her way to the bed.

"Did Dobby come by and make your bed?" She teased pulling at the pink chequered blanket.

"No. I wanted it to look nice in case anyone visited."

"Don't want to look like some hobo living in a van, huh?"

"I prefer 'accidentally homeless because I forgot my lease ended in the middle of the month' thank you very much."

"You're hopeless, Rí."

"To be fair, you're the one who keeps on top of things like that for me."

"You're going to be so lost without me."

Jordan went quiet. She let her eyes wander around the van, taking in all the changes since the last time she was inside Roan, still bare walls, no mattress, and an unbroken friendship. Ríona watched with a half smile creeping onto her face. This was nice, still awkward, but nice. Things would never go back to where they were before, and perhaps that was just life and the way things were supposed to be. Things change, time moves on, and so do we.

"You're really leaving, huh?" There was a resignation in her voice. This would possibly be the last time they see each other for months, possibly years. Jordan's future was set in stone, tuition paid, classes scheduled, books already occupying space on her desk. Her own was fluid, but like a river, it had a course it needed to run. Unlike Jordan's well charted course, her own was obscured behind hills and forests, even deserts and mountains. There was no way either of them could foresee where or when those waters would deposit her safely ashore.

"I guess."

"You guess? You can't stay after all the work you put into Roan."

"I just... don't want to lose you. It feels like I'm having to trade one for the other. Either I get the freedom I've dreamed about, or I get you."

"You'll always have me."

"Knock knock," Mrs McGraw announced with a rasp on the window. "Everyone decent in there?"

"Mom! Seriously?"

"Yes, Mrs McGraw. Here, let me open the top so all of you can check Roan out."

Zach chuckled. "You named your van?"

"Yeah. She's a part of my life now, so she deserved a name."

Jordan got up, grabbed Ríona's hand, and pulled her out of the van. "Why don't you two check it out? You too, dad."

"I'm good out here." He turned his head as if he was offended by the invitation. *Or by me*, Ríona thought.

"Oh honey, don't be like that. She did a fantastic job in here."

"I can't take all the credit. I did have a lot of help with it."

"Well, I think y'all did a wonderful job. Tomi sure knows how to transform cars."

Mr McGraw made a show of checking his watch before loudly announcing that they needed to go or else they'll be late. Ríona was amused he didn't add his usual spiel about the importance of always being on time.

Ríona knew she would struggle to hold back the tears. No amount of mental preparation, no amount of dreaming, could truly prepare her for the sting of emotions roiling in her chest. Staring at Jordan as the sun made her hair turn into translucent straw was all it took to unleash the outpouring of balled up emotions.

"Jordan..."

"Yes, Rí?"

"I know you don't want me to say this, but I need to. The reason I ran away that day you kissed me—," she wiped away the warm tears pooling at the corner of her eyes. "I had wanted you to kiss me for so long. I ran because I didn't want you to stop."

"I didn't want to stop."

"What?"

Jordan had a smirk on her face. "I wasn't mad that you were dating my cousin. I wasn't even mad at you. I was hurt that you chose her over me. I've been in love with you for so long—that kiss—I kissed you to see if all those times I wish I could were real. I needed to know if I liked you... and if you liked me."

"Like you? I love you, Jordan. I would give up Roan, give up the fiddle—everything, just to stay with you."

"I don't want you to. I can't be the reason you stay. I can't. Just promise me you'll come back for me, Ríona Kilbride."

"Of course I will."

Jordan leaned in, much like she had the first time she kissed her, and placed her sweet lips on hers.

"You go, sis!"

"Leave them be," Mrs McGraw said pulling Zach away.

Jordan's father huffed loudly, "dunno why you ha—"

217

"Honey, as much as I love you, right now just shut up and let your daughter be happy with who she is."

"This feels right," Ríona told Jordan, their hands still intertwined, foreheads resting against each other. This moment was theirs alone amongst a sea of former students leaving campus for the last time. A few people cheered when they noticed the pair. One yelled, "kiss her already".

Ríona smiled, for once not feeling ashamed of who she was, and did as she was told. The small group passing by cheered before quickly melting back into the ocean of bodies.

"I promise, when you're done with law school, I will come back for you, Jordan Kilbride."

"You better. Or else I'm hunting you down and forcing you to keep that promise."

CHAPTER 39

*R*íona pulled over into the tall grass beside the unmaintained fence. The fields were growing strong, stronger than they ever had those last few years before her mother passed. She wasn't physically able to work the fields like she used to, and she wasn't confident their finances would hold out long enough to keep the farmhands working.

Whoever had bought her house had one or the other, or quite possibly both. A farm their size needed a large family to maintain it. From the young boys next to the barn tooling around on the tractor, it seemed the house would be in good hands, even if they let a part of the fence fall into disrepair.

They didn't have the benefit of two wide-eyed girls so desperate for the other's company that they would happily spend hours walking the perimeter looking for any excuse to spend the day together.

"We all have our pasts, mo cailín. We've made our mistakes that will haunt us until our grave. We all have. But," she booped Ríona's nose, *"they are just a beginning. They are how your story starts. It is up to you now to figure out all the stories in between."*

She sipped her coffee, the smell of too much whiskey overpowering the sweet smell of the freshly brewed grounds.

"You'll never live those stories if you stay here. Out there," she waved her hand over the setting sun, "is where you can finally be you, not who all these people here want you to be."

Ríona sat in the driver's seat. The baby powder blue seat cradling her as the engine forced the black rose pendant to sway underneath the rearview mirror. A low hum of jigs played over her stereo, a well-crafted playlist she had been working on for years now in anticipation for this moment.

In a small way Ríona felt it was fitting that the place where her story as a shy Irish transplant was born would be the place where it died. She turned onto the endless road—the one that would take her past Jordan's vacant house one final time.

It hurt knowing that Jordan was already gone. By now, her flight would have landed in Boston. Her family would be waiting around the long carousel of baggage and tired travellers eager to return to their daily routines while Jordan struggled to settle into her own.

That day she first saw that beat up Volkswagen with the mattress thrown into the back, she imagined herself sitting in the driver's seat, like she was right then, waving goodbye to Jordan who waited for her outside at the end of their lengthy driveway. Nothing had turned out the way she imagined it would that day.

Her mother had once told her, "Your heart is trapped in longing." Like the Selkies whose heart was trapped by the cruelty of expectations. "They are trapped by the love of a man whom they want nothing of. It's only when they make it back to the rocky sea are they free to be who they are inside. Like ye."

ABOUT THE AUTHOR

Caitríona started writing when she was still a wee lass. Born mute, the way she learned language was different from most. She first learned to weave worlds and thoughts with an abandoned pen and stolen sheets of her mother's work printer. As she grew older and the world around her became real, discovering a world bigger than empty pages of a spiral notebook and online message boards, her passion for writing fell to the wayside. Life, as it's said, happened. Not always pleasant, as can be attested in her writing. That black dog will forever hunt its prey, no matter how strong she gets, always seeking the moment of weakness to pounce.

After living multiple lives, she found her way back to writing. And travelling. She now travels the United States and Canada in her self-converted van, named Gerudo.

Printed in Great Britain
by Amazon